Anthony Gilbert and The Murder Room

>>> This title is part of The Murder Room, our series dedicated to making available out-of-print or hard-to-find titles by classic crime writers.

Crime fiction has always held up a mirror to society. The Victorians were fascinated by sensational murder and the emerging science of detection; now we are obsessed with the forensic detail of violent death. And no other genre has so captivated and enthralled readers.

Vast troves of classic crime writing have for a long time been unavailable to all but the most dedicated frequenters of second-hand bookshops. The advent of digital publishing means that we are now able to bring you the backlists of a huge range of titles by classic and contemporary crime writers, some of which have been out of print for decades.

From the genteel amateur private eyes of the Golden Age and the femmes fatales of pulp fiction, to the morally ambiguous hard-boiled detectives of mid twentieth-century America and their descendants who walk our twenty-first century streets, The Murder Room has it all. >>>

The Murder Room
Where Criminal Minds Meet

themurderroom.com

Anthony Gilbert (1899–1973)

Anthony Gilbert was the pen name of Lucy Beatrice Malleson. Born in London, she spent all her life there, and her affection for the city is clear from the strong sense of character and place in evidence in her work. She published 69 crime novels, 51 of which featured her best known character, Arthur Crook, a vulgar London lawyer totally (and deliberately) unlike the aristocratic detectives, such as Lord Peter Wimsey, who dominated the mystery field at the time. She also wrote more than 25 radio plays, which were broadcast in Great Britain and overseas. Her thriller *The Woman in Red* (1941) was broadcast in the United States by CBS and made into a film in 1945 under the title *My Name is Julia Ross*. She was an early member of the British Detection Club, which, along with Dorothy L. Sayers, she prevented from disintegrating during World War II. Malleson published her autobiography, *Three-a-Penny,* in 1940, and wrote numerous short stories, which were published in several anthologies and in such periodicals as *Ellery Queen's Mystery Magazine* and *The Saint.* The short story 'You Can't Hang Twice' received a Queens award in 1946. She never married, and evidence of her feminism is elegantly expressed in much of her work.

By Anthony Gilbert

Scott Egerton series
Tragedy at Freyne (1927)
The Murder of Mrs
 Davenport (1928)
Death at Four Corners
 (1929)
The Mystery of the Open
 Window (1929)
The Night of the Fog (1930)
The Body on the Beam
 (1932)
The Long Shadow (1932)
The Musical Comedy
 Crime (1933)
An Old Lady Dies (1934)
The Man Who Was Too
 Clever (1935)

**Mr Crook Murder
 Mystery series**
Murder by Experts (1936)
The Man Who Wasn't
 There (1937)
Murder Has No Tongue
 (1937)
Treason in My Breast (1938)
The Bell of Death (1939)

Dear Dead Woman (1940)
 aka *Death Takes a
 Redhead*
The Vanishing Corpse (1941)
 aka *She Vanished in the
 Dawn*
The Woman in Red (1941)
 aka *The Mystery of the
 Woman in Red*
Death in the Blackout (1942)
 aka *The Case of the Tea-
 Cosy's Aunt*
Something Nasty in the
 Woodshed (1942)
 aka *Mystery in the
 Woodshed*
The Mouse Who Wouldn't
 Play Ball (1943)
 aka *30 Days to Live*
He Came by Night (1944)
 aka *Death at the Door*
The Scarlet Button (1944)
 aka *Murder Is Cheap*
A Spy for Mr Crook (1944)
The Black Stage (1945)
 aka *Murder Cheats the
 Bride*

Murder by Experts

Anthony Gilbert

An Orion book

Copyright © Lucy Beatrice Malleson 1936

The right of Lucy Beatrice Malleson to be identified as the author of this work has been asserted in accordance with the Copyright, Designs and Patents Act 1988.

This edition published by
The Orion Publishing Group Ltd
Orion House
5 Upper St Martin's Lane
London WC2H 9EA

An Hachette UK company
A CIP catalogue record for this book is available from the British Library

ISBN 978 1 4719 0956 6

www.orionbooks.co.uk

To Amy Webb with love

'Beggar that I am, I am poor even in thanks'

Hamlet

CHAPTER I

*A woman doth the mischief brew
In nineteen cases out of twenty.*
GILBERT.

I

SOME men are born public characters, some achieve
publicity and some have publicity thrust upon them. I
belong to the last class, on account of my association
with the unforgettable Fanny Price. I met this dazzling
creature for the first time at Z——'s Auction Rooms,
than which no better background for her beauty could
be devised. For of all the lovely and mysterious works
of art to be seen there over more than a century, none
eclipsed her for subtlety, wit or charm.

London—all big cities—can boast tens of thousands
of exquisitely turned-out young women, as hard-boiled,
as highly polished, as Easter eggs, but no man with an
eye for character could have included Fanny in that
casual category: which is not to say that she wouldn't
be at home in a speakeasy on Broadway or one of the
thousand road-houses that have ruined the countryside
from Kingston bypass to Brighton beach. But while
they would all be as alike as tin soldiers out of the same
box, Fanny had that quality of reality that is mankind's
chief attribute, and that no mere beauty or vivacity can

of itself sustain. And there was at the same time something else, something less noble, perhaps, but to me irresistible, that streak of original recklessness that be-
tokens the adventurer all the world over. I had no
reason at that first glimpse to suppose that she would
be either courageous or enterprising, though events
proved her both, but she would not merely take risks,
she would enjoy them. Danger was her daily bread;
she took chances as more cautious people take penny
tickets on buses; she never shirked an encounter or ran
away from a thing because it might involve her in unpleasant consequences. Her personal history, as I was
later to discover, was a kaleidoscope of ragged adven-
tures, brilliant opportunities, strange and original incidents. She sprang, lovely and irresistible, from her
obscure past as a flower springs from the withered seed;
even on that first day when I did no more than stand
back and listen to her talking with experts, herself one
of them, on what had been for years my own subject, I
felt that instant clash and its attendant sympathy that
convinced me this meeting was one of the momentous
occasions of a lifetime.

I was back at last after five-and-twenty years of
roughing it in practically every part of the world, and
on my first morning in London instinct led me into
Z———'s, that matchless treasury of beauty, as inevitably
as a pub-crawler makes for the door marked Saloon
Bar. As a younger man I'd preferred the philosophers
to the mystics; I'd plumped for the Baroque in art, and
always meant to end my days in one of those lovely
old Regency houses on the Brighton parade. But when
I was six-and-thirty, through a combination of cir-

cumstances that have nothing to do with this story, I fell in love with Chinese art, and since then I've never been unfaithful. Z——'s, as luck would have it, had that day a sale devoted to Chinese treasures. In particular, there was a Chinese robe, ancient, priceless, glowing with color, that could stand by itself and yet was supple as silk to the hand. There was a man standing in front of it when I came in, a little fellow who looked rather like a Chinaman himself, with a smooth, shrewd yellow face and the expression of a devotee. At a second glance I placed him. It was his expression that gave him away. I'd seen him, wearing precisely that absorbed look, in front of a pair of Chinese prints in Shanghai ten years ago. Sampson Rubenstein was his name, and at that time he had just turned his famous antique dealer's business into a limited company, retired with profits that would have shocked a pre-war coal-owner, and started the Chinese collection that every one today knows is the finest of its kind in the world.

I went to stand beside him, and he looked up vaguely, as men do when they feel some one else close at hand. To my surprise he knew me at once.

"Curteis, isn't it?" he said. "My God, have you ever seen anything more beautiful than that?"

He didn't wait for a reply, but broke into a reverent low-toned eulogy of the coat, reeling off details of its period, value, beauty, workmanship, in a voice that made me realize that I was in the presence of a mono-maniac. Naturally I was impressed. You can't meet blinding emotion like that and not get the reflex of it. This little Jew, his eyes nearly falling out of his head, for that instant blotted out the rest of the world. We

3

might have been standing together in a desert. His blazing enthusiasm seemed to re-create the ancient Chinese world.

Then Fanny arrived. She came and stood beside us, looking at the coat, without speaking. Other people crowded behind her, but I saw none of them. Her silence electrified the air; she was dressed in black—and she colored the world.

Rubenstein saw her an instant after I did. Perhaps my attention wavered. I don't know. But he jerked his head and discovered her, tall and elegant, her lovely face grave, her green adventuress's eyes bright as glass with the sun on it.

"You're here," said Rubenstein. "And Graham?"

"I haven't seen him," said Fanny in absorbed tones, without turning her eyes.

"Probably not, since you, presumably, are acting for him," Rubenstein went on. "What's your particular quarry today?"

"The same as always," said Fanny composedly. "Just my bread-and-butter." She waved a cool hand at the Chinese vestment. "Gorgeous, isn't it? You'll never be able to resist that."

Rubenstein didn't answer her; his eyes came back to the coat, as though guided by a string.

"It's worth whatever you have to pay for it," Fanny agreed. "After all, what's the good of money except to buy what you want? If you haven't money," she shrugged, "you have to get it other ways."

She saw some one whom she knew and went away, leaving Rubenstein staring after her. The room seemed suddenly darker than it had been.

"I'd hate to have to admit what that young woman costs me in a year," remarked my companion in gloomy tones.

In view of the few words that had passed between them, I hadn't expected this, and my treacherous eyebrows betrayed me, because I hadn't a complete hold on myself. Rubenstein saw my surprise, and exclaimed in impatient tones, "No, no, nothing of that sort. I'm a married man now. You must meet Lal sometime. No, that young woman is Graham's creature. I sometimes wonder what he pays her to act for him. I believe she knows as much as he does, as much even as I do. And her appearance is so deceptive."

"I asked for an explanation. "Who," I said, "is Graham?"

"He's a middleman by vocation," Rubenstein told me. "Anything that has a cash value gets sooner or later into Graham's possession. If you could buy permits to Paradise, Graham would sell you his. There would be no heaven for him if he thought of you stewing in hell with a thousand pounds in your stocking that might be in his wallet. He's got a nose like a rat and the manners of a ferret. I'm pretty sharp, but he beats me at my own game time after time. Look at this." He pointed to the coat. "Do you know whose that is? Graham's. And he's selling it. He knows I want it. He knows that, whatever price he runs me up to, I shall buy it. I can't keep away from it. And there are men in America who would give every penny—well, that's exaggerating, but who would stop short of nothing to get that coat away from me. That's why Fanny is here—to run the price up so that he can get top profits for it."

"Does he never overreach himself?" I asked.

Rubenstein shook his head. "Not with me," he said simply. "I made my pile by not taking risks. I never risked being cheated myself and I never risked cheating a client. It's the best policy, Curteis. And now I daren't risk Graham's sending that coat to America."

"He mightn't get his price there."

"No, but I should never be sure of that. And even if he didn't, he might hold it up for a year, and every day I should endure the torments of the lost, wondering if he had got a buyer, what he was going to do next. If it weren't, fortunately, that he can't bear to see money slip past him, he would be capable of keeping the coat himself. He's one of the acknowledged connoisseurs in the world of Chinese art—treasures of incalculable value are perpetually passing through his hands, and he lives in a little flat on the wrong side of the Park and tinkers with metal-work for a hobby. But he's clever," he added on a breath so long drawn out, it was a moan. "He'd have made a splendid King's Torturer. I wouldn't take a thousand pounds a day in exchange for the suspense he'd make me suffer."

"And unfortunately he knows it?"

"Unfortunately he does."

"He's a Scotsman?" I haphazarded, not too pleased at having to acknowledged him as a fellow-exile.

"And a Jew. He remembers all about the Scotsman, but as for the Jew—believe me, there's no one quicker to throw up a window in a club on Broadway to let out the stink than Graham when Jews are mentioned.

I dare say we shall see him about here somewhere."

And in fact we did. He came up just before the sale began. He was a tall, thin chap with a bony nose sticking straight out under a flat forehead. He had a bowler hat over thin sandy hair, and the top joint of the fourth finger on his right hand was missing.

"So you're on the scent again, my dear Rubenstein," he said smoothly. "There's no blindfolding you. By the way, I saw a rather nice pair of jade bracelets at a dealer's the other day. You might be interested." He smiled and the Jew eclipsed the Scotsman.

Then the real work of the day began.

II

Rubenstein bought the coat at a price that gave me goose-flesh. The bidding was between him and the girl, Fanny Price, almost from the start. That robe wasn't the kind of thing you can hang in your drawing-room, and there were no governments in the running for its possession. Rubenstein was interested in nothing else. Afterwards he asked me to come back to lunch to meet his wife. As we were edging our way out, Fanny's long, cool hand, glittering with a barbaric green ring in an ancient claw setting, came out and touched his arm.

"I hope you'll be magnanimous enough to ask me down to Plenders when you christen that coat," she said. "It's a jewel."

Graham's face peered over her shoulder, looking like a great starved cat. "How you rich men are to be envied," he said. "If I could afford to keep these

7

things. . . ." The bidding began again and he turned hurriedly back.

"Lal is Spanish," said Rubenstein to me, as we came out into the wet street and he looked about for a bus. Like a lot of rich men, he resented having to take taxis. "I wasn't married last time we met." That was all he said about his wife. For the rest of the way home he talked of Fanny.

"I've never been able to discover where Graham found her," he said, "or where she got her amazing knowledge. There's no Oriental blood there, and Chinese isn't a common subject among young women of her type."

I betrayed myself at once. "Should you say she was a type?" I asked.

"Perhaps not." Unquestionably Reubenstein wasn't interested in her as an individual. "By the way, don't, if you please, speak of her to my wife. Lal cannot bear her. She swears she's a bad lot. She believes that I'm in love with the girl. You never can get women to understand that a time comes when a man has had enough of that kind of thing."

But at that stage my sympathy was for the wife I hadn't met. Fanny, I thought, would make almost any woman tremble for her security.

Mrs. Rubenstein was a magnificent creature, big, dusky, with a voice like velvet, eyes like flame and the jealousy of the devil. She must have been lovely as a girl; now she ran to opulence. I had no chance of avoiding the subject of Fanny. Lal herself brought it up.

"You got the coat?" she said to her husband, who nodded.

"And Graham—he was there, of course?"

Rubenstein nodded again. "I hate that man," said his wife violently. "The way he looks at you—as if he wondered how much you would be worth to him on the market. And Fanny Price, that . . ."—the expression she used is quite untranslatable into English. In Spanish it didn't sound nearly so offensive.

Rubenstein didn't pay much attention to her; he told me not to, either. Quite regardless of us both, Mrs. Rubenstein continued to inveigh against this mysterious girl, to whose charge she laid every crime the mind of woman can conceive. She warned me to cut her dead if I ever met her again.

"She wouldn't know me," I objected.

Lal laughed. It wasn't a nice laugh. "She'd know any man just back in civilization for the first time in twenty years. She's as sly as a tiger."

"She's a very clever girl," said Rubenstein composedly, and at last managed to turn the subject. When I left he asked me to come down to Plenders when he took the robe down to add it to his collection.

That was the first step in the tragedy.

CHAPTER II

*Something will come of this;
I hope it mayn't be human gore.*
SIMON TAPPERTIT.

WHAT with one thing and another, the visit to Plenders didn't take place until after Christmas. And since that September meeting I had contrived to see a good deal of Fanny, spend a modest amount of money on her, track her patiently from gallery to gallery, tell her a good deal of my life story, and in return found myself almost exactly where we'd begun. It was like the mad race of Alice and the Red Queen. If you made your best pace you contrived to stay where you were; if I'd been a shade less enthusiastic I should have dropped out of the running altogether.

There was no snow that Christmas, and I traveled down to Plenders through a countryside of sodden leaves, drenched pasture-land, and the sullen smoke of chimneys blown by the gale almost at right angles. There was neither color nor light in the sky, but I was, as usual, thinking about Fanny, and I scarcely noticed the bleakness beyond the train window. I was totting up what I knew of the girl after three months' acquaintance. She was as individual as a play by Bernard Shaw and as brilliant as light; she was like a fire at which you could warm yourself perpetually, but with

which any definite contact was perilous. She appeared
to be without relations but had more friends than I
cared to count. She earned a living in a number of
ways. She acted for Graham; she had been the model
for an amazing set of silverpoint photographs for young
Norman Bridie, whose work, both in this field and
in color photography, had taken the town by storm; you
saw her face, her mocking green eyes, her chin resting
on her interlaced fingers, looking out at you under
fantastic hats at absurd prices from the advertisement
sheets of the more expensive fashion magazines; she
did country-house mannequin work; she had, she told
me, sung in cabaret shows in London and Paris; she
didn't seem to mind where you took her; she could
adapt herself to any surroundings, and at the end
of the time you knew as little about her, except such
insignificant surface facts as these, as you had at
a first meeting. I couldn't even gauge what her reputation was. Lal might be right; perhaps she was an
adventuress, making her bargain and keeping it coolly,
taking what she could get, cutting her losses, going
from one experiment to the next. I generally let her
choose the clubs at which we would dance, the cabaret
shows we would attend; always she was recognized
with a certain deference; waiters sprang to attention,
head waiters came and murmured honeyed words while
I glanced through the wine list. I think it more likely
than not that she got a commission on every order I
gave. I was told that she was a professional dancing
partner when it suited her book, and that might mean
anything. I admitted that it might—with Fanny. If
you'd told me she cheated at cards and got away with it,

I'd believe you; if you told me she'd done time for shop-lifting I'd hesitate—but only because I couldn't see Fanny getting caught. She, who lived so dangerously, was in her conversation the soul of discretion. I never knew when a personality was repeated to her, if she had heard the story before; sometimes I was almost certain that she had lovers, could identify them when I came face to face with them, but Fanny never gave me a chance to verify my suspicions. I was in love with her—I realized that and was exasperated by the truth. I'd thought vaguely about marriage, and had intended to find some homely woman of about forty, with domestic tastes. I'd had enough rovering and adventuring for the whole of my life, I thought. But the truth is, you can't live the kind of existence I had —and Fanny had—for years and then drop tamely into a hole and stop there till you die. Once the machinery has been wound up it goes on, and there's no way of stopping it. Not that I supposed that I need bother much about Fanny. The wretched machine could strut and posture for the rest of its days without her turning to look at it, if she so designed. Because there was Fanny's strength; she was one of the few people I've ever known who do give the impression that they can circumvent fate. I didn't realize then that it might also be her overwhelming weakness.

I had had, too, an opportunity of realizing exactly how reliable she was professionally. One evening we walked down Rochester Row, where the dark shops showed patches of light in their windows and were bulwarks of gloom above them. A prim rose-colored sky framed the roofs, giving an eerie quality even to the passing traffic. Fanny, who was not susceptible to natural beauty, talked warmly of this and that, her own vivid charm more brilliant than the shop-fronts. At one window she paused.

"They have rather nice things here sometimes," she said. They had something rather nice that afternoon—a pair of jade bracelets of ancient Chinese work. I pressed my nose against the pane.

"Genuine?" I asked.

Fanny shrugged.

"You can't tell with the glass between us."

"Let's go in."

So we did, and a tall, shadowy creature emerged and took the bracelets out of the window and put them before us almost without speech. We took one apiece and examined them. The man watched us, impersonal as fate.

"They're very fine," I murmured, looking sideways at Fanny.

Fanny behaved as though she were alone. I don't know what tests she applied, but after about eight minutes she said to the man, "Very clever, aren't they? But not the real article."

A smile, unwilling, admiring, crossed that parchment face.

"Very clever," he agreed, "but as you say, not genuine."

All Fanny's interest evaporated. She laid them down. "I'm ready, Simon."

I gathered up my gloves to follow her out of the shop. At the counter I paused.

"Are there many of those things going about?" I asked.

"Identical with these?" The fellow picked up the bracelets and began to put them back in a case. "I doubt it. They have to be done by hand. If they're not genuine, they're quite valuable."

"But not comparable with the real thing?"

"As you say, sir. . . ." He turned to the window. All his interest was for Fanny.

"You know a lot," I said a little enviously to Fanny, joining her on the pavement. "I might have been taken in."

"It's my job," said Fanny, carelessly. The yellow glow had faded out of the sky; the street was pleasantly dark and unpeopled. I asked Fanny what she'd like to do. She said, "See Nervo and Knox at the Palladium." So we did, and the Four Ginger Brothers, and then went on to that place in Dean Street where you get such good food so cheap, and can dance without having to change. Fanny didn't mention the bracelets again all the evening.

I found myself as perplexed at the end of my meditation as at its start. Even if Lal were proved right I would have backed Fanny against the world; she could have my last word and my last penny. She was a minx and a witch and an enchantment. She'd got into my bones as sunlight does, and I knew she'd never get out. While, so far as I was concerned, she probably only remembered my existence when I was actually with her.

I traveled down with two other members of the Plenders house-party—Norman Bridie, the photographer I spoke of, a compelling fellow, a bit under thirty, I judged, with a dark, clean-shaven face, a big, an unforgettable nose with a high, arrogant bridge, and a reckless slash of a mouth. He had dark eyes set very deep in their sockets, and black hair growing abruptly off a high forehead. You might as well think of reading Sanscrit without special knowledge as try to imagine what went on in that man's secret mind.

The girl with him was dark, too, small and pale, with a curious steadfastness of gaze that redeemed her face from mediocrity. She seemed to me very young, though I heard afterwards that she was six-and-twenty. It was clear that she was in love with Bridie, but like Fanny you couldn't guess how he felt about it.

"You seen the place before?" Bridie asked me. "Oh, it's worth seeing. A show place. I'm down for more or less professional reasons. Rubenstein's given me permission to do some color photography in the gallery. I've been itching for the chance for months."

The girl, whose name was Rose Paget, said unexpectedly, "I don't like that gallery. I'm glad it's Mr. Rubenstein who has to live with those figures, and not me. I'd be afraid."

"They're only wax," said Bridie.

"They're almost alive in some lights." She turned to me. "He's had wax models made for nearly all the robes, bridal and official and burial, and they stand about in groups. They watch you; they resent you." She shivered. "Do you remember a story by Mr. Chesterton about a man who disappeared, and he had a mechanical servant and people thought the servant had destroyed him? I always remember that when I'm in the gallery, as if at any minute a whole horde of people from another age and civilization, hating us for making them a show, would come sweeping down on us."

"Your imagination does you credit, Rose," said Bridie dryly.

"You don't feel it, I know. But Lal hates it too. You need to be a professional of some kind, I suppose, to appreciate the place. I wouldn't go up there alone for anything you could offer me."

"And you think they're going to be particularly irate with me because I dare to photograph them, and later exhibit them? Well, I hope you're wrong." He laughed and offered her a cigarette. She smiled as she took it, but I saw that her eyes were still very grave.

Plenders was an old Tudor Manor that Rubenstein's money had converted into something resembling a comfortable country house; in the summer he spent a good deal of time here, and Lal at one time had entertained her friends in the great hall and the enormous double drawing-room with its paneled walls and parquet flooring; but she had taken one of her whims that the place was depressing and she visited it with increasing reluctance. Now and again Rubenstein went down without her, but not often. A garrulous woman by nature, she couldn't understand a temperament that required solitude as humanity requires air and for the same reason—to preserve itself from death by suffocation—and she instantly suspected some intrigue. Her suspicions were always so baseless that no man of Rubenstein's intelligence could take them anything but lightly, and so her marriage, that with any other man might have crashed years ago, was preserved very little the worse for the storms her insane jealousy created.

As we reached the door I was conscious of a sudden feeling of faintness. I heard a man's voice say "Fanny," and Fanny's voice replying—cool, crisp and untroubled. In view of Lal's obsession I hadn't anticipated finding her here, and I hurried forward eagerly. Her companion was a tall young man with a mop of curling yellow hair, rather long above his ears, and a pleasant, cheerful face. I heard afterwards that he'd been in the war, but like Rose Paget, he looked considerably younger than actually he was.

"I didn't expect to find you here," I remarked rather tactlessly to Fanny.

"I've come professionally," said Fanny, giving me her hand. "Like Norman. He's come to photograph and I've come to admire." She turned her head over her shoulder as Rubenstein left Rose Paget's side and came towards us. "You've got a lot of new stuff, Sammy. I'm hungering to see it. It's more than a year since I was down here."

"And it would be a hundred before she came again, if I had my way," Lal confided to me, drawing me away from the group. "This is Sammy's house and he invites whom he likes. But she won't get into my flat in London and she needn't think she will. Sammy has no sense about anything except Chinese art and antiques generally. He thinks she's here because she cares for what he's going to show her. She's here for what she can get. And what she's out for this time is Norman Bridie."

I looked at that young man as he stood frowning

17

at his host, one tanned hand thrust into his pocket. He didn't look the type that even a woman like Fanny can twist round her finger, however enticingly she might stretch it forth.

"Not that he's any permanent use to her," Lal continued. "He hasn't enough money or enough influence, but she's got a bargain basement mind, that girl. Sees something going that somebody else wants and she pounces. She knows that Rose Paget is practically engaged to Norman. If she kept out of the way they'd probably settle things this week-end. But that would spoil her fun. Norman's rather run after at the moment, so she's determined to be the fastest bitch of the pack. I suppose you saw the photographs he did of her. Sheer publicity, that's all it was. Miss Fanny Price in a veil and a wreath of spring flowers leaning back against a crystal hoop. One thing, she'll have to mind her step with Graham about. That's a man who doesn't like to share his dinner with any one else."

Her racy vulgarity jarred at such a moment. I could not but observe the sparkle and the intentness of Fanny's manner as Bridie came to meet her. They were a striking couple, and it flashed through my mind that here perhaps was the one man I had so far encountered who might prove her master. That made me respect the fellow, but I didn't like him the better for the idea.

"Is Graham down here?" I exclaimed.

"He asked himself," said Rubenstein in a rather mournful voice behind my shoulder. "Naturally I couldn't refuse. He really does love these things of mine, and if only they didn't cost money he'd buy them himself. If he could steal them he'd jump at the chance, until he saw a reward offered and then he'd be torn in two as to his next move."

"You're such a fool, Sammy," cried his wife. "You credit everybody with the best motives. Graham is down here because Fanny is. She belongs to him, and he doesn't mean her to go giving away his goods when he's off the premises."

"One day you'll land me in the courts on a terrific slander charge," said Rubenstein good-naturedly. "Graham didn't even know Fanny was going to be here. And they haven't exchanged a dozen words since they arrived."

"Because she's already started to vamp Rupert. She hasn't met him before; he's more powder and shot to her cannon. And now you're here," she added, turning to me, "she'll have a really good week-end."

"Rupert Parkinson is Lal's particular find," Rubenstein explained. "He fell out of the blue. She thinks he's perfection."

"You said yourself you didn't want a better secretary," flashed Lal.

"Oh, he's good enough," Rubenstein agreed. "And he's tactful. He knows when to be out of the way. But all Lal's brooms sweep clean." Rubenstein, who was really devoted to his stormy petrel of a wife, put an affectionate hand on her arm.

"You wouldn't have kept him nine months if you didn't think him worth his salt," she insisted, and he laughed and said, "Oh, he pulls his weight. A knowledgeable chap." And then we all went up to discover our rooms and wash off some of the grime of the journey. When we came down we found servants lighting lamps and putting them about the hall.

"Something's gone wrong with the lights," said Rubenstein irritably. "Rupert's just telephoned to the village, but we can't get a man up before morning. You'll have to put up with country discomforts till then."

"They don't mind working here on Sunday?" said Graham.

"They'll make a favor of it. Well, it's a pity. We'd got the robe in place, and I wanted you to see the gallery tonight. But we must wait till tomorrow."

The wind dropped a bit during the evening, but the night grew raw and there were sharp spatters of rain flung against the windows. It reminded a man of all the evenings he'd ever been forced to spend out of doors, nights of open trench warfare, occasional nights in No Man's Land, even nights at home, when, in unfamiliar country, the road missed, he crouched under the lee of a hedge until dawn. It was all the pleasanter to be sitting round the fire in warmth and the golden lamplight. Rose voiced what a number of us were feeling, by saying in low tones, "It must be awful to be sleeping on the Embankment on a night like this," and she shivered.

"It's your own choice if you do," said Norman Bridie, that hard, logical young man. "As for Christina Rossetti's pilgrim, so for the down-and-outs, there are beds for all who come."

We played bridge that night. Fanny was uncannily brilliant; I began to find myself praying that she would lose. Lal partnered with me, and her attention was fixed so keenly on Fanny that she revoked twice and we went down to the tune of eight-and-sixpence. Bridie played with Fanny, and at the next table, Graham, Rubenstein, Parkinson and Rose Paget played a much faster and more accurate game. Saturday night ended pleasantly with the prospect of the Gallery the following day, and we woke to clear skies and pale sunlight. There was a faint misty haze over the flat countryside, and after breakfast Bridie and I and the two girls were driven out to play golf. Rubenstein obviously thought that our fever to behold the Gallery would be so frenzied that there would be no holding us in, and though his treasures could be seen by daylight, their beauty and the effect they produced was greatly enhanced by artificial light. That morning, walking over the Plenders golf course, partnered this time by Fanny, was my one unshadowed memory of that week-end. After lunch, Rubenstein gave us a chance to sleep off our meal and then he took us upstairs, with the air of a man approaching the Holy of Holies. So contagious was his mood that I almost expected to be asked to put on felt slippers over my shoes, as you do in the Potsdam palace to prevent the nails in your boots scratching the polished floors. When we actually saw the exhibition, however, I felt that any attitude he chose to adopt towards it was justified. It was more than impressive, it was, as Rose Paget had said, alarming. Most of the robes were exhibited on wax models but one or two hung on the walls. The very impassivity of those waxen figures, regardless of our presence, scornful of our civilization, created an indescribable effect. The spell worked on Rubenstein at once; he

21

moved slowly among the groups, sinking into long periods of reverie; Bridie looked about him with a keen eye, noting positions and the disposal of the lights; Graham sneaked round like a vulture hoping for a corpse, perching as near as it dares, bending his bony head to read inscriptions or examine particular carvings or embroideries. Besides those disturbing models were showcases of ornaments and decorations, beautiful little carved daggers and knives, embroidered sashes and ceremonial belts. The colors made one gasp; they painted the air all about them. The Gallery itself was a long room running from back to front of the house; the front windows had been sealed and were now hidden by tapestry panels; at the farther end the windows opened on to the lawns that fell into separate terraces, like separate levels of water, meeting at length the tangled woodland and orchard, beneath whose lush greenness ran a hidden stream.

I moved over and examined some of the cases. Suddenly to my surprise I saw a familiar pair of bracelets. "Here are the originals of our Rochester Row bangles," I said over my shoulder to Fanny, who came to look.

"Trust Sammy to have them," she exclaimed. "You know, those were a pretty good copy."

"They deceived me," I acknowledged frankly. "I envy you experts your certainties. I suppose Rubensteir is never wrong."

Fanny, the graceless, lifted up her voice and sang out, "Sammy, Simon wants to know if you're ever wrong."

Rubenstein came abruptly out of his brown study. "If you can show me a single faked piece in my collection," he said, "I'll give you a thousand pounds."

Graham's head came up with a jerk. "How you tempt the gods, my dear Rubenstein," he said, with his queer sallow grin.

Rubenstein was already ashamed of his impulsive wager. A certain Orientalism that as a rule he had kept well in hand was responsible for this momentary outbreak.

"Oh, I'm not afraid of ending the week-end poorer than I started" he said.

Fanny laid her hand on my arm. "Do look," she whispered, her eyes bright with malicious amusement, "Graham's going round like a dog turning out a dustbin in the forlorn hope of winning that thousand pounds."

And indeed, Graham, his color a little heightened, giving him an appearance of flushed parchment, his nose more aggressively pointed than ever, was hanging above every case and every drapery in the crazy hope of discovering some flaw.

CHAPTER III

I do begin to have bloody thoughts.
THE TEMPEST.

LAL, who had followed us reluctantly, was the first to tire. She had sat down on an embroidered chair near the door, idly watching Bridie fix up his apparatus. Rose Paget, who knew about as much of this subject as she did of Bridie's methods, was standing near him. The beauty and the mystery of her surroundings, robes and weapons embodying ceremonies thousands of years old, meant no more to her than if they had been a lot of fancy dresses from Selfridge's. She kept her eyes on Bridie, and I saw a curious sympathy in Lal's expression, as though she, too, found infinitely more value in the insignificant living than in the portentous and awe-inspiring dead.

Lal caught my eye as Fanny went to see what Bridie was about. "I'm cold," she said abruptly. "We needn't all stay. Tea will be ready." She opened the gallery door and I followed her out. No one else moved. Graham was still trying to earn his thousand pounds. Fanny and Rose both watched Bridie. Parkinson was downstairs attending to Rubenstein's secretarial chores. After an instant's hesitation I shut the door and we walked down together.

Lal made no secret of her mood. She was fuming.

"That—lady-dog!" she said. "It's infamous. She means to have him, of course. Rose Paget's nothing to her."

"And nor is Bridie," I urged, for if there was any emotional stress between the two it wasn't on Fanny's side; or so I believed.

Lal turned like a flash and laid a hand on my arm. "You're right, Simon. You're perfectly right. It's Sammy she's after and always has been. Catch Fanny being permanently interested in a poor man. Besides, he's honest, and she couldn't spell the word. She'll hang about up there, coaxing Sammy to talk about his treasures till everybody comes away and they've got the gallery to themselves. She has to make her hay quickly, that young woman, so far as Sammy's concerned. She knows that when we're back in London she won't have a chance of meeting him under his own roof."

I knew this mood; you couldn't argue with it or laugh at it or reason. You had to wait for it to pass. I tried to make casual conversation as we came into the big hall that no amount of lighting could wholly relieve from a sense of heaviness. There were innumerable corners where men might be lying in hiding, and the heavy ancient beautiful furniture it had pleased Rubenstein to put here threw pools of shadow that had the actual effect of blotting out the overhanging lights.

In a well-meant endeavor to turn Lal's thoughts from her husband and Fanny, I commented on an old monkish settle that stood alongside the wall. It was deeply scarred by fire, and badly scratched, but the carving was superb.

"Those old monasteries justified themselves," I exclaimed. "They were homes of craftsmanship, as well as educational centers. Did you ever see anything more lovely than that panel?"

"Oh, you needn't try and ape Sammy," cried Lal pettishly. "It's just an old bench. It doesn't become valuable because a lot of lousy monks once sat on it. I know Sammy thinks it does, and he thinks I'm a fool not to realize it. That's one of the things he admires in Fanny. She always knows the right thing to say to him about the things he buys. I must say," she looked round her at the magnificent proportions of the hall that had, naturally enough, a dwarfing effect on the tiny humans crouching over the fire, "when I married, I didn't expect to furnish my house from a second-hand shop."

I laughed; I couldn't help it. It was so typical of Lal to use that belittling expression of a place that Americans dashed to see as soon as they landed in the hope of picking up an antique that, without being so labeled, was really genuine.

"Well, what else is it?" demanded Lal, "Yes, we'll have tea, Benson. It's absurd of the others to stay up there watching that young man. They'll put him off his stroke."

"I doubt if any one could do that," I assured her dryly.

"Then they'll simply make him even more conceited than he is. Oh, they're impossible, all of them."

Fortunately, at that moment Parkinson put in an appearance and Lal turned at once to him.

"Do fetch the others down, Rupert," she said. "They're walking round the Gallery as if it were one of those shrines where you gabble a prayer forty times and save yourself forty years' purgatory. Sammy's mad on this subject."

"I'll get 'em," said Parkinson, whose hands were full of papers, "I want to put these letters ready for Mr. Rubenstein to sign."

He disappeared into the library and Lal continued to malign Fanny.

"She's only here to spy," she said. "You know, I shouldn't be surprised if Scotland Yard has her fingerprints."

"You might give her credit for a little wit," I suggested, and to my amazement Lal turned deathly white.

"You mean, she's too clever to be caught? That's true, isn't it?"

"It's only the clumsy who fail," I reminded her. I had a sudden vision of Fanny sleeving diamond brooches, pouching tiepins, regarding the whole affair as a reckless and thrilling game; just as she'd pitch every penny she possessed and perhaps even herself into the bargain, on a single throw. But I couldn't see her bungling so miserably that she would be hauled off to the basement and examined on suspicion.

Our conversation was interrupted by the arrival of Rose Paget, Bridie and Graham.

"I'm sorry," Rose apologized. "It was terribly rude—but I didn't notice the time . . . it was such a shock when Mr. Parkinson told us. We were so thrilled watching Norman."

Bridie was frowning. "I'm not altogether satisfied. I'd like to have another shot." He crumpled up a piece of bread-and-butter and ate it without, I think, realizing what it was.

"Why didn't you bring Fanny with you?" asked Lal.

"She was talking to Mr. Rubenstein," said Rose innocently.

Lal opened her mouth to speak, but at that moment Parkinson returned. He was a remarkable young man; in a couple of minutes the atmosphere was cool, witty and sparkling. I can't remember that he spoke of anything but the weather, the local golf course, a concert on the radio scheduled for that evening; but at once it seemed ridiculous to fret about Fanny spending a few minutes alone with Rubenstein or even to imagine that she wanted to steal Bridie from the girl whose eyes could never leave him, if he only went as far as the fireplace to knock the ash off his cigarette.

Fanny and Rubenstein didn't come down to tea. The rest of us finished at our leisure and moved as the spirit inclined us. Lal said something incoherent and went away. Rose said, "I have to start so early in the morning; I think I'll pack," and for the first time I realized what this week-end had done for her. I stayed by the fireplace; Graham went inquisitively into the dining-room that opened off the hall, and began valuing its contents. Bridie went off without a word and Parkinson returned to the library. I had the hall to myself.

I had been there some time, I think, reading fortunes in the coals and dreaming of Fanny, when I heard her voice ring out, low but unmistakable, from somewhere above me. There was a half-landing about a dozen stairs up from the hall, where was a deep window-seat and a window looking over the same view as could be had from the gallery. In the imperfect lighting of the place—for one of my memories of Plenders is of enormous rooms with little points of brilliance, powerless as candles to illumine those vast acres of gloom—it would be possible to pass up and down the stairs without realizing the presence of people in the alcove.

Fanny said, "Those are my terms, Norman," and he replied in his hard young voice, "I refuse to consider them, Fanny."

"Then it's stalemate," said Fanny.

"Don't think you've heard the last of this," Norman assured her.

There was the sound of feet on the stairs above the landing and then Lal rounded the corner.

"They're not in the gallery, either of them," she reported, her breath almost failing her for rage. "I don't know where they are. It's horrible. In this house. . . ."

"In Rubenstein's place," I told her, "I'd either get a legal separation or take a stick to you. You're abominable, Lal. I don't know where your husband is, but Fanny's talking to young Bridie. You can see the points of their cigarettes." I pointed upwards and she saw the twin glowing red tips through the shadows that thronged the house.

"If you can't have cake, eat bread-and-butter," paraphrased Lal viciously. "Why don't you do something about her yourself, Simon, since you're resolved to be a victim? Rose, poor child, is crying her eyes out upstairs, and Norman Bridie hasn't been able to string two words together all the afternoon. She's playing for safety, of course. Graham's her bread and butter and Graham's a rich man. If you ask me, he only came down here this week-end to keep an eye on Fanny."

There was a sound from the dark landing above us, and Bridie came down to join us. I thought he looked a bit fine-drawn, like a man who's just had a bad time and would die as soon as admit it. Fanny presumably went upstairs. We made the sort of three-cornered conversation that people do on such occasions and then Lal said something about Rose and disappeared, and Bridie and I were left together. I suppose the only interest we had in common was Fanny, and of her we couldn't very well talk. After a minute Bridie wandered into the smoking-room that opened off one side of the hall, and I followed him.

"It's going to be a filthy night," said Bridie, walking across to the window and looking out. "Fog's coming up." Rousing himself, he told me the story of a fog at sea in which he'd been involved; he told it economically and well, with that touch of individuality that marked all his work and gestures. "I've tried photography in fogs," he said. "You can get remarkably effective results. Half a dozen railings in front of one of those tall terrace houses you find all over London, the railings very thick, and a light behind a thin curtain just perceptible, and people moving like shadows. . . ."

From the hall outside I heard another voice—the voice of Parkinson, and it registered surprise. "Hullo, going off? What's up?" There was a mocking sound in the words.

Fanny wasn't easy to disconcert. She said, "I've had a call. I've got to go back tonight."

Instantly it seemed to me that all life, all excitement and romance, was departing from the house; my companions were as indistinguishable one from another as leaves on the same tree. The color and vitality of the world would be out in the black night with Fanny, who now stood by the fireplace in the hall, buttoning a long green ulster from throat to hem. She carried her hat in her hand.

"You can't go tonight," Bridie demurred. "Have you seen what it's like?"

"Sammy will drive me," said Fanny, who seemed to have shed any shred of conscience she had ever possessed.

"It's murder," said Bridie shortly.

Parkinson shrugged and moved on to the library. It wasn't for him to quarrel with his employer's whims. I came as far as the oval table on which the tea had been set and stopped. At that moment anger was my chief emotion. Here was Fanny with half the house in tatters—Lal and Bridie and Rose—oh, and myself, of course—and she didn't care a damn. She wasn't even upsetting the household out of devilment. It was just expediency.

"Finding the job of being Lal's confidante too much of a good thing?" asked Fanny lightly, drawing on a heavy gauntlet glove.

I said, "You're pretty rotten, aren't you, Fanny?"

She wasn't resentful; she waited for me to say more.

"Why do you want to spoil things between Bridie and Rose Paget?" I continued blindly. "It isn't as if you were proposing to marry the fellow."

"I am not," Fanny agreed.

"Then for decency's sake you might have left them alone. But you've never had much truck with decency.

31

If you were my wife, Fanny, I'd beat you. Will you, by the way? Be my wife, I mean?"

Fanny couldn't have been more startled by the words than I was myself. They hadn't been in my mind, or, I believed, in my imagination when I came into the hall. Nothing could be less like the kind of wife I'd intended taking, if indeed I married at all, than this electrical, untrustworthy, unattainable Fanny. Men of forty-eight want a little peace; marrying Fanny would be like importing a tempest into a walled garden. I'd as soon be married to an electric eel. Before Fanny could speak I had withdrawn the offer.

"I didn't mean that, of course," I said. "You wouldn't like it any better than I should."

Fanny stopped to light a cigarette, and over the tiny flame of the match her mocking eyes met mine with a brilliance that dazzled me.

" 'It's trouble enough to play with souls, And matter enough to save one's own,' " she quoted. "Suppose I'd said 'Yes' just then?"

"I'd have held you to it," I said recklessly, "and I should have had the sympathy of most people in this house, at least. And you wouldn't go back to town tonight."

Fanny laughed. "I'm not going to marry you, either," she said. "I arranged my life for myself years ago."

"And I don't fit into the scheme of things?"

"Nowhere, Simon darling. I wish Sammy would hurry."

"Is Rubenstein driving you back to town?" I demanded, aghast. "He'll break his neck. Have you seen the kind of night it is?"

"He's only going to take me as far as Kings Benyon. There's a six-twenty-eight from there."

"Which you won't catch," I warned her grimly.

"You obviously never went driving with Sammy. His idea of a nice comfortable speed is about eighty. He'll have to make it ninety, if he doesn't hurry, though."

"What about Lal?" I asked.

"For the first time in our acquaintance, she'll probably approve of me."

Parkinson came back saying, "Lal is just coming down. Are you sure you're wise?" He looked apprehensively at Fanny.

"Not a bit. But every gambler has his limits." She smiled. I admired the way she gave us absolutely nothing. I didn't know whether she'd had a genuine telephone-call or not. In any case, she had no intention of becoming involved in detailed explanations.

Then Lal came in. "What do you mean, Fanny?" she demanded. "Rupert says you're going up to town tonight."

"I've had a telephone call," said Fanny, still perfectly unmoved. "I ought to start."

Lal looked stubborn and incredulous. "I'm sorry. I couldn't foresee that. I've given Winton the evening off."

"That's all right. Sammy's going to drive me into Kings Benyon. He said we should catch the six-twenty-eight."

"Only by risking his neck. You certainly won't."

"Then we can go slow and catch the eight-three. It

33

isn't nearly such a good train and it means changing at Meadmore, and not getting back to town till eleven or after, but I must go by that if there's no alternative."

She was really intolerable, but Lal was no better. She stood beside the table, her eyes pits of fury. "Sammy will not drive you," she said. "I wouldn't let Sammy walk as far as the village on a night like this. It's murder to send any man into this weather. And he never could drive in the dark. If you must go, Rupert will take you."

Parkinson began a formal agreement, but at that moment Rubenstein came hurrying into the hall. He had a flat cap like a plate on his head and was wearing a double-breasted ulster. When he saw Lal he exclaimed, "Oh, there you are! I thought you were in your room. That woman of yours—Rita—said you were. Look here, Fanny's got to go back to town in a hurry, and I'm going to take her in to catch the six-twenty-eight. I shall be back before dinner."

"You're not going," said Lal woodenly. "You know you can't drive in the dark. You might kill the pair of you. Let Rupert drive her, if she must go."

Rubenstein was still pleasant; he shook his head and stooped towards Fanny's case. For all his money, he was a simple-minded fellow at heart, and was perpetually performing for himself small services for which he employed other people.

"Put that down, Sammy," cried Lal, and at her voice we all turned. She was like a woman in a masque; her face was chalk-white and her eyes blazed. She was as rigid as one of the Trojan women during the most magnificent moments of the play. "You will not take Fanny tonight," she continued.

That was the worst move she could have made. Rubenstein's face turned as white as her own; his eyes were as black as dark plums. It was years since I had seen a man so angry.

"We're going now," he said, and lifted the case. "If not, I shall certainly be late for dinner. It would mean hanging about in Kings Benyon until eight o'clock."

"Fanny would like that," said Lal softly. The scene was fantastic; none of us quite believed what we saw and heard. I once saw a fire spring up in the bush with the suddenness of a Maskelyne and Devant trick, and I stood watching it for some minutes before it occurred to me that there was reality—tragic reality at that. So this evening I stood staring from one woman to another, not actually accepting the truth, but rather like a man watching a melodrama from the stalls, interested to see the consequences. When they came, and we didn't have to wait long, they were so unexpected as to be ludicrous. Even Sammy didn't seem to understand them at first.

"If you take Fanny to the station tonight, Sammy, you needn't come back. Not probably that you meant to come back anyhow. Oh, I know you've no luggage, but in the circumstances that wouldn't trouble you."

All this time Fanny had stood in a remote silence. She looked the part of the theater-goer that I felt I was playing. I was reminded of what an American merchant had once said to me.

"Never allow yourself to feel insulted in business.

Let the other fellow say what he likes and when he's exhausted his spleen, get on with the job. You're not there to take compliments from the mouth but dough out of his pocket."

Rubenstein threw a glance over his shoulder. "Car ready, Rupert? Right. Then we'll go." He caught Fanny by the elbow. Lal dashed forward, catching Fanny by the arm. There was an instant of struggle: then, for the first time in his life using actual physical violence towards her, Rubenstein thrust his wife back and he and Fanny went out together.

I caught a glimpse of Lal's face as they went out of the door and I vanished up the stairs. The scene itself had been bad enough; the aftermath would be intolerable. Only, as I went round the curve of the staircase I stooped to pick up a half-burned cigarette, perhaps the one Fanny had been smoking while she talked to Bridie, and so I heard Lal say in a voice like a dying breath, "He's gone, he's really gone."

Parkinson said, "He'll be back before dinner. Would you like the bridge-tables out?" and busied himself with finding cards and scorers and drawing up chairs.

CHAPTER IV

Altogether it's very bad weather
And an unpleasant sort of a night.
INGOLDSBY LEGENDS.

THAT was one of the most anxious and disquieting
evenings I have ever spent. I didn't join the bridge
players; I said I had letters to write. I heard Graham
make the same excuse. About seven o'clock I came
down to find Parkinson, Bridie and Rose Paget playing
three-handed bridge. The sense of tension hadn't de-
creased and as I came into the hall they laid down
their cards.

"What's the time?" Bridie asked.

I said, "Seven o'clock. Rubenstein ought to be back
soon," for Kings Benyon was a bare half-hour's drive
from Plenders, which meant that if Fanny had caught
the six-twenty-eight, and from the expressions on their
faces I felt that both Rubenstein and she had intended
that she should, he should be back any minute. With
any one else you would have made allowances for the
weather, but Rubenstein in such a mood was beyond
caution or ordinary common sense. The card players
laid down their hands and stood up with an air of
relief.

Rose Paget said, "It must be nearly time to dress
for dinner. Where's Mrs. Rubenstein?"

Parkinson said shortly, "In her room. Her maid's with her, I expect. She lives for these situations. They're not only bread and butter to her, but meat and drink, too." He spoke with a certain dryness bred of experience. "She's Spanish, and despises Rubenstein for being not only an agnostic but a Jew into the bargain." He drew a deep breath. "God, those two women!" he muttered. He nodded abruptly to us and went off.

"Well," said Bridie equably, "if Rubenstein has any sense he won't attempt to get back tonight."

"Because of what Lal told him?" I asked.

"No, because of the weather. Just look at it." He crossed the room and jerked back a curtain. A fog had blown up from the sea, darkening a sky that was already deprived of stars; it would, we agreed, require more skill than Rubenstein possessed to maneuver the car round some of those greasy lanes and dangerous corners. I only hoped he'd have the sense to avoid the cliff road; it was supposed to be a short cut, but what with the landslides that had taken place there during recent storms, it wasn't likely to be a short cut to anything but Paradise, even to a good driver. And his best friend couldn't call Rubenstein that.

I left Bridie standing at the window and went upstairs; I heard a sound like a cat's pads and caught a glimpse of Graham moving in one of the corridors. In my own room I threw open the window and peered out. It wasn't possible to see much. I thought I heard the noise of a car, but it went by in the darkness and a little later I heard a motor-cycle chug past. I came down just before eight and found Parkinson shaking cocktails. His hair was tossed and there was a dead leaf on his shoulder.

"Lal's in no end of a stew," he said. "I've been down at the gate listening for a car. She's beginning to think he may have crashed. And," he added gloomily, "so he may."

"A car went by just now," I said, and he nodded. "I know. I spoke to the driver. An American tourist who'd lost his way in the fog. I bet he's cold." He poured out a cocktail and passed it to me. "I didn't dare ask him in for a drink with the weather what it is indoors. Lal says we won't wait. And God help the first man who mentions Rubenstein's name. This place is half-way to being a lunatic asylum already and by the morning we'll be lucky if it isn't a morgue."

The house felt like a mausoleum to me. That was partly the absence of Fanny, who for me would kindle brightness in the abode of the lost, but partly, too, that sense of unease occasioned by our position as guests of a man who had disappeared into the night and whose return seemed uncertain, and by the weather itself. I found myself thinking that Fanny was like the sun. You can live without it, but, my God, how you miss it.

Graham came down, fussily settling his tie, stared at me and Parkinson and said hurriedly, "Where's Rubenstein? Not back yet? Good gad, I hope he hasn't come to any harm. It's a crazy night. Still, he might have phoned. Yes, really he should have phoned. It's so inconsiderate." He took a cocktail and stood looking at it distrustfully.

"He may have had a breakdown," said Parkinson, giving me another drink.

"Or by taking Lal at her word," I chimed in.

Parkinson shook his head. "I don't believe he'd do that, whatever the circumstances. Not with guests of his own in the house. If you'd all come down at Lal's invitation it might be different. Still," he lifted his own glass, "you never can tell. This household, here or in London, is like a perpetual Guy Fawkes Day. You never can be sure when the next rocket will explode."

Bridie came down next, looking alert and business-like, and about as much troubled about his host's absence as a stray cat might have been. He took a cocktail, looked thoughtfully up the stairs, said, "Mrs. Rubenstein coming down? Or do we wait for Rubenstein? Oh, but surely he won't try and come back in such weather"; and then without giving any one a chance to answer, went on briskly, "What chance of my taking any photographs tomorrow morning before I clear out? I'm not altogether happy about today's experiment. But I ought to catch an early train."

Parkinson warned him dryly, "You'll have to wait for Rubenstein's permission. No one goes into that room without his knowledge and approval. Anyhow, I haven't got the keys. There's only one set, and he carries those about with him."

Bridie agreed and took up the Torquemada crossword. Rose Paget came down and said, "Is he back? No, thank you, I hate them"; this to Parkinson, who brought her a cocktail.

Graham turned back impatiently from the window. "I'll wager all I've got" (which showed you how moved he was) "that Rubenstein took that wife of his at her word, and he and Fanny are having dinner together tonight."

"Not on the sort of train that goes out from Kings Benyon on a Sunday evening in January," I assured him. "They'll be lucky if they find a refreshment-room open anywhere and get a brace of ham sandwiches."

Graham didn't care what they were eating; his mind seemed tormented with a vision of the two in intimate companionship. At that moment I think he wished he had Rubenstein's windpipe under his hands.

Parkinson came over and said, "Lal's just coming. For heaven's sake, try and prevent her talking about her husband throughout the meal. She's convinced he took her at her word and is probably lying under his car in a ditch somewhere."

"Of design?" I asked. "Surely she knows her husband better than that."

"She may be right," said Parkinson gloomily. "I wouldn't thank you for the chance of driving the car myself on such a night. The fog's like a blanket. And I say," he glanced round, lowering his voice, "do something about that girl, will you? She's getting steadily worse. Quite what the trouble is I don't know, but she looks as if she might go to pieces any minute."

At twenty minutes past eight, twenty minutes later than usual, Lal appeared in a magnificent white velvet gown. She had put diamonds in her hair, and there were diamond buckles on her shoes. She looked as if she were going to court.

"We won't wait for Sammy," she said. "If he has any sense he won't try and motor back."

We all refrained carefully from personalities during

41

the meal; Lal went straight back to her room, with the maid to sit with her, and, I thought grimly, to work her up into hysterics. She was a big dark creature, with a swarthy complexion. I had it on Lal's authority that she could work devastating havoc on the male servants and the tradespeople; personally I'd as soon try to caress a viper, but I had to admit she was a type that may be very successful in affairs of this kind. I pleaded an excuse and went upstairs. I had letters to attend to, I said. Rose was more honest. She said, "I've got a frightful headache and I'm going to bed." Bridie, Parkinson and Graham went along to the billiard-room. I could hear the click of the balls, but after a little while feet went past my door. I recognized that stealthy cat-like tread. That was Graham going to his room to torment himself afresh with visions of faithless, heartless Fanny. Parkinson came up to me presently. He said he'd left Bridie knocking the balls about by himself.

"This thing seems to be on every one's nerves," he said. "Bridie's as jumpy as a March hare, and I'd as soon look for feeling from one of his own cameras. It is queer, you know, that Rubenstein hasn't phoned. It does look as though . . ."

"He took Lal at her word?" I suggested as the fellow paused.

"No. I wish to heaven I could believe he had. I'm much more perturbed by the thought of him lying crumpled up somewhere in the dark. It's no use going to look for him; there are half a dozen tracks he may have taken. On the main road, if there'd been an accident, he'd be found by some one, and he has his name written in everything. I've seen Lal stitching the tabs into his pants. I don't know which, from her point of view, would be the better explanation. She's quite capable of murdering him if he did go up with Fanny; and of performing the same service for herself if he's done for on the roads. What a hell of a nuisance that girl is!"

I couldn't say a word in Fanny's defense. By this time my sympathy was all for the troubled house she'd left behind. Downstairs a clock struck eleven. Parkinson said, "I'd better go round with Benson now; lock up the place. He isn't likely to come at this hour. I'll sit up a bit longer myself. But Lal has the idea that the woods are full of thugs all waiting till she's asleep to empty their guns into her. There are enough bolts on these doors to protect the Crown Jewels."

I put down the pen with which I had been fiddling. "I agree with you," I told Parkinson. "It is a damned odd thing to do." Comment seemed futile, however. Parkinson, nodding briefly, went off on his job. Standing by the window, I could just see a shadow, equipped with a torch, make its way round the circular bed in the drive to the front gate. It stood there a moment, flashing the light this way and that, though it couldn't have been possible to see much. After about a minute he came back. It was Parkinson, still clinging to the hope that, after all, Rubenstein would turn up.

As he came into the house again, the ritual completed, I came down the stairs for a last whisky-and-soda. And Bridie, hearing our voices, joined us from the billiard-room.

"Does Mrs. Rubenstein say anything?" he asked laconically.

"We shall be lucky if we don't have her in a strait-waistcoat by morning," was Parkinson's cheering reply. "I went up to ask if she'd like me to ring up the police or the hospitals, in case of accidents. She was like a woman of glass. She opened the door of her room to me herself. That woman of hers has been playing her up all the evening. She's a malicious little devil, and she'd do anything to smash up the marriage. Rubenstein can't stand her, but Lal insists that she must have one companion in this land of her exile. Lal's face was per-fectly blank as she listened to what I had to say. She'd taken off the velvet frock and was wearing a dressing-gown. She must have been smoking solid ever since dinner. Her gown was gray with ash; the carpet was spattered with it. She said no. Sammy wasn't a fool, and he wouldn't thank us for making him one. Suppose it came out that he'd been off for the night with a girl, he wouldn't want the police making him a laughing-stock all over the country; and if there had been an accident we should have been notified. I had thought of telephoning the Kings Benyon hotels, but I doubt if it's any good. If he were there, I'm convinced he'd have let us know."

"He may have sent a wire from town," Bridie sug-gested, "and we haven't had it."

"In that case we shouldn't get it tonight at all. We're outside the postal area, and anyhow the nearest tele-graph station that could be open is at Kings Benyon."

"Wouldn't they telegraph it through?"

"Not so late. They're only open for two or three hours. All we can hope for is some message in the morning. I don't like Lal in her new part as Lot's wife. I'm feeling almost as jumpy as Miss Paget."

Graham's voice, like a demons' chorus downstage, suddenly broke in, "Is there no news yet?" and we all turned and assured him briefly that there was none.

"It's Fanny's fault," said Graham, his voice shaking. "She's a bitch, that girl. I ought to know."

Bridie knocked the ash off his cigarette. "Doesn't she give you a square deal, sir?" he asked, as silky as you please.

"If she does, it's only because she knows which way her bread is buttered."

Bridie shook his head. "There's more than that to it. There's something, a genuine artistic impulse—God knows where she gets it from. . . ."

I thought, "My God! The vanity of the fools. Fanny would cheat or lie to an archangel, if it suited her book." I put down my glass and went upstairs. As I passed Lal's room I saw that her light was still burning. Pausing for an instant to strike a match, I could hear the sound of her feet going up and down and to and fro, like a brooding panther, or the devil of Holy Writ, from the door to the wall and back again. I dare say that went on most of the night.

CHAPTER V

Be wary then; best safety lies in fear.
HAMLET.

I

I HAD a restless night myself. When I came down next morning I found Parkinson in the hall, sorting the post that had just arrived.

"Anything from Rubenstein?" I asked, but with no real hope.

Parkinson looked up. Insomnia seemed to have been contagious in the house during the past twelve hours. "What did you expect?" he asked.

I said nothing to that. It was ridiculous to say that he might have been compelled by the weather to spend the night at The Stag, Kings Benyon, because there was no excuse in that case for not letting us know his whereabouts.

"There's one thing," I suggested a bit uncertainly, "we could telephone Fanny and find out whether he traveled to town with her or no."

Parkinson looked at me with a pitying expression. "How well do you know that girl?" he asked. "Oh, there's no doubt she could tell us the truth, but she wouldn't if it didn't happen to suit her book. Ring her up by all means, but don't be sure that you're much further on when you have heard what she has to say."

That was a facer. I hated to acknowledge it, but the chap was right. Fanny wouldn't let a little thing like a lie stop her, if lies suited her book; besides, she had enough devil in her to pile on the suspense simply for Lal's sake. And if it came to taking sides, she'd certainly stand with Rubenstein, who mightn't be specially keen for any one to know exactly how he had spent the night.

"She'd like to keep Lal on the rack," I admitted, wondering how it was that I could see her so clearly and yet be totally unable to escape from her.

"Exactly," said Parkinson cynically. "Well then, what next? I don't mind admitting (*a*) that I'm anxious about Rubenstein, (*b*) that I'm not particularly keen on giving Miss Fanny Price an opportunity to make fools of us all, and (*c*) that I've no idea what to do next. I wonder if this sort of thing happened to my predecessor and if so, what he did."

"Who was he?" I asked.

"I never knew him, but I gather he came to a sticky end. Well, I don't blame him. This sort of thing is enough to wear any man's nerves to a frazzle. Here's Graham going about like a man who's seen a ghost, wondering, I dare say, if there's any chance of Rubenstein lying somewhere with a broken neck, and if so, what are his chances of buying up the collection for a song; and Miss Paget looking a wreck, while we shall probably need a strait-waistcoat for Lal if we hear nothing in the course of the next hour or two."

Some animal instinct, some indefinable urge towards self-preservation, made me turn my head, and I saw that Lal's Spanish maid was standing at the foot of the stairs watching us. I've seen similar gleams in the eyes of serpents, something peculiarly intense and malevolent. I didn't know how long she had been there or how much she had heard, but I felt selfishly relieved to think that it was Parkinson and not I who had to deal with that crazy pair. In fact, I felt so grateful that I was prepared to offer myself as escort to the sorrowful Rose, though I've never envied priests with their opportunities for hearing the griefs of women, and I thought, inevitably, that Fanny could break her heart, supposing she had one, and you'd never guess.

"Madam's letters," said Rita, coming forward.

Parkinson picked up a couple of envelopes and passed them over. Lal wasn't the type of woman who gets many letters. She never wrote if she could phone, and her friends were like her. Parkinson told me that sometimes he wondered how Rubenstein stood the sound of that modish white telephone in Lal's room ringing fourteen hours out of twenty-four.

"Ask Mrs. Rubenstein if I can see her for a few minutes," said Parkinson in an off-hand manner.

Rita said in reluctant tones, "Mrs. Rubenstein?"

"I've no instructions," said Parkinson briefly, and the woman, after one parting glance, went away. She wore native rope-soled shoes, which, I suppose, accounted for our not having heard her.

"There's a ray of sunshine for you to have about the house," observed the sorely-tried Parkinson. "I believe she suspects us of unmentionable practices and would like to see us all boiled in oil. How Lal manages to keep her with all the laws against foreigners, I don't know, but that woman's never been thwarted in her life."

"Does this kind of thing happen often?" I asked.

"Much too often for a man of my tastes. You know, in a way Lal rather enjoys a scene. I believe she'd enjoy it even more if Sammy were the kind who'd give her a black eye. But he never will; and he won't answer her in her own language either. One of these days she'll go too far, and there'll be a grand bust-up. By that time I shall be about ready for a strait-jacket myself."

He was sorting through the envelopes as he spoke. "What in heck I do now is beyond me," he confessed. "It isn't like Rubenstein to be out of the way when anything crucial's on. And these people," he tapped the envelope with his forefinger, "are at the parting of the ways. Rubenstein's heavily involved. It's a matter of something like a hundred and fifty thousand pounds, and something's got to be done one way or the other during the next twenty-four hours. He was going to see them this afternoon. Well, perhaps he'll keep the appointment without further reference to me. There's nothing to do but tarry my lord's leisure. If he doesn't turn up, it'll be proof positive so far as I'm concerned that something's wrong."

A door upstairs slammed and Bridie came down, his bag in his hand. He twitched his eyebrows at the sight of our serious faces, said to Parkinson, "Nothing to report? Looks bad, doesn't it. Look here, you won't want us hanging about with all this trouble, and anyway, I ought to get back on the 9.57. It's a pity about that photograph, but I can always come again if Rubenstein's keen. I'm up to my ears in chores this morning."

"What about some food?" asked Parkinson, his hand automatically reaching for the bell.

"I've had some coffee and stuff in my room, thanks very much. What about Mrs. Rubenstein?"

"I'll convey your messages," said Parkinson dryly. "I shouldn't suggest your trying to see her in person."

"I expect you're right. Well, I hope things turn out as you want 'em to." But you could see that the words were no more than a formula. By the time he reached town Bridie would have forgotten his host's existence in this or any other world. He might remember, regretfully, the photograph with which he wasn't satisfied, but Rubenstein, the man, would be dependent on his possessions, and his only value in Bridie's eyes would be those treasures he'd accumulated. I doubted if even the question of Rose Paget troubled him too much. As for Fanny, he didn't mention her name, and I still didn't know what had passed between the two, and whether that was the real reason for Fanny's sudden departure.

Winton, who had returned late the previous evening, drove Bridie down in the big Rolls. Rubenstein had taken the little Chrysler for Fanny, and, of course, it hadn't as yet returned. Winton hung about fishing for information.

"Mr. Rubenstein said he'd want me to take him over to Dunster this morning," he said.

"I don't know what Mr. Rubenstein's plans are," returned Parkinson. "If he does still want you for that purpose you shall hear."

Winton put another question and was as laconically answered, and the man sheered off, dissatisfied, not with the fact of the mystery, but with his own failure to elicit definite information. I heard a quick clatter of voices as he pushed open the service door at the bottom of the hall, and Winton's voice, surly with disappointment, hushing it.

"I might try his London flat. It's possible he went back there. And there's his club. He's always at one or the other when he's in town," he said.

But I could tell from his voice that he didn't anticipate getting news of Rubenstein from either source. Nor did he. At the flat the servant who answered the phone said that Mr. Rubenstein wasn't expected back till Monday night at earliest. Could he take a message, please? And what name?

"Thank heaven Traill didn't recognize my voice," remarked Parkinson, hanging up the receiver. "If there is some logical explanation, I don't want this story repeated all over London. Now for the club."

But the club hadn't heard of him for days.

"I'd better go up and see Lal, I think," decided Parkinson. "Look here, don't wait for me; go on and have some breakfast. I shall have to put in some telephone calls before I've time for anything else. If it gets round that Rubenstein has disappeared every kind of reason will be discovered except the true one. No one's going to believe that a flaming row with your wife, particularly a combustible creature like Lal, is going to make a man wreck his affairs. They're much more likely to think there's something dicky about the business, and that'll mean dizzy work on the Exchange. Rubenstein's honesty is regarded as being as safe as the Bank of England, but they'd never listen to our story. Fanny?

You try it on. Fanny would be an incident to them. They'd tell you that no man of Rubenstein's cash and social value takes chances for a girl like that. And I dare say they'd be right." He went off, exasperated, anxious, efficient as a dictator, and I set to work on bacon and kidneys.

He hadn't returned when Graham joined me, as yellow as a guinea and as jumpy as a hop-toad.

"No news?" he said. "My God, Curteis, this is serious."

I remarked with a coolness I was far from feeling that in my opinion we were all making heavy weather with very little justification.

"That's all you know about it," Graham squeaked. "Why, Rubenstein's one of those men you can set your clock by. And he wouldn't leave a parcel of his guests, most of whom scarcely know his wife, to be entertained by her and his secretary, if there weren't something pretty wrong. Has Parkinson thought of getting in touch with the police?"

I said I didn't know what he'd thought of, but he wasn't in touch with them yet. Then I asked what train he proposed to catch and he stammered vaguely about a Bradshaw and slow trains. I got hold of a time-table and pinned him down to travel by the 10.48. I didn't know what Rose Paget was doing; I thought we should make an odd trio. My one desire was to go round and see Fanny at once, and somehow shake the truth out of her.

Parkinson came back with messages from Lal and apologies for her absence. I told him the plan we had made for trains and asked about Miss Paget.

"She's staying for a bit. She's got a bad sick head-ache. We'll get her off after lunch. She won't be any trouble. She's just going to stay in bed. I'm to ring up Fanny," he added with a grimace. "Orders is orders, though I wish she had got some one else to do the job for her. What's Fanny likely to tell me?"

As it happened, he needn't have bothered about fram-ing his question. For though the bell rang for a long time there was no answer. Fanny, presumably, was already out.

Soon after that, Graham and I left together. I didn't see Lal, but happening to turn at the drive gate for a last glance of the house, I caught sight of the Spanish maid, Rita, standing at one of the windows, watching us go. The expression on that implacable dark face made my blood run cold. I'd rather—and mind you, I know what I'm talking about: I've been in countries where deadly snakes are as common as Dalmatian dogs in town—I'd rather, I thought, face one of them than such a woman if she'd made up her mind to do you a mischief.

II

As soon as I got to town I went round to Fanny's flat. There was no porter in the hall, and the house-keeper had a suite of rooms on the ground floor at the back. I went up to the second floor, up the drably-carpeted stairs with the dark-papered walls, the smooth banisters, greasy to the touch, past one imitation grained door after the next, thinking how dispirited an environ-ment was this for anything so flashing and vivid as our lovely Fanny. Never before had I felt the dreariness of the place; but then I had always come either with Fanny herself or in search of her, never with this weight of mingled wrath and anxiety in my heart. People who only knew the address thought what an expensive quarter of London Fanny lived in; it wasn't till you actually entered the building that you realized that the rents would be comparatively small. The accommodation was pretty second-class, but as Fanny once explained to me, "I never feed in the damned place, anyhow, and it's worth a lot to me to have a decent address."

I banged on Fanny's door, but I could get no reply. I waited a minute and knocked again, and, as if in response to my knock, the telephone began to ring. It rang and rang with that maddening reiteration of telephones that no one answers. I waited for it to die away, but every time that silence came down the voice at the other end must have pleaded with the exchange to have one more shot, for it would start again, cheerful and meaningless and enraging. At last, both it and I were silent, and I came down and hunted out the house-keeper.

Her name was Verity, and she was a solemn, troubled-looking woman with a brisk manner, and a habit of suddenly assuming an other-worldly expression that suggested that the manner in which the flats were conducted was no affair of hers.

"Miss Price?" she said. "Oh, yes. She was here this morning."

"She's out now," I said, trying to galvanize her into giving me a little spontaneous information.

"Oh, yes, she's out now," she agreed.

"Did she say when she was coming back?"

"No. No, she didn't. No, I don't suppose we'll be seeing her again."

"You mean she's gone?"

"Yes, she's gone. Bag *and* baggage."

That was an unexpected development, and for some reason it depressed me even more than Rubenstein's disappearance.

"Did she give any reason?" I asked on impulse. "I mean—I was expecting to see her."

Miss Verity laughed genteelly. "It doesn't do to expect anything where Miss Price is concerned," she told me. "She's one of these here-to-day-and-gone-to-morrow ones, I always say."

"She didn't leave an address?"

"She said she'd telephone for letters. Not that she has many. But that blessed bell of hers has been going all the morning."

I played for a minute with the crazy notion of renting the flat myself, so as to be on the premises if and when Fanny returned, but I abandoned that idea, as being about the most fatal thing I could do. There was nothing for me to stay for, and after a minute or two I cleared out. I did remember, though, to ask what time Fanny had arrived the night before.

Miss Verity clasped her hands and shook a smiling vacant head.

"I couldn't say, I'm sure. This is a block of modern flats, every up-to-date convenience, not a prison. Our tenants come and go *as* they please; no one spies on them. We don't even have a porter."

"Did you—did any one—see Miss Price last night?"

"I couldn't say, I'm sure. No, *I* didn't see her. P'raps some one met her on the stairs. P'raps she wasn't in last night at all. I couldn't say. All I know is she sent down a message at nine o'clock that she wouldn't be wanting the flat any more; paid a week instead of notice —they're furnished, these flats, see, and you take 'em by the week—nice for people up from the country or over from abroad—and out she went."

"By taxi, I.suppose?" I suggested a bit hopelessly.

Miss Verity giggled. "No one ever saw Miss Price walking on her own feet except it was up and down these stairs," she replied. "Yes, she went by taxi. But if you're going to question me like the police always do in the detective stories, and say did I know the driver, and was he my sister's son, and would I recognize him again—no, I would not. I did happen to see that she went in a taxi, but that was all."

In spite of her jibes, however, I followed the example of all the best amateurs and went round to the cab rank. The old man there told me that he believed he did remember a call coming from the flats, but he remembered nothing else. And in spite of all my efforts, I couldn't learn a thing. No one remembered Fanny at all, and I was forced to the conclusion either that the proper man wasn't on the rank or that she had, in her casual way, stood on the step and Providence had sent a cruising taxi for her convenience, the phone call from the flats being no more than coincidence. I left my name and address in case the man should return later, and went off to wait for further news. I half-expected to see the placards come out with great head-lines—MILLIONAIRE MISSING—but when I went into my club for a meal at midday there was nothing to be seen. I rang up Parkinson and asked for information from his end, but he had none. I told him about Fanny and heard his long dismayed whistle.

"That's not like her," he said. "Fanny gives you the impression of being the sort that enjoys facing the music. I should imagine no one likes a brass band better than she does. This is damned odd, Curteis."

I agreed shortly that it was. I didn't feel like discussing Fanny even with him. When I'd rung off I prowled about disconsolately. This sudden move of Fanny's troubled me more than I liked to admit, even to myself. If Rubenstein didn't put in an appearance soon or give us some idea of his continued existence I could see no alternative to putting the matter in the hands of the police. You wouldn't be able to help the thing leaking out anyhow. Rubenstein wasn't merely a marked man to connoisseurs—he was an exceedingly rich man, and rich men, like women, are always news. Parkinson had said as much. "I don't mind Mrs. Rubenstein in a paddy, but I'd gladly put a hundred miles between myself and the old man when he isn't pleased," he had added.

"He's only himself to blame," I had tried to console him, to which Parkinson said with a grim laugh, "If you'll pardon me saying so, you don't know quite so much about Rubenstein as I do. He always says that intelligence may be denied a man by Providence but discretion lies within the reach of us all."

I tried to explain to myself why Fanny should take such a sudden step, but even allowing for a volatile and impetuous nature I could find only one answer, and

57

that was that she was afraid. And the notion of Fanny driven out by fear made me shiver. I spent some time trying to think of any combination of circumstances that could defeat her. And taking her disappearance, without leaving a trace behind her, in conjunction with Rubenstein's, I felt myself grow cold with apprehension. But even at its worst, I had no notion of the long trail of tragedy and violence on which we were embarking or the deadful end of it all. Lal's undisciplined tongue had been, as the apostle observes somewhere, set on fire of hell. But neither she nor we had any idea of the furnace those spiteful words had kindled.

After my call to Parkinson, I left my club and walked about the city till it was dark. It's no use hanging about in the residential parts of London when you're as sick with anxiety as I was that day. Those remote picturesque squares Ernest Sheppard reproduces for *Punch* harbor heaven knows what resentments and breaking hearts; the city is a bustle of bright concrete activity. Stocks and shares are simple to understand; people are a mass of dismaying contradictions. I met one or two men I knew and stopped to talk to them, but all the time my thoughts were with Fanny. It didn't occur to me that, whatever her condition, she'd be tempted to do anything desperate. She isn't the sort to whom gas ovens hold out any promise of security.

Waking from a nightmare at about three the following morning I wondered, like a flash, if her disappearance had anything to do with the police.

CHAPTER VI

*There is a passion for hunting something deeply
implanted in the human breast.*
OLIVER TWIST.

PARKINSON rang me up next morning from town.
Lal had left Plenders late on Monday afternoon; there
was still no news of Rubenstein, and Parkinson was in
touch with the big commercial interest in which the
missing man was involved.

"If he doesn't climb out of his hidey-hole in the
course of a few hours, he'll find himself a lot poorer
than he expects," Parkinson added. "People are beginning to get nervous about rich men who vanish at
critical moments. I don't want to see the shares drop
about a dozen points, which is what certainly will
happen. It looks to me as though there's going to be
nothing for it but the police."

I asked about Lal. "Oh, she's made up her mind to
the worst possible. Rubenstein's dead and she's only
waiting to be notified. She's the widow all right.
Practically ordered her mourning and is wondering how
she can have Masses said for his soul, which wouldn't
please Rubenstein, who may not have been an ortho-
dox Jew, but who certainly didn't subscribe to her faith.
It's no use arguing with her, though I'd be grateful
enough if you'd have a try."

"What's the next step?" I inquired.

"Oh, the police. We can't avoid it any longer. I'm sorry because it will add to the current scare. But there are times when it pays to play for security, and if Rubenstein should eventually be found a moldering corpse somewhere, I don't want my career blasted by the suggestion that I suppressed the story until the last moment."

"What do you think yourself?" I asked, and he replied at once, "I think it's damned fishy, and I'm glad of the chance to pass on the responsibility. No news of Fanny, I suppose?"

I said "None," and put down the receiver, thinking how odd it was that two people, each individually so significant, should be able to disappear without a trace. I had the idea that wherever she went Fanny must blaze a trail behind her that would warn the world of her whereabouts. And yet she was gone and none of us had any idea where she was. Of course, in her case we weren't justified in going to the police, but they'd be on her track soon enough. She'd be the first person they'd want to question.

At first, naturally, the police didn't treat the affair as criminal; it was one more person missing from his home. They listened to Parkinson's story and they came to interview Lal, who sharpened their interest by dramatically declaring that she was convinced of his death, probably at his own hands, on account of her treatment of him. Already she had assumed the pose of the tragic murderess. The man in charge of the case, a little thick-set fellow called Burgess, with a blue dark-shaved jaw and the general appearance of a blue roan spaniel, except that his ears weren't so long, summed her up as the hysterical type and audibly wondered why Rubenstein hadn't planned a getaway before. When he heard that Fanny had vanished, too, he put two and two together, and made the handsomest four imaginable. Indeed, for some days no one took Rubenstein's disappearance seriously. Local hospitals and police stations were communicated with, and some local inquiries were made, but none of us were bothered with questions, and there were no headlines in the press. The local stationmaster said he knew the gentleman by sight and was convinced he hadn't taken a ticket on the Sunday evening; a porter and a ticket-collector corroborated the evidence. As a rule the 6.28 from Kings Benyon was a fairly full train on Sunday evenings, but the weather that week-end had driven people into the towns. All three men were convinced they would have recognized Rubenstein if they had seen him. The B.B.C. took their part on the fourth day and said, "Before the news this evening there is one police message: Missing from his home since Sunday...." The company to whom Rubenstein was a bulwark suffered a severe shock and the shares fell considerably. A mild panic arose but still nobody suggested anything but loss of memory, except for a few hazardous spirits who said darkly that there was more to this than met the eye, and wanted the police of other countries warned about the fellow. Meanwhile I kept in touch with Lal, who had fallen back upon her religion, to which hitherto she had sat pretty lightly, with the zest of an ogre devouring children. She and Rita were perpetually at Mass and Confession; they kept fasts and instituted a novena for Rubenstein's benefit. I heard all this from Parkinson, who was being driven half out of his mind by their lunacies.

I wish to goodness Rubenstein would give us an idea where he is or the police would get on with the job," he exclaimed to me. "I can't move backwards or forwards. There are things clamoring for Rubenstein's attention, and he never thought of giving Philpotts, his man of affairs, a power of attorney, so all I can do is sit by and see his money pouring down the drain. I can see three important investments at least he'd change if he were on the spot, but nobody seems to have the right to make a move for him. That's what convinces me something is definitely wrong. If he'd just gone off with Fanny he'd have wired instructions; he wasn't the type that puts a wench, even when it's Miss Price, above his securities."

The police meanwhile made the usual investigations in case of accident. No one turned up who remembered seeing the car, though two or three motorists had seen cars of an unspecified make on the road Rubenstein should have taken on the night in question. The notion that he might have tried to return by the dangerous cliff road was also mooted, but there had been such heavy landslides that no clews were visible, and it was thought too reckless to risk a man's life by making examinations from the cliff top. The Black Jack was a dour cliff overhanging black rocks, that were almost inaccessible even in good weather and quite impossible of approach in the gales that had been raging the whole week. Indeed few people could remember such a spell of storms; trees were blown down

in the parks and cars almost blown off the roads. Two
people were blown off the towing path into the river
near Richmond, and both were drowned; there was a
bad aëroplane crash and three people were killed by
falling slates. A big chimney came down in an East
End factory, luckily at night when no one was about,
but an army of men found themselves on short time
for several weeks afterwards. There were sundry mis-
haps on the high seas; a trawler went down with all
hands. Insurance companies were kept busy paying up
on policies. And on the eighth day the first actual clew
in the Rubenstein mystery came to light.

The police, by this time a little alarmed by Rubenstein's continued silence, had been impatiently biding
their time. They admitted from the first the possibility
that a car, traveling at a dangerous or even at a high
speed, along the surface of the cliffs in such weather,
might either pitch clean over the edge or be engulfed
in a landslide. There had been a number of dangerous
landslides in the neighborhood during the previous few
weeks, and dwellers in the district had been warned of
the danger of approaching the edge. But Rubenstein, a
comparative stranger to the district, might well not
realize this. And if a car did go over on that Sunday
night the subsequent falls of chalk and limestone would
obliterate all traces of the disaster. The cliffs at this
point overhung the rocks like a beetling eyebrow; and
all investigation would have to be made from the sea.
During the first week it was suicide to attempt to put
out from the shore, so for several days Lal and any one
else interested were kept in biting suspense wondering
if by some ghastly chance under those tons of fallen

soil lay all that was left of the enigma they had known as Sampson Rubenstein.

On the eighth day the wind dropped; in its place came clouds of rain, scurrying over a dirty sky; but even this change was welcomed. Anything was better than the destroying winds. The police sent out a boat to reconnoiter, and what they could discover from the ocean itself was enough to send them gingerly investigating at the actual cliff foot. What they found was the unmistakable remnants of a car. Digging out the remains was a dangerous job, but they tackled it. An authority, summoned for the purpose, gave it as his opinion that no further landslide would take place so long as the gale abated; and after a good deal of perilous digging the police's men uncovered a car that unquestionably was the one in which Rubenstein left the house on the night of Sunday, January the 6th. The car itself was smashed like an eggshell, but the number plate was undamaged.

I asked Parkinson if they'd found any trace of Rubenstein. "It makes you feel a bit sick to think of the poor devil lying all those days crushed under that weight of soil," I said. "Worse still, you can't be sure he'd be killed outright by the fall. He may have lain there till morning and heard the roaring of the approaching avalanche. It's a beastly thought."

"They've found nothing," said Parkinson blankly. "They're still digging, though. They haven't uncovered the complete car yet. And of course he may have jumped when he felt the car topple. Not that he'd stand an earthly anyhow. Pretty ghastly, isn't it?"

"How is Lal?" I asked.

"I never saw a woman make a worse impression on the police. She broke into hysterics, made them a present of her feelings for the poor devil. Burgess looked as though he'd like to vomit, and he can't be without experience."

"Can any one suggest why in such weather he came back by the cliffs?" I wondered.

"Sheer devilry, I suppose. The long road isn't very pleasant on such a night. And when he really is in a rage you can't hold him. I'd be sorry for the archangel that tried. I've known him work off his temper by taking quite unjustifiable risks in speculation. She gave him a rotten time, you know; and she really did matter to him. I know people wonder why, but he had all the family sense of his race, and he'd married latish in life for the sort of reason that drives men into matrimony in the early twenties. He didn't know much about women, if you ask me," added Parkinson. "I think he had the idea that sooner or later she'd conform to his notion of a wife. And of course she could no more see eye to eye with him than the man in the moon. Pity of it was she really did care, but she chose this odd way of showing it."

"If this were the whole mystery it would be bad enough," I said, "but it isn't. I still can't fit Fanny into the picture. Why at this critical moment should she clear out, leaving no trace? I had thought for a minute that the car might have been going into Kings Benyon, not returning, and they might both have gone over, but we know Fanny was alive on the Monday morning. I can't believe that in the event of an accident from which she was skillful enough to jump clear, she'd vanish into space and leave us to solve the mystery as best we could. But you can't take her out of the picture. She fits in somewhere."

Parkinson considered. "She may have had a hell of a row with the old man and then when they crashed, been afraid of a murder charge. But no, that doesn't hold water either. Fanny might do a lot of questionable things, but that isn't one of them. No, you're right, she may be our missing link. According to Philpotts, we can't presuppose death until we've got at least a bit of a corpse or get the permission of the courts to act; and that isn't done in a day. Lal is dying to get back to her beloved Spain where she can walk about in ample black and do penance for the rest of her days. She doesn't seem to be able to take it in when I warn her she won't be so rich as she's been accustomed to. She has no sense of money, that woman. I suppose there's nothing for it but to wait. The police are really getting going after Fanny now."

They might be, but they didn't find her. They didn't find Rubenstein either. After four days of careful digging, hindered by a further fall of soil, in spite of the expert's opinion, the police managed to uncover the wrecked car. It wasn't possible at this stage to move it away bodily, so innumerable photographs were taken of it from every angle, and pictures of the whole of the cliff face, both from the surface and from the rocks. They took some fairly reckless chances examining the face of the cliff higher up, in case he had jumped and the body had got caught on a ledge, but, of course, they found nothing. If he had jumped he'd have got swept down by the subsequent landslides.

"As a matter of fact, the odds are he would have made a leap if he felt the car rock under him. He always had his wits about him. But he wouldn't stand a chance, and anything that's left of him, after landing on those rocks," Parkinson shuddered, "has long ago been swept out to sea. Goodness knows when, if ever, you're likely to recover a body in such circumstances, or how much value it would be to you if you did. What hope has any one got of recognizing it, after the rocks and the sea have done their bit? To say nothing of the beastly creatures of the deep."

Meanwhile, of course, it wasn't possible to hold an inquest, and Parkinson was involved in maddening legal quibbles. He wasn't free to make other arrangements and there seemed to be a quite ridiculous amount of trouble about such trifles as the payment of his salary, which fell due on the 14th of the month, and the settlements of domestic accounts. What with the law, the police and Lal, I didn't envy the fellow.

"I'm trying to find out from Philpotts how long it will be before we're allowed to presume death," he confided to me. "This is playing merry hell with my affairs. I've got the offer of a peach of a job from a fellow who's going to America in less than a month, but I can't expect him to keep it open for me indefinitely, and I don't like to leave Lal stranded. She's been very good to me."

I asked if she had any plans, and he said, "Oh, she'll go back to her beloved Spain if she can. She's been at him to leave London ever since they were married."

"That means disposing of the flat and Plenders.

Surely you can leave that job to Philpotts? That's what lawyers are for."

"The flat will go easily enough. Plenders is a different proposition. Besides, I don't know what to do about the furniture. A lot of it's valuable, though Lal would sell it up to any junk merchant just to get rid of the stuff. She's always been a bit resentful of his preoccupation with his business. I don't see why Graham or any other vulture of his ilk should walk in and buy up the goods for a song, and sell them back to transatlantic millionaires at a hundred and fifty per cent. profit. Anyway, there's the Chinese room. I don't want to see that collection broken up."

"Has Rubenstein left no instructions in his will about that?"

"I haven't seen the will. Philpotts has it, and he won't move a step until he has a definite verdict. He's waiting for the police to move first. I think he imagines that Rubenstein is hiding somewhere in West Kensington or Clapham Common, enjoying this stink like hell."

Like me, he didn't by this time believe there was a chance of the fellow being alive.

"And still nothing from Fanny?" he went on.

I said I'd heard nothing.

"That's a mystery about as big as the other," he continued with a frown. "Of course, she may be sick." He said it in the voice in which a man says, "Of course, that sparrow may hatch out a roc."

"She couldn't have left the flats because she was sick," I pointed out, and my voice was as heavy as my heart.

"That's true. And you can depend upon it she had

some reason. How easy it is to disappear. Fanny's left the picture as completely as the vanishing lady of my childhood days at the St. George's Hall. In a way she's almost more of a mystery than Rubenstein, who may, poor devil, still be buried so deep in all that falling muck that they haven't uncovered him yet. There was another slide last night, by the way, rather a bad one. It's definitely dangerous to go on digging at present, and besides," he shrugged but his face was white, "I doubt if he'd be recognizable after all this time. One smashed lot of bloody bones must look very like another."

H turned away and hunched himself against the mantelshelf, with his shoulders against the carved deer and young women in bedgowns who sported among scrolls designed by the Adams brothers for better men, that now ignored their labors.

CHAPTER VII

Good wishes to the corpse.
QUALITY STREET.

IN addition to his other chores Parkinson was doing his best to scotch the persistent rumor that Rubenstein had engineered his own disappearance in order to avoid possible conviction for fraud in connection with the ———— Mining Company, of which he was director and a large shareholder. There was no evidence to support this, and Parkinson was at his wit's end to rebut the accusation until something happened to shut the mouths of all the panic-stricken busybodies concerned. This was the appearance of a boot that was washed up on the rocks some distance from Black Jack and was taken to the police as having a possible connection with the Rubenstein mystery. It was sodden with water and had lost much of its shape, but even so it was easy to see that it was small, beautifully-made, hand-stitched and obviously fitted for the foot that had once worn it. The makers' name, Russells, was clearly stamped in it. And Russells identified it without hesitation as one of a pair they had made some months earlier for Rubenstein.

"This puts on the lid, I fancy," said Parkinson, with a sigh of relief. I was relieved, too, more than I cared to say. "They can't argue that the boot walked off the cliffs of its own accord. Perhaps this'll stop some of the foul-mouthed comments that have been thrown at the poor chap during the past fortnight. And thank God, so far as I'm concerned, it means the end of Lal. She's through the disconsolate widow stage, and being a murderess by proxy hasn't proved very entertaining after all; so now she's the *femme fatale,* the woman men can't resist. Well, let her play that rôle in Spain. It'll suit her better there."

He spoke with a certain hard brutality, and I saw suddenly another aspect to the case. Lal was just the type to play Potiphar's wife; I agreed with Parkinson that the sooner he got shut of that connection the better.

But still Philpotts hesitated until on the 16th day after the discovery of the car we got what seemed to be the last link in the chain of evidence. The police came to see Parkinson for about the hundred and for-tieth time with the information that a body had been washed up about a mile below Black Jack, a body pretty badly mutilated but roughly corresponding in build to that of the missing man. The work of the tides dur-ing that stormy time and the persistent dashing against rocks that it had endured had made the corpse as beastly a sight as ever I saw even on a battlefield. It was generally agreed that Lal shouldn't be allowed to see it. The usual methods of identification were im-possible to apply. We couldn't examine the teeth be-cause, though an expert said the deceased had, he thought, worn false teeth, these were missing from the mouth; indeed, most of the mouth was missing. The face was a horrible sight, a kind of blur of features, all swollen and rotted on the bones. 'You can't, unhappily, at present identify a face by the skull, though that may come in time. And the usual birthmarks that help a man to speak definitely were so much damaged by the prolonged tossing and crushing and wounding the body had received that they simply didn't exist. One of the feet was missing, washed off by the action of the water, and the skull was crushed, probably, said the police surgeon, after death. The rocks would account for that all right. Or he might have drifted against a buoy. To identify such a find, I thought, must be a practical impossibility; you could only guess and hope you were lucky.

"It may be the man in the moon for all we know," agreed Parkinson. "All we can say is that the foot that's left is approximately the size of Rubinstein's, and that's a pretty poor way of identifying a man." The action of the water had stripped the body of clothes, and there was precious little likelihood that these would now be washed ashore, and on this very unsatisfactory evidence the local coroner, a man called Walpole, sat with a jury of seven to decide (a) the identity of the deceased, and (b) the manner of his death. You hear a lot about the age of miracles being past, but what else, if it wasn't a miracle, that coroner expected of his seven locals, I can't imagine.

I was spending the night at Kings Benyon, less because I was personally concerned in Rubenstein's death —I hadn't even been badgered by the police—than because Lal asked me to be there on her account.

"I couldn't come," she whispered, "and Rupert says it would be wrong, anyhow. But you know what people are like. To them one body found drowned is just like another. And poor Rupert's beginning to feel the strain so. It would be nice for him to have some one there."

Parkinson was coming down in the morning, and at about six o'clock the night before the inquest I had a wire from Bridie telling me he also proposed to attend, and would arrive for supper at eight.

"I suppose you wonder why my interest in this affair should suddenly be resurrected," he observed grimly. The shadows round his eyes were as heavy as soot, and he wanted a shave. "But this time Fanny can't escape. They're bound to ask again and again why she's disappeared."

"Does any one know?" I asked, and he nodded.

"I do. I had a letter from her the next day. It came during the afternoon."

I stared at him incredulously. "You've had that information all the time and you never came forward?"

"I couldn't have helped. She didn't tell me what she was going to do."

"But—she wrote."

Bridie stubbed out a cigarette savagely. "I'd better explain. I wanted her to marry me, you know, and she wouldn't. She didn't tell me why; it wasn't that she couldn't stand the sight of me—but she wouldn't. She'd have done the other thing, but that kind of mess has never appealed to me. I don't see that you're any freer to chuck a woman you're sick of because you don't happen to have gone to church with her. Besides, I shouldn't have got sick of Fanny. The boot would have been on the other leg."

"Would she stop with any man she was tired of, marriage or no marriage?" I asked doubtfully.

"Fanny's a queer creature. I remember we were discussing that murder case, the Kent one, Appleton; you recall that the fellow was betrayed by his wife to the police. He'd treated her abominably, and this was her chance of getting out of his clutches. It was a perfectly reasonable argument, but Fanny couldn't see it. She said, whatever the man had done, the woman should have stuck to him. She could have cleared out, she said, but she had no right to side with the community against him. Oh, there's no logic about Fanny, but there's something irresistible about her. If you could get her to marry you she'd never sell you. The difficulty is," he lighted another cigarette, "to get her to agree to the first step."

"And that's why she cleared out?" I was still a bit hazy.

"From Plenders? I gather so."

"I meant from London."

"She doesn't say definitely, simply that she's going away for a bit."

"With no reason at all?"

"In the light of her letter one understands her action."

"You'll be asked what was in the letter."

"My memory can be very inconvenient. I'll tell you this, Curteis, that letter dealt with purely personal matters; it didn't mention Rubenstein, it was nothing to do with Rubenstein. I've waited till the last minute to speak of it. I'm not going to speak of it in the court tomorrow if it can be avoided. There are going to be about forty reporters there, and a queue of interested hangers-on three deep down to the quayside. The vulture's a sedate and gentlemanly beast compared

74

with the human mob on grisly occasions like these."

The chops came in and we ate those and talked of this and that. But we couldn't keep off Fanny for long.

"I wish I knew where she was," Bridie admitted. "She may be hard-boiled, but this jam may be a bit tougher than even she allows for."

"I wish I had her here at this instant," I returned unsympathetically. "I'd grill her."

The door opened and Fanny came in. It was like something in a mime play. We both stood up and stared, and neither of us spoke. We might have been seeing a ghost. It was a wild and pouring night, and Fanny's golden helmet of hair glittered with the rain. She pulled off a fur coat and dropped it on a chair.

"Will you buy me a drink, Simon?" she asked me. "I haven't any money."

But it was Bridie who pressed the bell and gave the order. My senses were still whirling with the shock of her appearance. For that first minute I didn't even ask questions. I accepted her, delighting in her mere presence. I had forgotten what a radiant creature she was, even on such a night and in such a situation.

Bridie may have been as impressed as I was, but he didn't allow his feelings to betray themselves. Having ordered her a hot whisky and water, and told the waiter, in spite of Fanny's disclaimers, to bring another chop, he observed with a kind of malicious admiration, "Dramatic sense of values you've got, haven't you, Fanny? Lying low till you see your name in all the headlines, and then putting in a miraculous appearance at the eleventh hour."

Said Fanny casually, pulling off her drenched beret, "I didn't know. I've been ill."

"So ill you haven't even heard Rubenstein was dead?"

"Is he? I heard he'd disappeared and they'd found a body."

"By this time tomorrow the jury will have instructed us as to whether it's his or not. Till then we may honorably doubt. You haven't got him concealed anywhere, I suppose, in this mysterious place where you've been hiding?"

"I've been in bed in Paris," said Fanny. "And even you, for all your wit, can hardly suppose that's the kind of place where you'd find Sammy. Though I dare say Lal would crack half a dozen splendid jokes on the subject."

"You've been ill?" I interrupted quickly, but Bridie wouldn't let me talk.

"It's kind of you to turn up at all," he acknowledged, "and it's relieved me of the responsibility of finding some suitable explanation to offer the court for your prolonged disappearance; and why you chose to travel to Paris in a gale enough to blow the ship sideways."

"I went to Paris to get away from you," retorted Fanny without heat. "And it was the gale that gave me pneumonia. I ought to be in bed now. I dare say I soon shall be."

"Your last, if the bit about pneumonia's true," Bridie agreed. "Did you come down here to give evidence? To help the law? Really?"

"Really," said Fanny. She was haggard and exhausted, but even in this mood the light of her unforgettable personality flashed in her colorless face and slack limbs. "I seem to be the last person who admits to seeing him. He may have met some one else on his way back from Kings Benyon, but no one's come forward and anyhow, who goes for a nice walk in a fog?"

"Which is why you expect a rank bad driver to take you twenty miles in one for a whim." Bridie's voice was acrid with bitterness. I wondered more than ever what was in her letter; I thought I could guess a good deal. No, Lal was right. Those two could never make a match of it. There was the harsh core of intolerance in Bridie that you find in most artists; he might not stop loving Fanny but he wouldn't stop resenting her either, and that's no basis for happiness.

"We shall be in the news tomorrow, Curteis," the fellow went on, turning to me. "I hope you've had a nice picture taken of yourself lately. The crowd will christen us Maskelyne and Devant, popping the rabbit out of the hat, after we've assured every one it was empty. And ye gods, what a rabbit!"

He regarded Fanny with critical malice. He couldn't forgive her for being what she was and at the same time enslaving him so that he couldn't forget her either.

"If any one expects me to be able to help, they're mistaken," remarked Fanny, sipping hot whisky and water. "He said good-by to me in no end of a hurry at the mouth of Kings Benyon—you know that road that widens into the market square with the station at the further end? We were held up there—there'd been a traffic accident—and I was so afraid of losing the train, and Sammy was in such a stinking temper I only wanted to get away from him. He was just as keen as I was; he slammed the door of the car almost before I was out of it, and I wrenched myself off the step and ran like a hare. I caught the train by the skin of my teeth, and that's the end of my evidence."

"You'll be asked what he said to you in the car. Do you think he was contemplating suicide?"

"Of course he wasn't. Only fools and cowards kill themselves. Sammy was neither. Besides, he really thought the earth of Lal—God knows why. If I'd realized he was missing, I could have told them to look by the Black Jack."

"Why?·Did he say he was coming back that way?"

"He wanted to take me that way. I told him I'd jump out of the car and risk a broken leg first. I don't think he'd have cared at that minute if the whole shoot had gone into the sea. As it appears to have done. What does Lal think about it?"

"She told the police she was responsible for his death . . ." I began.

"She would," said Fanny viciously. "And probably the first time she's told the truth for years. She was devilish to him."

"He doesn't seem to have had much luck with his women," Bridie agreed. "By the way, if you're thinking of telling any particular story as to why you went to Paris, perhaps you'd instruct me first. I always approve of sympathetic witnesses telling the same truth."

"I had an invitation unexpectedly from friends, and a chance of work," said Fanny glibly. "That's gospel. But thank you for warning me. Oh, is this my chop?" She got up and I drew out a chair for her.

"The police may suggest other reasons," said Bridie.

"They can have 'em. There was you, for instance. And you." She turned and blinked at me like a great tawny cat.

"You didn't have to worry about me," said Bridie. "London's large enough for the pair of us."

"I have a point of view too, though."

"And what brought you back?"

"The news about Sammy. A girl who was looking after me told me. Is it true? Is he dead?"

"I've told you we're going to learn that officially at tomorrow's inquest. What about phoning the police?"

"What for?" asked Fanny.

"You weren't thinking of walking into the inquest tomorrow as inconsequentially as you walked in here tonight? You, after all, are the principal witness."

"We'll get Burgess to come up here," I said hurriedly. "Fanny's in no state to walk down to the station. The landlord'll give us a room."

"And be glad of the chance," amplified Bridie. "You're a gift to him, Fanny. It's nice you should do some poor devil good."

Burgess came along within a few minutes of our call. His manner to Fanny was civil, but that's the most you could say of it. He scarcely attempted to conceal his hostility. He kept on asking her why she hadn't let the police know where she was.

"I tell you, I was ill. I probably shouldn't have known Rubenstein's name if I'd heard it. I can give you the doctor's address—or, look here," she dived into her flat scarlet leather bag, "there's his receipted bill. Now you can get in touch with him. And here's the address of the house I stayed at; you can cable the landlady."

"And your friend's address?"

Fanny gave that, too. Then Burgess put her through a long questioning as to her motive for going to Paris. Fanny repeated the story she'd told us.

"You had obligations in London," said Burgess, who seemed to have provided himself with every available scrap of information.

"You can get back from Paris between lunch and tea," said Fanny. "I couldn't know I was going to have pneumonia. And there was plenty of work for me in Paris, only, as it happened, I didn't do any. It wasn't till my friend said, 'I suppose you know the English police are combing the country for you,' that I knew anything had gone wrong. She brought me papers. And I came over."

He kept her some time longer but he got nothing more out of her.

"I wish you'd been more discreet," I told Fanny, after she'd sent him away with a flea in his ear. "That man could make things very unpleasant for you!"

"Even the police can't invent a situation that doesn't exist," Fanny expostulated. "Sammy's about the only man I know who's never attempted to make love to me. Only a fool like Lal would think it likely. That woman's a devil, Simon. Did you know Sammy once had a cat he was devoted to? She made him get rid of it. She said it smelt. But it wasn't that. Only—the cat was a female. Like the story of the convent of nuns and the pet lamb that was a male. It's all pretty beastly."

She leaned back and shut her eyes. Now that she was still, all her radiance was shut off, like an electric current when you press a switch. It was like seeing a wax model of her lying in the chair. But sympathetic though I assured myself I was for her weariness, I couldn't leave her alone. Bridie went upstairs, leaving us together, and no sooner had the door shut behind him than I surprised both of us by saying, "Fanny, tell me the truth. Why did you go to Paris?"

Fanny opened her eyes. "Because I was sick of you all," she said, "sick to death."

I asked no more questions. Her voice was convincing in its weary passion. The memory of her lovely, disturbing, unhappy face remained with me throughout a sleepless night.

The coroner was a man of sense. He had no intention of allowing his inquest to degenerate into a publicity stunt. He crushed a juror who seemed to suggest dark motives behind Rubenstein's death—because it was obvious from the start that the jury meant this to be the body of Rubenstein.

"It's the old Chestertonian theory," whispered Parkinson to me. "You find in life what you expect to find. You don't look for hamadryads in the side-board or murders in postmen's uniforms. Rubenstein's car fell into the sea—ergo Rubenstein fell with it. A body has been washed up from the sea—ergo, it is Rubenstein's corpse."

The affair took very much less time than any of us had anticipated and from the newspaper point of view was disappointing.

Evidence was called to show that Rubenstein had been in a reckless mood when he left the house, which would account for his mad attempt to return by the cliff road. Fanny was called, but the question of her absence only lightly touched upon. Her explanation was accepted at once, and her story of the journey to Kings Benyon called for little examination. The result was obvious from the start. Rubenstein had been a fool and had paid a heavy price in consequence. It wasn't for the coroner or the jury to blame any one. Domestic brawls weren't suitable subjects for open debate, unless a criminal charge was involved. People might take Lal at her own valuation and consider her morally guilty; they might cast sly looks at Fanny, who, her color returned to her smooth cheeks, made no show of emotion. But the verdict was "Found Drowned" with no suggestion of suicide. There was a quantity of water in the lungs, though the state of decomposition made it difficult to speak with certainty of the precise manner of death. The fall from the cliff surface might have been sufficient in itself.

"Well, I'm glad for Parkinson's sake," remarked Bridie, as we came away. "He doesn't want to be kept hanging about for this wretched affair for the next three months. And I dare say it won't matter to Rubenstein that some one he probably never set eyes on lies in his grave."

"What do you mean?" I exclaimed, a bit alarmed. "We can't prove anything."

"I beg your pardon," retorted Bridie. "We can't prove who that poor devil was. But we do know it isn't Rubenstein. Did you notice the foot that hadn't been pulped off by the water? It was swollen, I grant you; it wasn't a very pleasant sight, but that man didn't have his boots made for him at Russells. He wore ready-mades and cheap ready-mades at that. The foot was mis-shaped and calloused like the feet of nearly all working men and people in a small way. I ought to know. I'm an authority on the subject. I can get the most magnificent models so far as, the head and torso are concerned, but when it comes to the feet, time after time they're cramped, ill-used, crooked—and generally the boots are to blame. But as I say, it's of no matter. Probably Rubenstein did go over the cliff and is lying where he won't be recovered until the sea gives up its dead."

He and Fanny went off together. I wondered at her wisdom in having him as her sole companion, but she threw cold water on my well-meant efforts to preserve her from embarrassment.

"So far as Norman is concerned I'm a mirage, something he believed for a little while he saw, but now recognizes as a delusion," she told me. "By this time next year he'll have shelved me altogether in his mind and when he's suitably married, as eventually, of course, he will be, he'll talk about green slickness if my name's ever mentioned. As for me, oh, I can take care of myself."

So they departed to town together, and I stayed a little longer with Parkinson in Kings Benyon, where he, poor wretch, had to arrange to have the battered remains coffined and brought up to town, where Lal proposed to have them interred at Kensal Green with all the ceremony available.

At her invitation I attended the funeral. The day streamed with rain, and we stood in that distressing welter of monumental achievement — headstones,

crosses, broken pillars, anchors, marble angels and re-
cumbent cherubs, while a priest intoned the burial
service and, to the tune of "Now the Laborer's Task Is
O'er" we committed to the earth the body of a man
whose name none of us knows to this day.

CHAPTER VIII

Glory's blood relation,
bastard murder.
MACBETH.

I

THE day after the funeral Parkinson rang me up to
say, "I've seen the will at last. Philpotts can deal with
most of it. But Rubenstein, I'm thankful to say, left
the Chinese collection to the British Museum. They're
sending a lad down to go round and make lists, and
I shall have to be down there for form's sake. Philpotts is a good chap but he knows less about Chinese
art than I do of darning socks."

I said, "Has Graham heard?" and he said, "I don't
know. It doesn't matter anyway. If Rubenstein hadn't
done this, the house might have been shut for months.
Lal has conceived the idea of regarding it as a shrine,
a sort of second Fotheringay, with herself for the most
devout of Scottish Catholics. Once this little job's done,
I'm free. I've wired to Sandeman that I can sail next
week."

But he didn't.

Unexpectedly I was with the party when the gentleman from the British Museum, whose name was ap-
propriately Tester, made his rounds. Lal had asked me
as a last favor to go down. "Rupert is so worried up

about this new position of his he can't spare any time for Sammy's affairs," she declared. "And I don't feel I can visit the place again, not at present, anyway. But I don't trust these experts. Sammy did, and I expect they cheated him over and over again. I can't prevent their having the contents of the Chinese room, but I want to make sure they don't go anywhere else in the house."

You might have thought Philpotts would be enough to guard her interests, but Lal liked all the ceremonial she could get. And since Fanny was keeping out of my way and refusing my invitations, and London was like a desert without her, I agreed to Lal's suggestion and went down to Plenders with the others.

A rather ridiculous embarrassment arose at the moment of our arrival. No one had been near Plenders since the morning following Rubenstein's disappearance, and though Parkinson had the keys of the front door and the living-rooms, it hadn't occurred to any of us, until this moment, that the only keys belonging to the Chinese room had been on Rubenstein's key-ring and were at this moment presumably at the bottom of the sea. The door shut automatically, but from the outside could only be opened by a key. Parkinson went off for a locksmith and Philpotts and I talked together, while the man from the British Museum prowled about the hall examining the musum pieces with which Rubenstein had furnished it.

"If you have any influence with Mrs. Rubenstein," said Philpotts, who clearly hadn't, "it would be a kindness if you could make her see that her continued

86

slanders against Miss Price will land her for heavy damages if that lady chooses to bring a case."

"I don't suppose she will," I said. I could see Fanny making money in quite a lot of rather disreputable ways, but not this one, which would be quite legitimate. She wasn't spiteful.

"I think Mrs. Rubenstein regards Miss Price as partly responsible for her husband's death," I murmured ungrammatically.

"That," said Philpotts, speaking like a lawyer on the stage, whom indeed, with his thick, curling, gray hair, his stock and his diamond pin, he greatly resembled, "is absurd. If any one is responsible, it appears to be the poor lady herself. In any case, accusations are now quite out of place." Having opened the ball with personalities, it seemed ridiculous to sink to comments on the weather and we hung about rather uncomfortably until Parkinson's return with a locksmith from the village. It was a dank day in February, and a miasma seemed to hang about the whole house and to be concentrated on the locked gallery. The lock was an intricate one and took some time to force; the man from the British Museum looked several times at his watch in a meaning manner. When at last the door was flung open it released an atmosphere of decay that affected me very unpleasantly. The tapestries over the front window blotted out the light from that end of the gallery and only a steady sheet of half-hearted rain could be seen through the tall window overlooking the lawns. In that ghostly gloom the wax figures were endowed with a curious new life. I am not an imaginative man, but I could have sworn that more than one inscrutable Chinese head turned to watch our movements; there was a rustle of silk, a swaying of garments, a general air of malevolence that I found overpowering.

Philpotts seemed similarly affected. Parkinson said, "Give you the creeps, don't they, in this light?" The gentleman from the British Museum afforded us a little satisfaction by being obviously astounded at the wealth and rarity of the collection. He began to go slowly from group to group, stooping to examine the robes, consulting a small book he carried, making notes. Once he turned to us to say, "Gentlemen, I had no notion— this will indeed be a valuable acquisition. . . ." At any other time it would have been a delight to watch that utter absorption. Now I resented so much attention being paid to the relics of a past age

"Is he going to make an inventory of everything in the place?" I asked Parkinson, who shrugged and said, "Well, it's the Government way. I suppose. . . ."

But I never heard what he supposed. There was a shrill thin cry from the farther end of the room, where the expert was examining a very beautiful lying-in-state robe. Startled, we turned to discover the source of his terror. For that cry was not one of awed delight, of an excitement too great to endure silence. It had been an ugly cry, full of fear and incredulity. And when we came to stand beside him there broke from our throats, also, varied sounds of horror and amazement. Those sounds rose and broke against the aloof ceiling, filling the room with their echoes. For a full minute we stood there, speechless, except for those animal and witless cries. For we knew then that what Norman Bridie had said as he walked from the inquest to the station at Kings Benyon was true, that the committal in Kensal Green had been a farce, and here at length, beyond all doubt, under our eyes lay the shriveling, the dreadful figure of what had once been Sampson Rubenstein.

II

There are occasions in life when reality seems so improbable that the human intelligence is moved to mirth. This was one of them. The face of the gentleman from the British Museum, the riven appearance of Philpotts who had, I believe, genuinely cared for the dead man, and the contrast between his expression and his Regency buck appearance, Parkinson's mutter of, "Then who the devil did we bury in Kensal Green?"—the feeling of tension that had accompanied me down here, made so grotesque a background for the sickening thing at which we all stared, that I felt an hysterical desire to giggle. The expert stiffened, and lifted his head, abandoning a momentary attempt to look as though he were accustomed to discovering corpses in a considerable state of decomposition in priceless Chinese robes in empty houses. Philpotts put his hand over his eyes.

"We must get the police," he muttered. "My God, this is murder—or may be? ..." Even at such a moment his habitual caution asserted itself and that, too, seemed funny.

Parkinson proved his priceless qualities as a secretary and aide-de-camp by twitching the cloth back over the discolored face and saying, "We'd better get out of this, I think." And then, "How the devil is any one going to tell from that how he died?"

III

It was murder all right. Rubenstein had been stabbed by a thin-bladed knife or dagger, a number of which were found among the collection in the glass-fronted cases. The knife had been thrust with some violence into the side, though the cloth was discolored and rotting—indeed the whole discovery was so revolting that even the body from the sea paled in horror—the jagged edges of the cut could still be discerned. The police surgeon thought death would be practically instantaneous, and it was improbable that Rubenstein would retain consciousness after such a wound. Parkinson, checking up the collection, said that no knife was missing, and the most careful examination could not discover a mark of blood on any particular weapon.

"He wiped the knife on the man's clothes," said Burgess. "There's a mark here that's blood, or I'm a Dutchman. All the same, we'll have the stuff analyzed. All this delay is going to make things pretty difficult for the police."

Up to the present I really hadn't suffered much inconvenience at their hands, but now each one of us had to account in as much detail as possible for his movements during that fatal night. It was difficult to remember the sequence of events, and almost impossible to put definite times to them, but we did our best. It seemed to me the police were going to be pretty clever, if they were going to find a culprit now. Any clews must be obliterated and no man in his senses was going to come into court and swear on oath that he could recall this or that detail that occurred on a night six weeks ago.

We spent—wasted, rather—a good deal of time, sometimes singly, sometimes in pairs—trying to reconstruct the murder. According to Fanny, she had said good-by to Rubenstein just before half-past six. He would be back, we supposed, at about seven or a little later. At about seven-ten the bridge party had broken up, and the members scattered, reassembling again at about eight. It seemed then that Rubenstein must have come by his death between those two periods. He could return quietly enough. When he first went to Plenders Lal had entertained tremendously, and every time the poor chap emerged from the library he found himself engulfed in a sea of feminine acquaintances. There was an austere side to Rubenstein's nature; he genuinely did want to shake free from luxury and fuss, and only at Plenders did he have opportunity. Lal was an attractive woman with very little brain. Solitude she didn't understand; she thought it synonymous with sulks, and she would either throw a temperament herself or do her utmost to persuade "Sammy to be loving." Poor Rubenstein, there must have been times when he envied the Thibetan monks their savage seclusion; he kept the fewest possible servants at Plenders and whenever he could he went down there alone. But because this wasn't often permitted to him, he had made himself a secret entry and exit by reopening an ancient door in the side wall of the house, admitting to a narrow corridor, whence sprang a flight of mean stairs by which he could gain access to the gallery. He had had a second aperture made in the wall of the library itself, so that he could go in and out of the house, up to the gallery and to his own room without being disturbed. On this, then, the last night of his life, suppose him to come stealing through that secret door, of which he alone possessed the key, and mounting the stairs either to his own room, that was as small and bleak as a cell —in sharp distinction from Lal's, that was enormous, steam-heated, luxurious and enveloping, with its multitudinous rugs and cushions—or more probably, direct to the gallery. It was a habit of his, as all of us knew, when he was at odds with his world, to refresh himself by silent hours among his particular gods; it's a primitive instinct in man; you find it in saints and artists all through history. Here, then, the assassin must have found him. The first difficulty any one would encounter would be that of motive. Why should any one want to murder Rubenstein? There might be a sudden row; there might be jealousy; there might be accusation and counter-accusation. No one bar the murderer could say. In this field everything must be supposition. You'd need to know the inner spiritual ramifications of the household to reach any definite conclusion as to the identity of the criminal.

The police were reticent; I dare say the affair of the inquest stuck in their gullet. Burgess had popped up like a Jack-in-the-box, and was checking and counter-checking every uncertain statement that we made.

"Hang it, man," I remonstrated with him once, when he was in his most grueling mood, "you can't expect us to remember anything definitely down to the minute and second of its taking place."

"There's one at least that remembers," was Burgess's grim retort, "that's the only one I want."

"Have you no clews?" I asked him.

He looked at me queerly. "Interested, aren't you?"

"Of course I'm interested," I agreed hotly. "I or any of my friends may be accused any hour of the day. I think we've a right to know something."

"Go on," said Burgess. "Now say the bit about an innocent man not understanding how he can be an object of suspicion to the police."

"Oh, I've no doubt we're all that," I returned in bitter tones. "Only, I think we should know what you're working on."

"All right," said Burgess suddenly, after giving me a long look that I felt might have a disintegrating quality if it were bent upon me too often. "Have you ever seen the head from which this comes?" And he opened his hand and showed me a long red hair.

I looked at it carefully. "No," I said, "so far as I know it's no one in this household."

"Maybe it isn't," Burgess agreed. "But if a stranger is mixed up in this he was let in by some one who knew the lie of the house, most likely some one living in it. Now—what about this?"

He showed me the second clew, and for an instant my head reeled. It was a green wooden button of peculiar pattern. I recognized it at once. It was one of a set from Fanny's green ulster, the one she had worn when she left Plenders on the night of Sunday, January 6th. Fortunately my experience had given me a lot of opportunity to acquire the prime virtue known as saving face, and I don't think that I batted an eyelid.

"That?" I said in puzzled tones. "I don't think I know that."

"Not very observant, are you?" said Burgess cheerfully. "Lucky for me I've got other witnesses. I mean to say, at least four people are prepared to swear that came off a green coat Miss Price was wearing on the night she left the house. We found it in the dead man's hand."

"Even so, Miss Price hasn't the monopoly of such buttons," I exclaimed, but God knows I hadn't much confidence that that cock would fight.

"We know that," Burgess's voice was steely. "Don't get it into your head that we want to jump in the dark. All we want to do is find the owner of the button."

I suppose they were satisfied later on that that's what they'd done, because thirty-six hours afterwards they arrested Fanny as being concerned in the murder of Sampson Rubenstein.

CHAPTER IX

It was a maxim with Foxey—Always suspect everybody.
OLD CURIOSITY SHOP.

I DIDN'T obey my first impulse to fly to the prison where Fanny was incarcerated, with offers to help and splutterings of fury at her position. That, I knew, would cut no ice with Fanny, who, even in such circumstances, wouldn't lose her head. She had been brought before a magistrate and formally charged with the crime, and had announced with calmness that was part of her official manner that she was innocent but would reserve her defense. As soon as I got the news I went to see a friend of mine, one Arthur Crook, a slow-speaking, pot-bellied lawyer, with a great circular face and a crafty eye. He had an eyrie of an office— he never spoke of it as chambers, though his address might be the Temple—and he wore snuff-colored clothes. He suffered from gout and had to walk with a stick. He had a tongue like vitriol and a voice like velvet.

"Curteis?" he said as I came in. "What's your scrape? If it's blackmail, don't pay a penny. Go to the police. What the hell do we maintain the police for? Tell me that!"

"It isn't blackmail," I told him. "It's murder."

His roving eye settled on me with a peculiar colorless

95

intensity. "Don't use that word," he said. "Accident, if you like. Death, if necessary. Not murder. Murder's a hanging matter."

"That's just what I'm afraid of," I said.

He put up his great freckled hands and fitted them snug as a collar round his own thick neck. "Not a nice sensation," he observed. "You won't like it, Curteis. It may not last long in actuality but in the imagination it goes on for ever."

"It's not my neck I'm thinking of," I explained. "It's a girl."

He looked dubious. "I don't like these women cases. Who is she?"

"The girl who's been taken for Rubenstein's murder."

His eye swiveled round to me. "She's a baggage," he said. "What's she to do with you?"

I said flatly, "If she gets out of this I hope she's going to marry me."

He shook his head. "My dear boy—oh, my dear boy —you don't have to marry that sort."

"It's cheaper in the long run," I told him cynically, and he grinned.

"You know your way about. Well, go on. You don't think she did it? Or do you? Or you know she did it and you want to get her out of the jam?"

"I'm convinced she didn't," I told him. "Well, why should she?"

"Ask the police that. What is their case, by the way?"

"Oh, I dare say they'll argue that there was an affair between them."

"And was there?" asked Crook, cutting the end of a cigar, and opening and shutting his eyes thoughtfully.

"Fanny says not; says Rubenstein's one of the few men who have never wanted to make love to her."

"If she's my client I hope she won't say that in court," returned he. "Most damaging admission. It provides a motive right away. Nothin', according to the public intelligence, which, as you know, isn't high, so inflames a woman as bein' ignored. What's the girl like?"

I tried to tell him, but after a minute he stuck out his big powerful jaw and told me to shut up. "You're no disinterested witness," he said. "What does Rubenstein's wife think of her?"

"She'd quote you whole sentences out of the Old Testament."

"And she might be justified. All right, all right. Don't argue. I shall have to see the girl and I can judge for myself. Anything missing? Money or anything?"

"Not so far as I know. Of course, I'm not the police."

Then he asked me if I'd seen Fanny since the arrest. "No," I said. "I doubt if I'd be exactly *persona grata* at the prison. I'm thanking my stars I haven't got red hair, or they'd probably have me in the next cell as the accomplice."

"Even you," observed Crook austerely, "ought to know that in this country, whose purity is a byword all over the world, we do not jail male and female prisoners in adjoining cells. Why should the police pick on you?"

"Merely because I disagree with their present verdict."

97

"You have an alternative to offer?"

"It seems to me there were half a dozen people in the house with better motives than Fanny, who was seen by us all to leave and who had told a perfectly consistent story about six times as to her movements. I thought you might go and see her."

Crook puffed thoughtfully at his cigar. "No good my going till I've smelt round a bit and discovered how the land lies. Give me twenty-four hours. Any suspicious strangers seen wandering about the place at the time?"

"There were two cars in the neighborhood that night. The fog was so dense a man could have walked up to your front door without being recognized."

"And even more easily have approached the side door and been let in by an accomplice. How does your pretty Fanny explain the button?"

"She says she can't, so far as I can make out. My own theory is that it's all part of a put-up job."

"This is the coat she was wearing when she left?"

"Yes."

"And she hasn't been back to Plenders?"

"No."

"Was she wearing the coat at the inquest?"

"No, she wore a fur coat, I remember."

"Where was the green one she had worn that night?"

"You'll have to ask her."

"She's going to have her work cut out explaining how that button got into the old man's hand if she didn't go back to the Chinese room after she'd left the front door. After all, the house was shut up the next day." Then he considered. "There's another point," he said. "It won't pay to ignore the police's case, y'know. It may be that she's guilty in the sense she knew Rubenstein had been murdered, that she was an unwilling accomplice. The police are arguin' obviously that the fellow never got to Kings Benyon at all; never got further than his own side door—for some reason, either because the girl urged him, or because of something he'd forgotten or some suspicion we don't know anythin' about—he got out of the car and came back by the side door. From what I've heard it seems to me all Lombard Street to a boiled hen against any one seeing him if he did. Suppose he went up to the Chinese Room where he was murdered. Perhaps he found some one tampering with his treasures. . . ."

"That won't wash," I said abruptly. "No one but himself had the keys, and he always locked the Gallery when he left it. Nobody went there alone, and he was always the last to leave. Why, when we went down the other day we had to wait while a locksmith was fetched to unfasten the door."

"Doors aren't the only ways into a room," said Crook coolly. "Aren't there any windows?"

"There are long windows reaching from floor to ceiling overlooking the garden."

"An active feller could get in through them, I dare say. How are they fastened?"

"A patent lock on the inside," I told him grimly. "Not much hope there."

"What about the glass panes? Removin' them has been heard of."

"What about the time it would take?"

"Time's no object in this job. The feller knew it was

a foggy night, knew he couldn't be seen, even if there were lovers in the shrubbery, which you wouldn't expect in that weather, knew he wouldn't be disturbed—except by Rubenstein himself. No one else could get in."

"That's true," I had to acknowledge. "And it's easy enough to get into the garden."

"Could a man get up to the windows?"

"The Gallery's over the veranda. A child could climb those posts. And the veranda leads into the billiard-room, but, as I happened to notice that night, there are dark blinds and very heavy curtains which would be drawn early. It isn't probable that in such a gale a sound would be heard."

"There's one line of defense then. X climbs into the Gallery with the object of helping himself to goods he knows he'll be able to sell—not in this country, I dare say—but England's not the world, in spite of what they taught us at Eton a generation ago. He's interrupted by Rubenstein, who proposes, naturally, to give the alarm. X strikes in self-defense, say, and your young woman, growin' impatient and seeing she isn't going to stand an earthly of catching her train, comes bounding up the stairs, breaks into the Gallery and finds Rubenstein murdered and the fellow who did it standing over him."

"Why doesn't she give the alarm?"

"Would you give the alarm with the threat of a knife in your ribs? She's absolutely helpless. She's got to agree to the murderer's terms or join the long brigade of corpses. The criminal is safe enough; no one knows his identity, no one knows he has been in the place, he can go out as he went in, either through the window, or he can slip down the back way. Most likely he'd go back through the window, having compelled Fanny to help him to arrange the body in the most realistic way possible?

"And Fanny goes through the door, back to the car, carrying a pair of boots with her—she'd be pretty safe not to be seen by servants at that hour—shoots the car over the cliff, and then walks into Kings Benyon?

"How about distances? Could she catch the late train?"

I considered. "She ought to, with time to spare. Well, Fanny might be coerced into doing that, but I don't feel she'd keep quiet about it."

"Don't be a ruddy fool," said Crook inelegantly. "What chance has she got of telling the truth now? She's made herself accessory after the act at best. And what proof has she got that any one's going to believe her story? This fellow will have disappeared; she doesn't know his name or where he can be found; a likely story to tell the police, isn't it? They know too much about these vanishing murderers. Oh, he's got Fanny trussed up like a fowl, and she knows it. She shows her sense when she insists on reserving her defense."

"And it would explain her clearing out like that," I was forced to admit. "Of course, from her point of view, the longer we could postpone the discovery the better. No one is going to be too certain of his movements within a few minutes one way or the other several weeks after the event."

"They'd drop on him like a ton of bricks if he was," Crook agreed promptly. "Well, that's one explanation. There may be others."

"Let me give you some," I suggested, for I had studied this subject in detail. "Rubenstein wasn't killed at six, but between seven and eight. He came back unobserved and left the car in the path by the side of the house. Winton was off that night, and he's the only person who would be likely to walk up that path. There were three indoor servants and Rita, Lal Rubenstein's maid. Rubenstein goes up to his room, discovers he has a few minutes before he need change, and goes, for quietude's sake or because the mood takes him, or for some other reason which doesn't much matter at the moment, into the Chinese Gallery. Here he is found by his wife, who immediately starts a fresh storm about Fanny. She's told him he can clear out, and she means it. He gets furious, says he will—says—oh! anything, what does it matter? Lal is enraged, and mark you, when she was in a tantrum she wasn't a sane creature. There's a row; she seizes the dagger and says, 'Either you swear to give up Fanny or I'll finish you off with this.' That sounds melodramatic, I know, but you've never been present at one of their scenes. She'd throw things at him, use language that would make a prophet of old blush. She's a woman with any amount of physical strength, and, of course, rage would add to it. She's crazy enough to do a thing like that and almost be incapable of realizing what she did. She loathed all his interests; she'd always been jealous, even of the Chinese Gallery; if a fire had broken out and destroyed it, I'd have been pretty sure in my own mind who fired the petrol trail."

"She'd want an accomplice," Crook pointed out.

"She'd got one: Rita, the maid. She detested Rubenstein. More important, she adores Lal. She doesn't regard English people, and particularly English Jews, as being quite human. I can see her standing over poor Rubenstein's body discussing its disposal. I'm sure the idea of dressing it up like a doll would come from her."

"The wound had been plugged with cotton-wool," said Crook. "Where would that come from?"

"The police found a roll in Rubenstein's room. That's another argument in favor of Lal. A guest wouldn't know where to turn."

"He might in a panic dive into the first room he came to. Whose would that be?"

"Rubenstein's. He slept close to the Gallery."

"For the same reason as the faithful slave slept across the threshold of his master's door?"

"I don't think so. But I remember Parkinson telling me that when he couldn't sleep, and he suffered badly from insomnia these last two or three years, he used to steal into the Gallery and stay there, rapt and enchanted, until morning."

"Well, *chacun à son goût.* It isn't the way I'd care to spend the night. Still, it isn't my corpse they're arguing about. To come back to the point about the cotton-wool. Wouldn't a murderer instinctively bolt for the nearest room?"

"He's much more likely to staunch the blood with his own handkerchief, and afterwards burn it, as is the habit of ninety-nine per cent of criminals in detective yarns. If a woman committed the crime, though, her handkerchief would be too small to be of any value."

Crook looked impressed for the first time. "That's a

point," he said, "though I dare say the Crown will tear it to rags. Still, it's something to bear in mind. Who shoved the car over the cliff?"

"Rita, of course. And here's another point. Parkinson went up to ask Lal—about ten o'clock this would be—if she'd like him to try to get in touch with any of the hospitals—I don't suppose there was more than one and perhaps a nursing home or so—in case of an accident, and she came to the door of her room herself. Now, Benson said afterwards that Rita had spent the whole evening in Lal's room. Then why didn't she answer Parkinson's knock?"

"Couldn't say," growled Crook. "Can she drive?"

"I don't know," I had to admit, "but I could find out. She's got the nerve and she's got the strength."

"Could she get out and back without being seen?"

"No one would comment on her roaming about the house at any hour of the evening. No one would notice her. She was attending to Lal Rubenstein. The passage into which the secret door opens is only used by the servants; she simply had to wait for one instant while the coast was clear and then dive out of the door. The lighting in that passage is pretty bad, and the door had a soundless apparatus so that no one could tell when Rubenstein went out. He was put to quite a number of similar shifts by that wife of his. No one would be at that side of the house during the evening; it would be simple enough to start up the car and drive it off. Rita was as strong a horse. Her pedestrian abilities are well known. She's about as moral as a tom-cat. If she were seen creeping about in the dark no one would think anything of it. If her shoes were found caked with mud the next morning no one would find it peculiar. I should say they were oftener caked than not. She could come in by the side door and go straight up to Lal's room without going near the main part of the house at all. If she did meet any one she could say she had walked as far as the gate to see if there were any sign of Rubenstein."

"Sounds very pretty," Crook agreed. "I suppose you do realize that Rita's amoral propensities cut both ways. If she was seen sneaking in late that night it will be easy for her to say she'd been meeting a friend. I dare say, too, she'd find it easy to produce one if necessary; if she were the kind of woman who's terrified of a fog, her being out in one would help a lot more."

"If she were that type (*a*) Lal wouldn't have kept her, or (*b*) she wouldn't have stayed with Lal, and (*c*) she certainly wouldn't have had the nerve to drive the car to the Black Jack, which every one knows is dangerous."

"I don't say that isn't a possible explanation," Crook allowed. "But I won't vouch for what the police will say."

"I'll give you another: Rubenstein came back and went into the Gallery and was there discovered and murdered by Parkinson."

"Why?"

"Because Parkinson had been faking his accounts —forging his signature on a check—was embroiled in a love affair with Lal Rubenstein—I don't know. Whichever it was, Rubenstein had learned the truth and none of the three is the type of thing he'd forgive. I should say myself it wasn't the last, but the first two—

Philpotts may be able to help us there. Parkinson would know where to look for cotton-wool; he'd think of dressing up the body; he had the chance to move the car to a safe place that evening when he went to the gate and spoke to the American driver who had lost his way; he might drive the car over the cliff in the middle of the night, using the side door that didn't have a bolt. Rubenstein might want to come in late and not be anxious to rouse the whole house. Parkinson's a poor man and deadly ambitious."

"He made a point of staying in this country until the body was conveniently found."

"Bluff, pure bluff. You can label any sort of candor bluff, and half the time you're right."

"And Mrs. Rubenstein's sudden religious fervor? You don't think that a bit suspicious?"

"Oh, not necessarily. She's the kind of woman who would adore to stand up in the market-place and expose her sins. However, if you don't like Parkinson, what about Graham? He's insanely jealous of Rubenstein's possessions."

"He crept into the Chinese room and stabbed Rubenstein—why?"

"Opportunity of buying the things back at a tithe of their face value and making himself something approaching a millionaire. I don't argue anything premeditated in his case, of course, but if he saw Rubenstein gloating, and perhaps taunting him. . . . There may have been a row. Rubenstein's been trying for years to buy Fanny off, and neither Graham nor Fanny would budge an inch. There was bad blood between those two all right. The question is, if Graham's involved, who's his accomplice?"

"Your beautiful Miss Price," was Crook's immediate retort.

"There's one thing you seem to have forgotten in this case," I reminded him. "How did Graham get into the Gallery in the first place? I don't see him shinning up the posts of the veranda."

"That seems to rule out Graham," said Crook composedly.

I was frowning. "Whoever's concerned in this, I'd say it was a two-man job," I said. "If a stranger came through the window, some one unbolted that window from the inside. The police can find out who that is."

"The police won't trouble," said Crook patiently. "The police have got their theory. Your Fanny coaxed old Rubenstein to go up to the Chinese Room, followed him in, engaged his attention, and then her accomplice came in and finished off the job. By the way, what reason does she give for clearing out on such a night, when the chauffeur had been given the evening off? Did she know that, by the way?"

"I—think—so," I had to admit. "Lal said something about it during the afternoon. I think Fanny was there."

"Another plank in the police platform. It isn't after all, very reasonable to take your host, who's a notoriously bad driver, out on such a night unless you've got some strenuous reason. What is her excuse?"

"She said she had a telephone call."

"From town? They'll be able to check that up."

"Oh, I never believed that from the start. The fact

is," I hesitated, "she wanted to get away from a chap staying in the house. . . ."

"That won't carry her far," prophesied Crook with a kind of cheerful melancholy. "The prosecution will argue that she could have left first thing next morning and gone to bed with a headache, if she felt so badly about it. And quite right. She could. But I suspect that a solitary pillow at eight P.M. isn't much to that young woman's taste. Her one hope, as I see it, is to show that she was actually in town at nine P.M. on Sunday evening. That'ud clinch it, because she couldn't have helped to dispose of Solomon and caught the six-twenty-eight. Short of that, heaven help her!"

"Through you," I reminded him grimly.

"Providence moves in a mysterious way—or so we sang in our Sunday school when I was a smitchy urchin of about six. What does she say about that?"

"I haven't discussed it with her, but I should say the police have, and she can't prove a thing. They're not likely to make jays of themselves just to give us the fun of showing them up."

"You think of nearly everythin'," approved Crook. "Not quite all, though. There's the red hair. Chauffeur red-haired by any chance?"

"Dark as an Italian. Besides, Rubenstein was wearing a wrapover coat. He wouldn't have picked up that hair in the car."

"Stalemate for the hair, then. We have to fall back on your mysterious stranger. I hope you'll make him materialize. What about the button? That's rather important."

"Perhaps it fell off in the car and Rubenstein found

it and came into the Gallery carrying it in his hand." I suggested feebly.

Crook leaned over and patted my shoulder. "Your feelings do you credit, my boy," he said, "but don't take a story like that into court. The button was violently torn off, remember. No, I prefer our original version, however difficult it may be to discover our man. We'll have the veranda posts and the window frames gone over, though after all this rain we're not likely to scratch up much. No hope of footprints, of course, but that's no odds. Nowadays the intellectual murderer don't wear his own shoes; he puts on rope slippers or buys a noticeable kind of boot you couldn't miss, and gets rid of it the minute his job's done."

"We'd better get round the neighborhood," I said warmly. "Find out if there are any stories of a red-headed chap being seen there...."

"If you like," Crook agreed, without enthusiasm. "But remember the police will have done that. Never do any job an expert can do for you. Anyway, they're more likely to get the facts."

"And if I do unearth the fellow?"

"They'll suggest you made him out of a pocket-handkerchief and the art of Willie Clarkson. Still, good luck. I'm going to work over the job for a day and then we'll go down and see the little lady together."

CHAPTER X

*Get your facts first and then you can distort 'em as
much as you please.*

MARK TWAIN.

CROOK was right. I learnt nothing fresh from my
visit, though at first I thought my luck was in. I
dropped into the pub and inquired during the second
round of drinks whether any one had found the red-
haired chap who was supposed to have done the little
Ikey in. This was at Kings Benyon, where I was quite
unknown, and I had no fear of being recognized. It's
true I had stayed there for the inquest, but not at
this inn, and one man is very much like another. Anyhow, nobody did know me. They knew a lot about red-
haired men, though. There were several in the neighborhood and they hadn't been chipped, had they, when
the story got round? Red-haired men got shy of coming into the Coach and Pair. It was acknowledged local
wit to stand up and point a beer-mug and exclaim,
"Why, haven't they caught you yet?" and one wag had
raised a laugh and endowed a story by solemnly lifting
his pint-pot and saying, "This beer's where you ought
to be by rights, Henry Foster, in jug." Poor Foster,
he didn't know when he'd live that down, because he
really had been an object of suspicion for some days,
ever since it was shown that he had been seen lurking

in the neighborhood of the house for several days prior to Rubenstein's murder. But at last he had sheepishly admitted that Rita was the attraction, Rita whom he couldn't resist, to meet whom he had learned to lie and scheme and deceive his sharp-tongued black-haired wife. At first he had shrunk from admitting the truth, but was driven to it by the ugly choice between acknowledging the situation and standing his trial for murder. Rita, questioned, had had no scruples about confirming his story. Foster was one man in a crowd to her; the fact that he was married with a family of young children, whom he had to keep on a frugal agricultural laborer's wage, was nothing to her. The district was full of possible or actual conquests; but the rest of these, rubbing sweating palms together, had thanked whatever gods they served that they'd been gifted with raven or flaxen polls.

Crook had warned me that it wouldn't be much use my applying for permission to examine Plenders outside or in. He would get a private inquiry agent—he recommended one called Marks—for that purpose. But first of all he wanted Fanny's story.

We met near the prison at Robertstown, where she was being kept until the trial, and on the way Crook wondered whether it would be any use to apply for a transfer to the Central Criminal Court, supposing the case got that far.

"The odds are the powers that be wouldn't consider we had enough ground, and I'm not sure we have. But give me the Central Court any day. I've got a lot of murderers off there. The atmosphere suits me," he said in a blithe voice.

111

"Whom are you thinking of getting to lead?" I asked, not much caring for the significance of that. "The Crown will get Rubens or O'Malley, I suppose."

"And you want some one of the same size? They cost money, you know. If it comes to that, I'm damned expensive myself."

"That'll be all right. Do you think ... ?" I hesitated. "What are your impressions of the case so far?"

"I haven't any—yet. Wait till I see the girl. Everything will depend on her story. Mind you, I think she may be involved, guiltily involved, I mean. That type of woman is scarcely ever reliable, in my experience."

"That's a damned unfair thing to say before you've met her," I protested.

"And another thing—don't let the Court realize which way the wind blows so far as you're concerned. You're—what? Just a guest at the house. And don't forget it."

"You can trust me," I said shortly. I've found myself in so many diplomatic entanglements, told so many magnificent lies, fought my way out of so many compromising situations since I left school, that I rather resented his suggestion that I'd let the whole thing down with a smack.

"How long do you say you've known her? four months? That's quick work. Still, a lawyer is like a doctor—he can't be shocked. By the way, this is between ourselves, but, in case inquiries are made, what is the actual relationship between you?"

"So far as I'm concerned she's a candidate for the watchers round the vestal flame," I told him, more huffily than before.

Crook grinned. "You've quite the poetic touch, my boy," he said. "Who's to get the credit for that, though? Ah, well, here we are."

Fanny looked, as usual, as though she had come out of a bandbox. She was wearing black and her hair might have been set that morning. I introduced Crook and she gave him her hand.

"I'm glad to see you," she said. "I'd like some official advice as to my next step."

"Couldn't come before," boomed Crook chattily. "Had to get the police story first. No use wasting time talking till I saw the kind of thing we were up against. Now, my dear, let's hear your version. I may as well tell you I know the statement you made to the police. Do you want to add or subtract anything?"

"No," said Fanny, coolly. "It was all true."

"So far as it went," Crook nodded. "But are you sure there's nothing else that might help us?"

"I don't think so," remarked Fanny after a minute.

"Then perhaps you'll fill in a few gaps," said Crook blandly. "This letter now, that you wrote to Bridie. What was there in that that he shouldn't have come forward at once and told every one about it?"

"It's what wasn't in it, and that isn't anything that could throw any light on the mystery. It was a purely private letter."

"And this being a purely private conversation, it would be helpful to have the truth."

"All right." It was pretty difficult to disconcert Fanny. "He had asked me to marry him. Simon knows that." She glanced at me. "I couldn't. For one thing, it wouldn't work, and for another, I'm not the sort of

113

woman that, in cold blood, he'd want to marry. I'm too—experienced. I don't know how much of my past life will be raked up in Court, but if they dig out everything that's happened to me since I was sixteen I'll be hanged in advance. I've fought my own way for fourteen years, ever since I got tired of mixing ice-cream sodas for first-year boys from Princetown. I've lived hard and made my own way. You have to make up your mind right from the start what you're going for. I went for security—oh, yes, I did, Simon, and so would any one who wasn't a moron, who'd begun as I did. You," she turned candidly to me, "called me an adventuress to my face, once."

"No need to tell the Court that," rumbled Crook. "Well, what of it? Did you suppose this young fellow —what's his name? Bridie?—was a Galahad?"

"That wasn't the point. What really mattered was that I wanted to marry him—and naturally I couldn't. So I wrote a letter telling him my story—expurgated, of course—and posted it from town after my arrival. I should be out of the way when he got it, which I thought was important." She made her bald statement without any trimming of explanation and we accepted it at its face value. But I could see Crook didn't like the story much.

"Of course, there was the chance that he wouldn't want to see you again," said Crook a bit brutally, "and that'ud be hurtful. I know what it is to sit with your eyes glued to the window-pane, and your ears growing as long as the princess's nose in the fairy tale, listening for the postman and then finding it's nothing but another blame advertisement after all."

Fanny smiled faintly. "Yes. I don't need to explain much to you. And then there was Rose Paget. She really cared for him, she'd be the right sort of wife for him. There's something Oriental in Norman's outlook really. He wouldn't expect a wife to be a partner, he'd expect her just to be a woman. You know what I mean? That would suit Rose to perfection. So I thought I'd clear out. I had friends in Paris; I could get work there; you can borrow money anywhere. I didn't leave an address, I just went. I didn't want Miss Verity writing to me to tell me who'd telephoned and who hadn't. I didn't want to know how much interested Norman was, or if he wasn't interested at all. It's true, the story I told the police, I did get pneumonia going over, which was no part of my plan, and I did lie sick, knowing nothing about Sammy until Dorice told me."

"You've got proof of all that, of course?"

"Yes, the police have had it."

"They'll have to produce that in court. Now tell me, what did actually happen that night after you and Rubenstein left the house?"

"We drove hell-for-leather to Kings Benyon. It was touch and go whether we caught the train. Sammy was livid with rage; he really wasn't fit to drive. I kept my hand on the switch of the door the whole way so as to leap if we really did look like crashing. He was like a devil. We didn't speak half a dozen words the whole way, except that he asked me if I'd like to chance Black Jack. In good weather it takes quite ten minutes off the journey, and I didn't want to find myself stranded at Kings Benyon at six-thirty-five with

115

an hour and a half before the next train went and only Sammy for company. All the same, I preferred that to the thought of a violent death, with the same company. Sammy didn't argue; he said, 'I dare say it's pretty dangerous up there in this weather,' and then we whizzed on. We may have passed some cars on the road, but I scarcely noticed them. You remember the motorist who asked his friend what cemetery they were passing, there were so many headstones, and was told they were milestones? I was reminded of that. There had been a minor crash a bit earlier on when we arrived at Kings Benyon, and it blocked the market square. The station lies just beyond. I told Sammy not to bother about me, and I jumped out. I caught the train by the skin of my teeth. Being a foggy night there weren't so many people traveling as usual; there were two women in my carriage and a man in a bowler hat. I shouldn't recognize any of them again and I'm sure they wouldn't know me. We each sat in a corner and one of the single women put her feet up on the seat; but no one's coming into court with a story of that kind. When I got to Victoria we were late in. We were due at eight-twenty but it was getting on for nine. I was very hungry—I hadn't had any tea—and I had no food in my flat. I bolted for the brasserie —it's called the Parnassus, it would be—and went down and had a meal. I told the police that, too. They asked me if I remembered in which of the two rooms I sat. I said the front one. There were still quite a number of people there. I had a table to myself and ordered Scotch woodcock and lager. I didn't notice what the waiter looked like. I didn't actually notice the time."

"Did the police expect all this detail?"

"Apparently. Another thing that troubled them was that I hadn't noticed anything odd about Victoria Station when I got out. I said it looked much as usual, dark and drab and uninspired, and all the least appetizing people in the world were meeting acquaintances or waiting for trains. Burgess pressed me quite affectionately to remember any outstanding incident, but I said there wasn't one. Was there, by the way?"

"Apparently some chap was traveling with a young monkey and the beast got off its chain and went careering madly round the station. There was a press photographer there, and a crowd collected to watch it. It is," added Crook dryly, drooping his left eyelid, "the sort of thing you'd expect to notice."

"If I saw the monkey I dare say it wouldn't look much different to me from everything else on two legs on Victoria Station on a foggy Sunday night," said Fanny grimly. "Anyway, I didn't. And it can't have been on all fourteen platforms at the same time."

"Which platform did you come to?"

"I don't remember. I never do notice numbers."

"And you dived straight for the brasserie?"

"Yes. It's fairly new, by the picture theater."

"Then the odds are you came out on platform fifteen?"

"Perhaps," said Fanny vaguely. "Does it matter?"

"It may be quite important. I don't want to prejudice you and it's not my job to assist your memory, but if you could recall alighting at platform twelve it would help us quite a lot."

"Why?"

"Because the six-twenty-eight arrived at number twelve and the eight-three at number fifteen. Well, go on. After the brasserie—you went home?"

"No. I went into the Prince Edward Cinema House in Vauxhall Bridge Road. They were showing 'Only a Child'—it was pretty maudlin. They had the girl wonder—Topsy Barrett—and she always acts as an emetic on me. However, I didn't want to go back to the flat. I knew it was impossible, but I kept feeling that somehow Norman might ring me up. And if he didn't other people might. So I stayed in the dark. A cinema is a good place for a pickup, too, and I would have welcomed any company that night so long as it took my mind off Norman."

"Did you pick any one up?" asked Crook.

"Yes. A little suburban cad—one of these men who think they're no end of a rakehell if they stand a girl eightpennorth of offal at a sandwich bar. He spoke to me as the lights went up. Oh, he was a little rat but what did it matter? He said, 'What about some supper?' His idea of supper was two saveloys and a cup of coffee. In return, I listened to his telling me how he was married but separated from his wife; she was such a cold woman. I didn't stop long. I was home before twelve."

"Twelve o'clock isn't an hour that matters much," said Crook. "If, as the prosecution is going to claim, you traveled not by the 6.28 but by the 8.03, you could still have been home by 12. It was due in at 10.50

and it was forty minutes late. By the way, what a
rat of a station Meadmore is."

"Is it?" said Fanny. "I've never got out there."

"Did Burgess say the same thing to you?"

"He tried to trip me up. Then he could have said.
'If you didn't change there, how do you know anything
about it?'"

"You could have said you passed that way twelve
months ago."

"The station wasn't open twelve months ago. It's
one of those new branch lines."

Crook nodded. "Well, and after you'd said good-by
to your friend—you didn't exchange addresses, I suppose?"

Fanny shook her head. "He asked for mine, but I
said I was leaving town in the morning. I got a taxi
back. If I'd gone in a bus he'd have come with me,
and I wasn't going to bring a tick like that back to my
rooms."

"You wouldn't know him again?"

Fanny laughed shortly. "Do you know one louse from
another?" she demanded. But Crook didn't know what
a louse looked like. You could tell that from his expression.

"If he sees this report in the paper he may come
forward," he suggested.

"There's a lot to be said for caution," observed
Fanny derisively. "But even so, he has taken rather
a long time to think it over."

"The chances are that when this case is thoroughly
ventilated you won't get too little evidence on that head,
but too much," Crook warned her. "The world's full

of vain lunatics who're aching for a bit of limelight. There'll be dozens of men you've never set eyes on coming forward to swear they bought you eggs and bacon in every hostelry from the Berkeley to the Star in the East on the night in question."

"That'll cut a lot of ice with a jury," said Fanny scornfully. "They'll ask at once how any one remembers a special evening. Fog? Don't talk as if half the nights of January in this country weren't either foggy or wet. They'll think you and Simon shoved a fiver in his hand."

"Send all the applicants along to me," murmured the graceless Crook unperturbed. "I'll sift 'em. If there is one who can help us, he's worth his fiver. Well?"

"I don't think there's any more to tell you. I rang for Miss Verity in the morning and told her I'd had a letter. As a matter of fact, that was true. I did have a letter from France suggesting my going over."

"Did you keep it?"

"I kept it till I got to Paris because it had an address in it where I could get a cheap room. I don't remember destroying it. It may be among my papers. They'll be in my suitcase."

"Anyway, you could probably produce the writer of the letter," I suggested.

"Not nearly so satisfactory," pronounced Crook, sliding his eyes round to meet mine. "Well, that's the whole of your story?"

"Unless you want to coach me," said Fanny coolly. "I don't know what the police case is yet—except the button, of course."

"Let me help you. First—that accident among the

traffic at Kings Benyon that you say held up Rubenstein's car. According to sworn local police evidence,
as well as the evidence of eye-witnesses, also sworn,
that accident didn't take place until after 6.30, so if
you caught the 6.28, you couldn't have seen the smashed
car."

"Mine wasn't a car," said Fanny coolly. "It was a
horse and van. And when I say accident, I only mean
the horse had come down. I dare say that isn't so
picturesque as seeing two cars playing at being serpents,
but it blocks a road quite as well."

"You think of everything, don't you?" said Crook
admiringly. For the life of me I couldn't tell whether
he believed her or not. "The button's your particular
snag at the moment."

"Well, that's what you're here for, isn't it?" said
Fanny with her cool impudence. "I don't know how to
explain it, except by saying it isn't a patent of my own
and presumably other people have similar buttons."

"Unfortunately, no one else staying in the house at
the time. In a murder charge opportunity is practically
everything, with motive an extremely poor second."

"That's illogical if you like," I protested heatedly.

"I would refer you to the case of Rex. v. Hearn,"
said Crook in his most pedantic manner, "where learned
counsel pointed out to the jury that if their inevitable
conclusion was that Mrs. Hearn did administer poison
deliberately and kill both named victims, it need not
cause them to hesitate for one moment if they were
not able to assign a motive. There was no motive that
justified murder. The sting," he added dryly, "is in
the tail. Now, Miss Price, that button was found

clutched in Rubenstein's hand. Can you remember if all the buttons were on the ulster when you left the house?"

"The police took me over this ground," said Fanny. "They were. I remember buttoning them right down to the hem."

"And I remember watching you," I put in dejectedly.

"Moreover, when the police took possession of the coat, they gave me every chance of explaining how the button got torn off it. Short of suggesting that Sammy and I had had a bouncing bout in the car, I couldn't think of anything."

"Did you notice that evening when you reached your flat that the button was missing?"

"No. I just tore the coat off. I didn't think anything about it till the police came along. I took the coat on deck, but I only just pulled it on over my traveling suit. I'd no idea a button was missing till the officials pointed it out to me."

"You realized the significance of their question?"

"Oh!" cried Fanny airily, "they did all the proper things. Like comic detectives on the stage. It is my duty to warn you that anything you say—you know the old gambit. It was like watching a play. Somehow I'd never believed they really were like that. They said they'd consider any explanation I could offer, but they took me by surprise, and on the spur of the moment I couldn't think of a thing."

"And you said?"

"Oh, I registered blank ignorance. What else could I do?" Suddenly she put her hands together. "Oh, God!" she said, "I wish they'd let me smoke."

Crook was frowning. "That won't get you very far," he said. "You can't think of anything better?"

"I can't think of anything at all," said Fanny. "On the whole, isn't it better that I shouldn't? If I'd had some glib explanation all ready when they popped the question, wouldn't that have made them doubly suspicious? You oughn't to be able to explain away incriminating circumstances, not off your own bat, I mean. Lawyers do it when they're defending you, because that's their job. You see, if you can't offer any suggestion at all, you really give your man a much better chance. He hasn't got anything to explain away. And if you tell lies, somebody'll be clever enough to find you out. Anyhow, when my life's the stake, I like to be on the safe side."

Crook looked at her with real admiration. "Do you consider you're on the safe side now?" he asked.

"When I want a frock," said our wayward Fanny, "I don't buy a sixpenny pattern and put the stuff on the floor and cut round the edge and then cobble it together myself and expect it too look as if it were created by Victor Stiebel. I go to an expert and have it built for me. It's the same here."

"Only, when you go to the expert, you do provide your own material," Crook pointed out.

"I've brought you all I've got," Fanny defended herself.

I could see Crook wasn't sure whether to believe that or not.

"It'll make no more than a sun-bathing outfit and a short cut at that," he warned her, none too gayly, "unless we can match up a bit more of the material. What about the letter to Bridie, the letter you wrote in the train? Why didn't you post that till after eleven o'clock, if you got to town at nine?"

"Because I didn't want him to get it till I was out of the country. He wouldn't get it before midday, and I meant to catch the eleven-something boat-train."

"This is like a game of my childhood: here we go round the mulberry bush, round and round and round, and never get anywhere else. You have an answer for everything, and none of them advances us a step. But if you meant to go to Paris anyway, why did you bring in the bit about the letter on Monday morning?"

"I did have a letter on Monday morning."

"But that didn't make up your mind for you."

"It gave me an address to go to."

"What was in the letter? I mean, was it worded strongly enough to convince a jury that it really was a lure?"

"I've told you, I don't think I tore the letter up. It said, 'When you've nothing special on in your town, why not come over to ours? There's always a chance to make a bit.' "

"That all?"

"As near as I remember."

"Not exactly a pressing invitation?"

"Dorice doesn't press. She just says something and you can do what you like with it."

"What did she mean by making a bit?"

"On the side," explained Fanny, and neither Crook nor I was really any wiser. "You can make the same money in London that you can in Paris," Fanny went on, "only in Paris you make it more elegantly."

124

Crook gave that up. "Nothing to do with our case," he observed austerely. "Anyway, you admit you meant to go abroad anyhow. That'll look a bit thin to the jury."

"They'll argue that if I had anything on my conscience I wouldn't stir a foot," contradicted Fanny. "It's a confession of guilt, clearing out."

"Of course it is," said Crook patiently. "But you don't suppose you're going to be credited with sufficient intelligence to realize that."

"If you don't have intelligence, how do you pay your own way from sixteen to thirty?" demanded Fanny.

"Ask the jury that," said Crook in a rather hurt voice, as if he didn't much like being treated like a moron. "They'll answer you easily enough."

"Oh, well"—-Fanny was debonair as ever—"I'm not being tried for any of the commandments but the sixth."

"Remember that, and remember, too, you'll be in the dock, not in the confessional. What you want to appeal to is the hearts of the jury, not their heads. I've known an old gray-haired father and a sacred medal pull off a case when all the prisoner's friends had begun to feel in their pockets for something towards the wreaths. You want to get them saying, 'A girl like that couldn't have murdered Rubenstein.' That's your job."

Fanny shook her head. "My job is to answer questions. It's my counsel's job to get me off."

"I'll say one thing for you," exclaimed Crook sincerely, "the fellow, whoever he is, will earn his fees. Now, listen to me. You've told one yarn and the police are going to tell another. I'm going to suggest a third," and in a good deal of detail he put forward the solution he'd already outlined to me, by which Fanny was neither a murderess nor completely innocent, but an unwilling accomplice.

Fanny shook her head. "I can tell a good lie and get away with it," she acknowledged. "But I'd hate to go on telling lies for four or five days without any one to whisper the right answers to me when I got bunkered. You never can tell what new notion they may not shoot off, and I mightn't have an explanation ready. I'd better stick to the facts I know; it's less confusing."

"Have it your own way," said Crook a bit huffed, thrusting his great jowl close to her face. "I'm only here to take instructions. I can't write out the whole story for you to learn by heart. But I want to save your neck, if I can."

"Do you suppose I don't?" said Fanny. "But I don't see that I'm helping myself much by making myself the accomplice of some one I either can't or won't betray. Which, by the way?"

"That would depend on your evidence."

Crook looked like a man who has at last scored a point, but Fanny didn't appear to notice it. She went on coolly, "All right, we'll suppose I've told your story. Now hear the jury's version. In this one there's nothing accidental at all about Sammy's death. I cajole Sammy into the car, having engineered a scene with Lal—that's so suspicion shall fall on her, you see—then I remind him of something he's forgotten—that he hasn't locked up the gallery or something of that sort—he goes bounding back, and X is waiting for him, stabs him neatly; I follow—we dress up the body, and so forth.

Which version do you think will be the most popular? Oh, you don't have to hesitate. It's one of those absolutely certain tips where you simply can't lose."

Crook nodded thoughtfully; his great strong fingers stroked his blue chin. "You've got your wits about you," he acknowledged. "Only you do have to remember that the burden of proof lies with the prosecution. They might disbelieve your story; I don't see how they could disprove it. . . ."

"Don't forget my accomplice. He mightn't be so agreeable to swing just to get me out of jug. Well, it's a triumph for the moralists this time. Be sure your sin shall find you out. If you will be dressed by exclusive people whose bills you can't pay, even a button can identify you. If I'd shopped in a Kensington bargain basement, no one could have traced me."

"You've rejected my ideas," said Crook. "Have you anything fresh to offer?"

"I stick to my original story. This is all part of a put-up job. No, don't ask me to explain how Sammy got my button clenched in his hand. It's part of your job to explain that so that I don't hang. It does give you scope," she added kindly. "You simply have to trump up another story that might be true, and the jury give me the benefit of the doubt. I never read detective stories," continued this amazing Fanny, "but I'm nuts on crime, and that's nearly always the way it's done."

"If she's a murderer," said Crook thoughtfully to me as we came away from the prison, "she deserves to get away with it. All the same, it's a pity she won't listen to reason. It's a tall story to suggest that some one ripped that button off her coat and hid it in the Chinese Room in order to put suspicion on her. What was her motive? Don't say money. A girl like that can have all the money she wants without having to commit murder for it. I wish I saw a bit of light. Look here, how well do you know her? Would you have any idea which member of that party, if any, would have any hold over her?"

"I could find out," I told him.

"How?"

"The usual way. Making inquiries."

"We can get a private detective for that," said Crook.

"I'd do it better. Oh, don't think I'll scamp the job or waste chances. I've done a lot of queer things in my time. And for your information I was in the Liaison Department—otherwise a bloody spy—during the greater part of the war."

"Get on with it," said Crook. "I'll work it from my end, too. Let me know when you discover anything definite. I suppose," he added, as we separated, "you do realize that our greatest enemy in this case isn't the police or the real murderer, or even the button that's going to take the devil of a lot of explaining. It's the young woman herself. Everything's against her —her manner and her appearance and the way she makes a living—these freelance women are always suspected by the honorable citizens who compose our muddle-headed juries—and her assurance and the fact that she was guilty of that unmentionable crime, separating a husband and wife—and the fact that she doesn't care a damn for any of them. The kind of clients I like," he put his hand on my arm, saying confidentially, "By jove, they're open; and I'd forgotten. That shows you how this case has shaken me; the ones I like, I repeat, are the trembling wretches who daren't conceal a thing. This wench may try and pull my leg as well as the judge's."

"And get away with it?" I suggested.

"Even that," he agreed in gloomy tones. "It doesn't do in this country anyhow not to conform to type, and the Court will be full of people who are stuffed with detective stories and know that any one who doesn't have hysterics in the dock is guilty. All the old safeguards are down," he added, putting the beer down, too. "You daren't look a man in the eyes or have an alibi or be strong and silent—it's the day of the whimpering rat and the ferret. The dog, the trustworthy British, dependable dog, is simply nowhere."

He called for more beer.

CHAPTER XI

I only ask for information.
ROSA DARTLE.

CROOK told me to leave the routine side of the affair to him. He would get a man—the invaluable Marks, if possible—to go over the house, inside and out, with a tooth-comb, "though," he warned me "that's a mere matter of form. The police don't miss things." He would also follow in their footsteps at the Parnassus, the snack-bar where, according to Fanny's own story, she had been so unsatisfactorily entertained by her anonymous rat, "and that's a matter of luck," said Crook, "you never know whether chance will be with you or not." Being a gambler he felt characteristically and, from his experience, far more hopeful about discovering something useful from this direction.

I said I was going to follow up my other suspicions, and he smiled at me, a wide sly smile that made me feel the damned amateur so familiar to film fans, who, in the intervals of running a business, supporting a home, standing for Parliament and competing with the Poet Laureate in the superior weeklies, also contrives to run to earth subtle and supernaturally intelligent criminals.

"What's the use?" he asked softly. "That's not our cup of tea. All we have to do is raise enough doubt to get your pretty Fanny acquitted. You haven't got to present a complete case against some person or persons at present unknown. Why do the authorities' job for them? Particularly," he added with a grin, "as the odds are they'll do it so much better."

I let that pass. "I wish I knew what Fanny's concealing," I said.

Crook jeered openly. "You'll have to rely on your wits for that. The conceit of the creatures, Curteis. It happens every day. Men and women come in and tell half a careful story and think (*a*) that they can pull wool over my eyes, and (*b*) that a few lies will help the case along like anything. Your Fanny's one of them. Mind you, I don't say she isn't speaking gospel truth; I only mean that it wouldn't occur to her not to lie if it suited her book. It's a pity because it makes our job twice as long and twice as difficult. We've got to sift the chaff and wheat before we can start work, and that's a delicate operation and takes time."

I made a movement of intolerable impatience, seeing which he laughed. "You don't know much about the law," he told me—for the second time. "That kind of preliminary is so common we're surprised when we don't get it."

Nothing, however, could persuade Fanny to add to what she told us, or to qualify a word of her story. She knew nothing. Therefore to all intents and purposes we knew nothing, too. From there I began my research.

Immediately I was up against the problem that had first of all faced the police. Everything depended on the hour of Rubenstein's death, and so far no evidence had been sufficiently weighty to make us certain what that was. If he had been killed before seven o'clock the irresistible conclusion was that Fanny, if she hadn't had a hand in it, at least must have known about it. But if he wasn't killed till later, that is, after his return from Kings Benyon, then practically every member of the household was suspect, and only Fanny got off scot-free.

Instinctively I tested my second theory first. The great snag here was Fanny's button. It was impossible to blink the fact that that would be the first piece of evidence to jam in a juror's mind, and once jammed, it was difficult to see how it would ever become unstuck. You couldn't say casually, as I'd said to Crook, that the button could be accounted for in some quite insignificant fashion, not necessarily because that wasn't true but because it wouldn't satisfy their sense of justice. I went through the list of the guests, and I could find only one possible explanation, which was that when Lal, like the tiger-cat she was, flew at the girl waiting so coolly for Rubenstein to pick up her case and come down to the car, she had torn off a button that Fanny hadn't noticed in the heat of the moment, but that afterwards Lal had discovered and turned it to her own uses. That theory definitely named Lal as Rubenstein's murderer, and there were a number of points to confirm such a suggestion. One of these, though this perhaps would hardly be arguable in law, was her extraordinary religious fervor since the fellow's disappearance. This might be so much dust thrown in the eyes of the world, or she may suddenly have experienced a real terror of the final consequences of her act. For I didn't for one moment believe it was a premeditated crime. I could see Lal, still furious at Rubenstein's behavior, storming into the gallery when she saw the light under the door, accusing him of the most extravagant practices in connection with Fanny, rousing him at last to one of his moods of rage that alarmed even the imperturbable Parkinson, so that he said something—I didn't suppose we should ever know exactly what—that maddened her beyond control, and seizing the dagger, she stuck it into his side. She was a big woman physically, and though normally she was slow-moving, passion could rouse her to frenzy. It was one of Rubenstein's tricks to concentrate on some particular specimen of his collection, handle, even fondle it, in complete absorption. It was, presumably, his bad luck that made him choose the dagger that particular night. He might just as well have been playing with the bracelets that were adjacent to it.

Of course, if Lal were mixed up in this, that presupposed Rita as her accomplice. I could see Lal, stricken and appalled at what she had done, yet preserving a certain clarity that is perceptible in nearly all violent criminals. It is your cautious and normally hesitant man who makes a mess of crime; your hothead, having plunged, goes through with a swashbuckling gesture to the end, and his are nearly always the crimes for which only the victim and the victim's relatives suffer. Here then were the two women bending above the body, plugging the wound, taking down a robe from its place on the wall, dressing the corpse—and here Lal would have her magnificent inspiration about the button. It would be Rita who would suggest throwing the blame in another direction, and both, I think, would be glad to see Fanny inculpated. Perhaps Lal had spoken of the button to Rita, whose malicious mind would at once turn it to the best possible use. Lal had been distrait enough for the rest of the evening; she had come down to dinner late, and had returned to her room, accompanied by Rita, as soon as the meal was over. She wasn't seen again that night, but she hadn't been able to sleep. She had refused to have any local inquiries made; she had assumed from the first that Rubenstein would not be returning; the next morning she had closed the house and returned to town; she had wanted to keep it closed indefinitely. I remembered Philpotts saying that Plenders wasn't a national shrine, whatever the widow liked to think. But granted that Lal was involved, you saw her point easily enough. The house should remain shut as long as possible, for ever, no doubt, if she could have arranged it; anyway, long enough for the body of Rubenstein to crumble to a skeleton and delay the possibility of arrest. She might even have gone back to Spain, and left that room perpetually locked, but for the provision in Rubenstein's will regarding the contents of the room. I couldn't pick a single hole in the theory of the two women's guilt. I remembered that when Parkinson went to speak to Lal later in the evening, it had been she herself who opened the door, instead of the servant, Rita, as you would have expected, and indeed Rita didn't seem to be in the room at all. Where, then, would she be? I could ask the servants, Benson and Mrs. Rutter, both of whom were now in London, and if they didn't know, it might be possible to assume that she had been disposing of the fatal car. It would be safe to leave the car in its place in the lane until approximately eleven o'clock, when Winton might be expected to return. Therefore, I argued, the car had been removed between, say, eight o'clock and eleven. Rita was a capable woman, with great physical energy. The walk back from Black Jack, even in such a fog, would present no terrors to her; I didn't think she had any sensitivity, nothing but an insatiable animal passion that disturbed the senses, and destroyed the peace of any number of homes in her own walk of life.

There, then, was my case, and I added to it the twin facts of Lal's eagerness to establish the unknown drowned as Rubenstein and to bury him with a ceremonious finality that seemed to give him a right to the dead man's name, and her desire to shake the dust of England off her feet as rapidly as possible and return to her beloved Spain where, in ample widow's weeds, she could wreak any havoc that suited her jealous, passionate spirit.

There, I repeat, was my case. Now I had to get some proof. Manifestly I should learn nothing new about Lal's movements. It was through Rita that I must try to establish my thesis. I saw Benson, who had been terribly upset by the news of Rubenstein's grotesque death and who was as anxious as Lal herself for the widow to clear off to Spain or Timbuctoo, or hell for that matter, and leave him free to seek decent and honorable service elsewhere. Both he and Mrs. Rutter, indeed, all the household staff except Rita, had been Rubenstein's servants, and now he was dead all were eager to "make a change." Lal didn't treat them as human beings; she'd have sacked them all at a day's

notice, without caring whether they were provided for
or not, if it had suited her and if the law had permitted
it. It was easy enough to get Benson to speak of that
fatal night.

"There was a feeling among us downstairs that some-
thing was going to happen," he said solemnly. "Mrs.
Rutter, she's sort of got second sight, and she said,
'If this evening goes through without some disaster
I'll be surprised.' "

"But this kind of scene wasn't precisely unfamiliar?"
I said as delicately as I could.

"That's just why Mrs. Rutter, saying what she did,
seemed so queer, sir," explained Benson. "I know there
was a lot of ill-ease in the kitchen quarters that night."

"Shared by Rita?" I asked.

Benson made the sort of face a man makes when
he bites on something that's gone putrid.

"She wasn't with us. Not likely. She was with Mrs.
Rubenstein the whole evening."

"You didn't see her at all?"

"Only when she came down and fetched something
or other."

"Did that happen often?"

"Every half-hour by the clock. There's a woman
might be on the stage. Never was like a proper human
being."

I asked idly what sort of things, and Benson said,
"Once it would be a cup of tea. Then it would be a
hot-water bottle; then it would be some coals for the
fire; then it would be hot milk. In and out she was
like a mouse in its hole." He hesitated a moment, then
broke into a spate of indignant speech. "And it isn't

even as if she was that much gone on Mrs. Rubenstein. It was just play-acting. She was out meeting her friend as usual about eleven."

My heart leaped. Inquiries had shown that Winton had returned at eleven-fifteen. If Rita had made some excuse to clear out at eleven it looked as though I might be able to make a case.

"Which one was that?" I asked as carelessly as I could.

"I couldn't say." Nothing I could put on paper would convey Benson's disgust.

"I wonder if Mrs. Rutter would know," I said.

Benson said, "All cats are gray in the dark," which showed you what he thought of Rita's promiscuity.

I had to explain. "It may be rather important," I said.

Benson looked stubborn. "I couldn't say," he replied in that obscure idiom popular among his kind, that may mean anything or nothing. "Come to that, she'd do anything. Knife the master as soon as not."

"You've no proof she's involved in that," I said hurriedly.

"No," agreed Benson rather sullenly. "Too occupied with this plowman chap."

I got the man's name from him eventually. He was a spindle-shanked, artful, gray-eyed fellow called Masters. I found him at his own home. He looked at me sideways.

"My affair," he said.

"What you don't answer now you'll have the chance of answering in court," I warned him.

"When's that?" he demanded in sharp tones.

"When Rita is asked to account for her evening. If she wasn't with you, as she says she was, there may be questions asked."

Masters' answers ruined my hopes. Rita had slipped out to meet him at eleven. They had parted at one. Both Rita and the man had alibis for the latter hour. Rita had been stealing along to her mistress's room; Masters' brother had sat up—he was a sick man, querulous and resentful of other men's opportunities. I tested both stories most thoroughly. I couldn't find a leak anywhere. With infinite reluctance I abandoned this answer to the mystery and fell back on the second theory that inevitably involved Fanny.

It also involved some one else in the household. Some one, moreover, whom Fanny either could not or would not betray. I surveyed my list of suspects. Bridie she might refuse to betray, but Bridie, to my mind, was out of the question. One, he wouldn't, given any provocation, stick a knife in his host's side; two, if he did, he'd raise the alarm himself; three, even if he didn't, he wouldn't allow Fanny to be arrested, while he kept quiet; four, he hadn't any motive. Parkinson she had only met that week-end; which left only Graham, and Graham lay open to a good deal of suspicion. He had known Fanny for years, though in what circumstances I as yet had no idea. I didn't know either what link there might be between them, or whether he had information that would effectually seal his lips. Graham was insanely jealous of Rubenstein, and might, at a pinch, lose his head and express that jealousy in the most unguarded fashion; he was perfectly capable of blackmailing Fanny into silence and of letting her be arrested or even hanged without intervention on his part. The fact was, I discovered ruefully, I knew absolutely nothing about Fanny's life before I met her, and it was clear that I should learn nothing from her own lips. Nevertheless, along this line I had to work.

The obvious source of information to tap was Lal, but Lal wouldn't have Fanny's name mentioned, so I did the next best thing and got hold of Parkinson. Graham had known her much longer, of course, but I had Graham in my mind as a suspect, and I decided to leave him for the moment. Luckily for me—since he was to be more useful than I had at first recognized —Parkinson's prospective employer, Sandeman, had delayed his departure for the States for some weeks, and Parkinson was available for such assistance as he could render.

He said at once, "Lal's convinced it's Fanny. She said the day they took her that it was the best day's work they'd ever done. I wonder how subtle Lal could be."

"Not subtle enough to realize how dangerous subtlety can be," I told him.

"No. Well, I dare say we're lucky she hasn't pitched on either of us. Had you, by the way, thought of yourself in the dock?"

"No," I said, "I hadn't. Odd how ridiculously innocence can blind you to possibilities. What would be my motive?"

"For killing Rubenstein? Fanny Price."

"What, jealousy?" I stared. "But that's absurd. Rubenstein never made love to Fanny."

"I'm sure he didn't. And you weren't jealous. You

hadn't any cause. But you might find it mighty difficult to prove that." He flicked at a fly that had settled on the side of his plate. "Of course, I'm even more open to suspicion than you are. Which makes me even more eager to see you discover the truth. How do you propose to start?"

"I want some information about Fanny. Do you know how Rubenstein got in touch with her?"

"Graham could probably tell you, though he'll have a heart-attack if you start asking questions. It's suddenly occurred to him that he may be suspected, and he's spending his time preparing little diagrams proving that he can't be involved."

"That'll help him a lot," I commented. "Why, no one knows within a number of hours when Rubenstein was killed. It isn't like one of those neat country-house murders where you can draw a map of the house, with a dot placed accurately to indicate the movements of every member of the party at a given moment."

"Ring him up and tell him that," begged Parkinson. "He telephones me morning, noon and night thinking up new reasons why no one should drop on him. If the telephone girls liked to listen-in they could get a packet. No one ought to be so scared for his skin unless he's guilty. Oh, I admit it seems improbable, but nothing's impossible in crime. I suppose that's why all the psychological novelists who used to deal with marriage dilemmas have now taken to murder and violence. Gives 'em even more scope than the other when you can combine the two."

I went off to see Graham, who lived in a block of chambers and suites called Ravenswood Mansions. They were second-rate flats; I'd been over one myself when I was looking for a hole after my return from South Africa, but it was typical of Graham to be attracted by the low rent and the neighborhood of cheap eating-houses.

I hadn't cared for what I had seen of the fellow, and what I had just heard about his eagerness to preserve his own skin increased my distaste, but I couldn't afford to be over-nice about any possible avenue for information, so I swallowed my feelings and went along to see him. He jumped six inches when he heard my name and came half-way across the room in a long, shambling step to meet me. His great beak of a nose jutted like the Black Jack cliffs as he put a cold hand into mine.

"You've brought news?" he blurted out. "My God, Curteis, this is a bad business."

"It's bad for Fanny Price," I agreed. "It's about her that I've come."

"What do you mean? I can't help you."

"You've known her longer than any of us...."

"It's no good blaming me for what she's done. I didn't guess she'd be capable of this. I knew she was, as they say, hard-boiled, but murder ..."

"It's the privilege of her friends to prove that she didn't murder Rubenstein," I pointed out.

"But the police say she did."

"And Fanny says she didn't. Personally, I back Fanny."

"Well, but how do you think I can help you?"

"I thought you might tell me a little about her. Where, for instance, did you meet her?"

"I don't see how that helps you. It's years ago. And anyway, the fellow's been dead for I don't know how long."

"Isn't there some member of the family who could remember Fanny, who might know her back history?"

"Well, but even if she could—Mrs. Hammond, I mean—what's that got to do with Rubenstein?"

"The history of a murder doesn't start with the crime," I explained. "Sometimes it goes back years. It may in this case. That's what I want to find out. Did you say the name was Hammond?"

"Yes—well, the lady took her own name after her husband's death. He was partly Chinese—Chinese father, English mother. A very striking man—highly intelligent. But people are queer. Most of her friends urged Leila Hammond not to marry the fellow, but she would, and as it happened there weren't any children to complicate matters. In fact, I believe everything turned out very well. Still, she dropped the name of Wang and now she's known as Hammond again. She does a lot of social work," he ran on nervously, "and having a Chinese name is apt to give wrong impressions. I don't suppose she knows anything about Fanny, though. In fact, I don't think she ever liked the girl."

"How did she meet her?"

"Oh, Fanny was Wang's secretary. Where he picked her up I can't tell you. But Fanny learned everything she knows, which is a good deal, about China and Chinese art from him. He was writing a book on the subject; it was a mass of notes when he died. I doubt if he'd ever have shaped it. Impatience, that was his weakness. When he knew a thing himself he wanted to go on to something he didn't know. He couldn't wait long enough to tell other people about it. I dare say Mrs. Hammond has the notes somewhere, but I doubt if any one could make anything of them. He was a lecturer, too. Fanny used to go round with him. That's how I met her. She wasn't much use to me in his lifetime, he kept her so hard at it. But after Wang died about three years ago I ran across her again— Mrs. Hammond sold most of his stuff and I picked up one or two pieces—and I found Fanny there, and she's been quite useful to me from time to time ever since. She's good," he added grudgingly. "As good as Rubenstein. I don't believe I ever found her wrong. A knack like that is inborn; you can't discover it, you can only develop it."

I wasn't interested in his prosy reflections and I asked for Mrs. Hammond's address. Graham warned me that it might not be the same, he hadn't kept up with the lady, he didn't think Fanny had, but when he knew them they lived in a flat at Hampstead. I drew him on to talk a bit about the night of Rubenstein's disappearance, but he refused to say much. He said he'd been writing letters; as you remember, he added.

"I was writing letters, too," I told him. "I can't vouch for any of you."

When I got to the address in Hampstead I found that Mrs. Hammond had moved. I wasted the rest of the day discovering her whereabouts, and when at last I got to the right house she was out at a meeting and wasn't expected back till late. I left my name and a note, and a message that I'd ring up next morning. Mrs. Hammond said she could spare me a few minutes between a delegation of shop-girls and a committee of inquiry into the conditions of rag-pickers in East London. I must be at the house on the stroke of 11.30. I got there at 11.25, and as the clock chimed the half-hour the door opened and Mrs. Hammond came in. She was wearing a hat with half a shot bird in it, and something pepper and salt that gave her a very square appearance. She had a handclasp like a grizzly bear and a voice that matched it. She wore rimless glasses, and her eyes were hazel. I realized at once that she was quite ready to label me the type of man who has had a bad time and wants a bit of help— or possibly justice. Or I might have been a collector. She said immediately that her time was very limited and she couldn't undertake any fresh responsibilities or subscriptions. She detailed the work she did and the demands it made upon her, and having used most of the time she'd allowed me, to make these explanations, she waited for mine. I mentioned Fanny's name and she looked suspicious at once.

"I've seen nothing of Miss Price since my husband's death," she told me briskly. "And in any case I know nothing of her private affairs."

Years of dealing with blackmailers, scoundrels, deserting husbands, unmarried fathers and the more unmentionable members of society were helping her to put me in the right category. I said, "Mr. Graham of Ravenswood Mansions gave me your name. He said you might be able to help me."

She said again, "I have no idea where she is."

I stared. I wondered if I were dealing with a lunatic.

When a thing matters enormously to you it's incredible that any one else should remain unaware of it.

"I can tell you where she is," I told her. "In jail, waiting to be tried for murder."

"Oh, is she?" I can't reproduce for you the cool voice in which Mrs. Hammond received the news. "I'm hardly surprised."

To most people it's a shock and to many an excitement to discover an acquaintance charged with a capital crime, but Mrs. Hammond might have been meeting murderesses or suspected murderesses four days out of seven. "I never did think her a reliable sort of girl, and it stands to reason that if you play fast and loose with men sooner or later you'll get into trouble."

"Which men?" I asked baldly.

Mrs. Hammond loftily couldn't answer that, not in detail. She merely said, "She was perpetually out and about with men of every kind and class. She seemed to have no discrimination at all. One day she'd be off to the Berkeley with a man in tails, and the next to some cheap dance hall with some one in a lounge suit from the forty-five-shilling tailors. Oh, she was mad for pleasure."

"How long did she work for your husband?" I asked.

"About two years and a half."

"And why did she leave him?"

"He died," said Mrs. Hammond, unemotionally.

"Otherwise she might be working for him still?"

"I dare say. He thought a good deal of her work."

"Then, in the circumstances, don't you think it rather dangerous to describe her as an unreliable person?"

"I didn't mean professionally. She knew her job. She was that type of young woman. But—well, I always saw the mark of the adventuress in her. They have a glittering time for a while, but they generally come to grief in the end."

"The point," I explained politely, "is that we—her friends—don't think she's guilty."

Mrs. Hammond stared. "In that case, what have you come to me for? I can't help you. I wasn't there. I don't know anything about the case. Do you expect me to come into court and say I'm sure she's innocent becouse she was my husband's secretary for two years and a half and she's not the type of young woman to resort to violence? I'm sure she's exactly that type, if necessary."

"We don't want you to come into court and say that either," I warned her dryly. "I want to know where your husband came across her."

"I don't know the name of the man," said Mrs. Hammond. "My husband and I had separate interests and we kept them apart. We neither of us cared to talk shop; he had his affairs and I had mine. I do a good deal of social and committee work, and his research—he was writing a book on oriental art at the time of his death—often kept him up till the small hours of the morning. He told me one day he had met a girl at a friend's house who, he thought, would make an efficient secretary. She knew nothing of his particular subject, but he thought she would learn. She apparently knew shorthand and he seemed impressed by her intelligence. Well, she was intelligent all right. If I were asked for a reference for her, I should say that so far as I knew, she was quite satisfactory at her work."

"Was your husband easily pleased?"

"No. He suffered a good deal of pain from an accident in his youth and that made him irritable and exacting."

"But he didn't complain of Fanny?"

Mrs. Hammond was thoroughly honest, with that candor that is often so much more disagreeable than downright bad manners.

"No, he always spoke very highly of her. I've told you that already. Of course, it's my experience that a woman can be an extremely good worker and a thoroughly bad citizen."

I got angry. I said, "You've nothing to go on, but instinct."

"And my knowledge of human nature," said Mrs. Hammond smugly. "Remember, I have spent most of my life dealing with individuals, particularly with young women."

This conversation was getting us nowhere. I asked if she could give me Fanny's address during the time of her employment by the Chinese scholar, and she gave me the name of a house in Fawcett Street.

"It stands to reason that a girl earning what my husband could afford to pay her couldn't possibly afford a flat in that part of London unless she had some other means of support. And I know the hours she kept with him. She couldn't have done any other work."

Mrs. Hammond's meaning was obvious. I said, "You're discounting private means, aren't you?"

"There's one other thing perhaps I should tell you,"

this truthful, detestable woman went on. "A rather unpleasant thing happened while Miss Price was here. I lost some rather valuable jewelry—insured, of course —but one's possessions have a certain personal value that can't be commercially assessed. Miss Price was most hepful in making inquiries and suggestions, but— the jewels were not found."

"And you think she was involved in their—removal?"

"That would be slander. But the police said obviously it had been some one in the house, possibly in collaboration with some one outside. And I had had my servants for years and years."

She looked at her watch. "I'm sorry I can't help you more, and now—I have a committee." She crossed the room and pressed the bell.

CHAPTER XII

But I will wear my heart upon my sleeve
For daws to peck at.

OTHELLO.

ON that pleasant note we parted and I went to Fawcett
Street. I saw that once again Fanny had had the wit
to choose a good address and put up with indifferent
comfort. Fawcett House had a good, even a handsome
exterior, but inside it was all shoddy, licks of white-
wash, curtains hung to conceal bulging walls, cheap
flats with a good appearance. There was no porter, and
the housekeeper was out when I arrived. I went up
to No. 8, which had been Fanny's flat. A cheerful
young woman in a cretonne overall opened the door.

"If you want Bill," she said, "he's gone to fetch his
boots back. Got a couple of guineas unexpectedly this
morning, and at last he can pay for the soling. Come
in and wait if you like. I'm just frying some kippers."

I explained that I didn't want Bill. "I was given
this address as being a flat occupied about two years
ago by a Miss Price."

"That gorgeous girl? You knew her? I suppose you
aren't in touch with her now?"

I was more amazed at this ignorance than I had
been at Mrs. Hammond's. "She's in jail," I said.

My woman friend stared. "That's not the same one?

149

Good heavens! What rotten photographs they've had in the press. And what rotten luck that Bill never did that portrait of her. Bill's mad, you know," she added confidentially. "He just mooned about after that girl from the first instant he set eyes on her. He wanted to paint her. We only saw her twice. This was a sub-let and she had some sticks here we thought we might take over. We had to talk about price—no, that's not meant to be a rotten pun. I was the only member of the three that had any sense. Fanny Price was ready to take anything we offered—she said she hated the things anyhow—and Bill would have given her anything she asked and popped everything except his easel to pay her. He was crazy about her. He'd let everything else go, trying to make crayon sketches of her. There was some talk of a picture in oils, but nothing came of it. If he'd had that he'd be able to ask anything he liked for it now, thanks to the morbid streak in human nature."

"You didn't keep up with her?" I asked hopefully.

"We weren't Fanny's money. Besides, she knew so many people. Though she had her bad times like the rest of us. After she'd gone I was clearing things up one day when I found a pawn-ticket. A diamond brooch —twenty-five pounds. You know what these brokers are. If you can't produce your ticket they pinch your goods. I nearly blacked a man's eye once because he wouldn't let me have Bill's only decent suit out of pawn. And he had to go and see a prospective client. Well, I thought of wretched Fanny Price looking for that ticket and seeing her twenty-five quid go up the spout. Because if a broker will give you all that on a brooch you can take your davy it's worth about four times as much."

"You never managed to get in touch with her?"

"No. I asked the housekeeper and I asked them at the letting office—you take these flats on an annual lease, unfurnished—but they hadn't heard anything more of her. Well, p'raps she'd found some one to whom diamond brooches and twenty-five quid were no more than the skin on the apple."

"What happened about the ticket?"

"Oh, we kept it in an envelope for a long time, months after it had run out, and then one day it got swept up or something—it wasn't worth anything then." Suddenly her fair face colored. "You don't think we redeemed it, do you? Why, we never have £25 for one thing," she began to laugh, "and anyhow, I always say it's not worth going to hell for that much money. If it were six figures you might be tempted. But twenty-five pounds wouldn't begin to pay our bills, so why wreck your soul to pay your creditors?"

She couldn't help me any further, so I went downstairs and this time was lucky enough to catch the housekeeper at home. I didn't very much like that story about the brooch, coming on top of Mrs. Hammond's story about the jewel robbery. You see, one of the things that had attracted me to Fanny in the first place had been my recognition in her of the very streak of the adventuress of which Mrs. Hammond had spoken. If she'd told me, laughing and head-high, even a bit complacent, that she'd engineered that robbery, I'd have believed her. It wasn't that she hadn't a moral code, but she hadn't got a conventional one. I could see her pinching brooches and even patting herself on the back for her own intelligence in not being caught. What I couldn't see was her stabbing Rubenstein.

The housekeeper was a sallow, embittered, over-worked woman, with no pretensions to education, a driving employer, driven in her turn by the people who probably made a quite handsome income out of these wretched flats. She said she remembered Fanny; she had been at No. 8 and had gone pretty suddenly. No, she couldn't say why, but she wouldn't be surprised to hear there was a man behind it. There was a fellow in a reddish beard that came to see her sometimes. Proper roughhouse they had once. No, she didn't know who he was, but it just showed that it paid you to live decent. Once you got yourself messed up with men you might end anywhere. Anyhow, Fanny had sublet in a hurry, let her furniture go for nothing, and disappeared. She couldn't give me any idea where she'd gone to.

"Come up in the world coming here," she said. "Come out of Railton Street. Well, we know what that's like. All bed-sitting-rooms, and they say the amount of money that changes hands in some of those houses of a night would surprise you. All the colors of the rainbow that street is."

I managed to get the number of the house and went to Railton Street. It was a terrace of gaunt disfigured houses with peeling porticos and shabby façades. Dingy lace curtains hung in the windows, mostly a sooty laurel stuck up its dishonored head in a patch of earth in front of the basement window. I counted nine of those laurel bushes to twelve houses; the others hadn't even the enterprise to produce that handful of grimy leaves and splintering stem. This was so definite a step in the downward scale that I was surprised at a man of Wang's culture taking a girl from such a district; and then I remembered Fanny and thought that she would transfigure even this intolerable environment. The landlady said at once, "If you've come after 'er you've come to the wrong 'ouse," and would have shut the door in my face if I hadn't shoved my foot in the crack.

"I'm inquiring for the police," I told her with indirect truth.

The door opened wider; something approaching affability showed on that tattered face.

"And I'm not surprised neither. If I'd known the sort of girl she was I'd never 'ave 'ad 'er in my 'ouse. No one shall say I'm not broad-minded, but when it comes to 'aving doings with yellow men, then I'm through." She spread her pudgy hands, the broad wedding-ring sunk deep in the discolored flesh. "I wouldn't 'ave nothing to do with 'er, not after she took up with that Chink."

"That Chink, as you call him, was a very famous philosopher and author," I told her, straining truth as one strains the elastic of a catapult to get as much force as possible behind the blow. "Miss Price was his secretary."

" 'E may be the Prince of China for all I care," said the stupid woman obstinately. "All I say is, there's plenty of white men for a girl to go and work for. I never did stand for these funny foreigners. When 'e come calling for 'er one day, saying, 'I'll wait in 'er room if she's not in,' I soon sent him about his business. My lodgers don't 'ave gentlemen to their rooms,

I told 'im. This is a respectable 'ouse and so long as I'm in it it'll stop respectable. And when she did come in—three in the morning, if you'll believe me—I told 'er straight out: 'If you want to play your dirty games with yellow men you can do it in somebody else's 'ouse,' I said. It wasn't as if that was the only Chink she was ever with. I saw 'er with another with my own eyes, sitting in the pictures. Well, I got my own living to get and I got to think of my other lodgers. 'Out you go, my lady,' I told 'er. 'And never mind about the week's rent. You'll cost me more than a week's rent staying 'ere.' "

"And she went?" I asked, wondering what on earth had happened to my lovely Fanny to have got her into these squalid surroundings.

"Oh, she went all right. I saw to that. Where did she go? 'Ow should I know? If you're looking for 'er, I'd try Jermyn Street about dinner-time."

That led me nowhere, simply gave me a picture of a Fanny I'd never suspected existed, a Fanny in a pretty bad way. Still, I was comforted to think that she had moved up the ladder when she went to Fawcett Street.

My obvious job was to discover the name of the red-bearded fellow who had, clearly, driven her out of Fawcett Street, and the time that he had entered her life. It might be sheer coincidence, he might have nothing to do with Rubenstein at all, but this was the first clew I had found. And why had Fanny had a rough-house with the fellow? That didn't sound like her tactics at all. More and more I began to feel that this man had some hold over her. I went back to my line of inquiries like a bloodhound after a corpse.

Mrs. Hammond had told me that she didn't know the name of the man at whose house her husband had met Fanny, but she had added that he was a famous Chinese authority of English birth. She said he had written a book in the Ancient Civilizations series on that country. I went to the *Times* Book Club and asked for information. They discovered that the book in question had been written by a man called Ellison, and told me the publishers. The publishers, cautious folk, promised to forward a letter, and a couple of days later I found myself traveling down to Brighton to interview my quarry in one of those fine old Regency houses for which Brighton is famous and that once sheltered the more picturesque bucks who regarded the place as a kind of spa, and with whose disappearance so much of the grandeur of the place has departed. I thought of them as I plowed doggedly along the promenade. It was a wild sort of day, with the spray flying over the parade, and the place seemed inhabited by a queer sort of dwarf as people went by doubled against the wind. Ellison was in and was expecting me. He was a thin, ascetic sort of fellow with a wandering manner. He said he remembered Fanny quite well and kept breaking off his answers to recount incidents that occurred to him about her, that in the ordinary way would have delighted me but that now drove me almost to frenzy.

"A most interesting woman," he observed, joining his finger-tips. "I recall her perfectly well. She had had a very unfortunate time, I believe. A scoundrelly husband, I heard. Or perhaps a husband by courtesy. In any case I understand he treated her abominably, left her high and dry, and sponged on her whenever he could. She wouldn't speak much about it. I discovered her singing—French songs in a very French costume— in one of the night haunts of London. A superb creature; she gave you the impression that she snapped her fingers at the whole show, the bawdy words and the fourth-rate audience. I got hold of her afterwards— oh, it wasn't difficult in that kind of place; a bottle of champagne would have bought any girl the management was displaying. She told me a bit, not much, but she said she had learned shorthand and she seemed intelligent. I knew my friend, Wang, wanted a secretary, and I wanted to do something for her if I could. I asked her to come to my house and arranged for Wang to see her. He gave her the job at once, and she stayed with him till his death. I saw her from time to time during that period, but not enough ever to become intimate with her. She wasn't actually my type of a girl at all. I mean to say, I should never have been at ease with her. I simply don't understand that kind of woman. I've sometimes wondered what were her antecedents. Good blood on one side, the wrong side of the blanket, I've always imagined."

"You never heard any more about her private life?"

"Never. I didn't inquire, naturally, and Wang wouldn't have been interested."

It seemed to me that my researches were leading me farther and farther back into the past. This husband, whether courtesy or real, seemed to play a considerable part in Fanny's life. I began to wonder if that was why she had refused Bridie. She hadn't told him the truth, because he had quoted the letter. But I had a vision of this ruffian preying on her till she hurriedly threw up the Fawcett Street flat and went to Armitage Road, where no amount of inquiries had elicited any information about a red-haired man, and thence to the place where she'd been living when I met her. Miss Verity couldn't help me, either. She reminded me again that this was a block of modern flats, not a prison, and said that no one kept tabs on the movements of tenants. She could recall nothing about a red-bearded or even a red-headed man, though she added cheerfully that Miss Price might have had half a dozen such friends for aught she knew. My one hope, therefore, seemed to be to go back and back until I discovered something tangible about this creature. I hesitated about attacking Fanny directly at present; the stubborn creature was capable of sticking in her toes and swearing she hadn't got a husband; and perhaps she hadn't. Like the woman of Samaria, she might have had any number and not been too meticulous about legal ties.

Ellison was able to give me the name of the cabaret where he had first seen Fanny, "though," he added, coloring a little, "there isn't any need to mention my name. It was quite by chance that I went there. . . ."

Ellison's name didn't matter to me any more than the man in the moon, so I gave him my promise readily enough; and at the night-club—for that's what it really was—I was lucky enough to get the address of another girl who had done entertaining there at the same time as Fanny. I tracked this woman down and discovered that she was now in music-hall shows in the

157

suburbs and smaller houses of entertainment, at Hammersmith and Chiswick and Hendon Park. I went to
a show at Hammersmith and afterwards waited patiently in her dressing-room till she came in. She was
a common little thing, with a vivacious manner and
a bad skin. But she had a kind of cockney charm and
a good deal of vitality. I took her out to supper and
bought her champagne; she'd just as soon have drunk
ginger-pop, but she knew champagne was the right
thing, so she had a couple of glasses and got quite
talkative. It was easy enough to get her going on Fanny.

"When I opened the paper," she said, "you could
have knocked me down with a feather. Not that I'd
put it past Fan. There was a lot of devil in that girl.
And, of course, the fellow was rich. Well, we all knew
Fan wouldn't end in small letters like the rest of us. I
mean, just to look at her—she never was quite like
any one else. Even Mr. Politi, whatever his real name
may have been, treated her different."

I asked how well she'd known Fanny, had she ever
had anything to do with her outside the night-club.

"I can tell you quite a bit," said Miss Allen eagerly.
"Well, it was me really that got her into the Half-
penny Bun. We were lodging in the same house, and
she had a job in a Euston eating-house washing dishes.
Ten bob a week and your food—what the customers
leave. You know the kind of thing—or no, p'raps
you don't. She had a room in the Euston Road first,
and there weren't any keys to the doors, so if you
wanted a night to yourself you had to shift the dressing-
table across it, just to be sure. Fanny always did, anyhow. Well, she was quite right. The sort of men you

meet in lodging-houses in the Euston Road aren't any use to a girl. I liked her looks so I spoke for her to the boss—we'd talked now and again, you see—and he, Mr. Politi, that is, sent for her and took her on right away, just on her face value. 'You be careful,' I warned her, seeing this was her first job of the kind. 'The Half-penny Bun isn't the same as a church.' She laughed; I dare say she knew more about cabarets than she did about churches. But she was right when she laughed. What was the good of Fanny being careful? Made for trouble, she was. Had all the men after her from the first night she sang there. She could have taken enough to set herself up for life, if she'd liked, in a small way, the first month she was there. But Fanny looked high. Took a lot of chances the rest of us would have blinked at. If a toff that took her fancy asked her out, out she'd go, never mind where she met him. 'Aren't you never afraid of your luck?' I'd ask her, and she'd laugh again and say, 'Who knows what luck is? Here today and gone tomorrow. I'm more afraid of staying here all my life.' She didn't neither. Took up with a Chinaman or so I heard. Very respectable, you know; married to a white woman. Lived in ever such a posh flat, Hampstead way. Of course, I never went to see her there, but that's what I heard. No pigtail or anything and he wore clothes like you might yourself. Well, you've got to look after yourself in this world. No one's going to do it for you. I saw her again about three years afterwards. She was walking through the streets with a proper gentle-man. Little red beard he had, I remember. That's funny, you know. It isn't like gay Paree, where there's beards on every corner. You notice 'em more here. I remember there was one of these street photographers turning his little handle at the time, and when she'd gone past I went up and said, 'I used to know that lady; I'd like a picture of her.' He wasn't half saucy." I filled up her glass as she fell into a reverie and her eyes brightened and she went on. "Yes. What do you think of this for cheek? 'Out to make easy money, I suppose,' he said. But I got the picture just the same. Not that it was anything to me who Fanny went with or what she did. It isn't as if I'd ever really known her. What? No, I didn't try and speak to her, of course. She was always a bit above me, even when she was washing dishes—in a way—though that was funny, sort of—and by that time she'd gone a lot higher in the world."

I said, "I suppose you didn't keep the photograph," and she giggled and said, "You've got it bad, haven't you? Matter of fact, I did. I come across it only the other day when I was turning out a box. I remember showing it to a friend of mine once. 'That girl's born for something big,' he said to me. 'Queen, p'raps,' I laughed, and he said, 'Yes, or hanged. Never can tell.' Queer, wasn't it?"

I went back with her to her rooms and she found the picture for me.

It wasn't a good picture, and it was yellowed with the years; but I'd have known Fanny anywhere. The man with her had a little beard and horn-rimmed glasses. To the best of my knowledge, I'd never seen him before.

~ ~ ~

CHAPTER XIII

Everything's got a moral if only you can find it.
ALICE IN WONDERLAND.

WE had a bit of trouble running the red-headed chap
to earth, and Fanny didn't help us. I can't say we gave
her a lot of opportunity—Crook saw to that—but she
didn't even take advantage of the rope we did pay out.
When I went to Crook with the handful of facts and
rumors I'd gleaned he scratched his head and told me,
"If all my cases were like this I'd retire into the country
and plant potatoes. We've been running all we know
since the day we met and we're exactly where we were
at that time. We've tried the picture-house, the station
officials, the bartender, and we've got what I anticipated
—an army of half-wits panting for publicity and none
of 'em even able to pick out her photograph from a
row on the table."

"Why didn't Fanny tell us herself about this man?"
I asked.

"Either because he has nothing to do with this little
job and she's not the type of young woman that wastes
your time for fun—which is a pleasant change—or because she has, and she knows it."

"How does she know?"

"Because she's in with him, say." Crook's eyebrows
forked like lightning; he looked like that fellow that

does stunts on a ladder at the London Music Hall. "She may have been keeping up with him, professionally, ever since the marriage. This tale about Mrs. Hammond's jewelry—I wouldn't be surprised if she was mixed up in that. She and the red-headed gentleman."

"Do we ask her outright—about the husband, I mean?"

But Crook was nothing if not original. "As I see it," he said, "it's no use our tackling Fanny Price about this doubtful husband of hers at this stage. If he's in it the irresistible conclusion is that she's involved, and our case is that she ain't. We'll play our cards carefully here, my boy, with no more admissions from the lady than we can help. Nelson's blind eye must have been a whale of an advantage some of the time."

I agreed rather stiffly that we didn't want to give Fanny the impression that we were trying to drag the fellow in.

Crook clicked with his tongue. "We don't drag any one in," he said severely. "The pattern's made. All we have to do is uncover it. It seems pretty obvious that our lovely Fanny's marriage was a bit of a scunner. Looks as though this fellow battened on her whenever he had the chance."

"I'd no idea she had a husband," I said uneasily.

"Well, she's hardly the type that wears her heart on her sleeve, that is, provided she's got one to flaunt anywhere. But there are these casual references to the feller from more sources than one." He began to jot down some notes. "Miss Allen saw them together in 1931.

162

The woman at Fawcett Street talks of a red-bearded man at the end of that year. He seems to have put the wind up Fanny properly; she cleared out practically at a day's notice and left no address. Remember that pawn-ticket? Looks as though she'd been put to it, don't it? Perhaps it was Mrs. Hammond's brooch. I don't know—and anyway, it's nothing to do with the case. We've tracked her to Armitage Street since then, and apparently he either didn't find her there or he'd got some other source of supply. Anyway, we don't hear anything of him after the early part of 1932. She may have been sending him money, of course, but with any luck she'd shaken him off. It's noticeable he hasn't come forward with any offers, and she's keeping mighty dark about him for her own reasons."

"We don't know what those are," I said sharply.

"No." Crook almost laid his finger against his nose, "and just at present I don't want to. I'm all for a bit of light myself."

"If you aren't going to get it from Fanny," I said uncomfortably.

"Oh, I'll just pop along and see Fanny and tell her the rumor's going round that she's actually a married woman and the court will want her proper status for formal reasons. That way I ought to get the chap's name, and we can start working from there."

"Finesse," I murmured, feeling rather like a man who sees an inexperienced doctor hacking away at a helpless patient on the operating table. And sure enough Crook roared. He had about as much finesse as a lobster that grabs you with a claw first and asks questions about your identity afterwards.

I didn't go down to the prison with Crook, but I waited eagerly enough for his return.

"The fellow's name is Randall, and they were married in '27 or '28—no details—but we ought to get those easily enough. Fanny's not exactly forthcoming about the fellow. I gather they didn't live together after the first few months, after which she seems to have kept out of his way all she knew. No information as to present whereabouts."

It took Marks some time to get the facts, and even when he'd got them we were still only at the beginning of our chase.

Fanny married this chap Randall in 1927 in London; three months later they were in Paris, where they don't seem to have stayed long, and then they were heard of in London again. There was nothing to show how he got a living, or whether she did the job for the two. It would be typical if she had. You couldn't imagine any circumstance downing Fanny; even a rotten husband she'd take in her stride. Randall appeared to have described himself as a man of independent means.

"I know all about that," said Crook with his sly sideways glance. "So blame independent you never see 'em."

From all accounts he kept good company, drank and dressed well, and bought his wife expensive presents. At all events witnesses said she wore handsome jewelry and fine furs and silk stockings.

"Whether any of them were ever paid for is another matter," observed Crook, grinning. He was beginning to like this case. After the return from Paris the history of the pair became more sketchy; the next definite information about Fanny was her dishwashing period that, admittedly, didn't last long, and then her experience at the Halfpenny Bun. We had definite dates for that. In 1928 she was at the hash-house; in 1929 she was singing at the Halfpenny Bun. In the autumn of that year she got the job with Wang, who died in the beginning of 1932. At the end of 1931 Fanny had abruptly cleared out of Fawcett Street, which sounded as though the husband might have turned up again. Since 1932 she had been living her free-lance existence, and though she had been seen out with any number of men we had no definite information about a man with a red beard.

"Though that means nothing," Crook pointed out. "He may have shaved it off; they may have arranged to meet where they weren't likely to be recognized. As it is we haven't a single witness who, if she met the fellow face to face, would dare to identify him.

"Where was he during those three years when he seems to have vanished as completely as though the earth had done its famous swallowing act?" meditated Crook. "Living with some other woman, on some other woman, in the workhouse, abroad, in jail—by jove, Curteis, there's one line we can get on to. The police keep a record—it's a slim chance but no end of a gift to us if it proves right."

I was less hopeful. "Provided he was arrested in his own name, or is using it still. Even if they have his fingerprints, how does that help us?"

Crook hit me hard on the shoulder. "Take each stile as you come to it," he said. "You're not a professional athlete, are you?"

I wondered aloud whether Burgess might help us here, but Crook said, with some violence, that he didn't fancy putting all his cards into the hands of the opposition, not until he was compelled. There were other men at the Yard. I left it at that.

That night he telephoned in triumph. "Randall was pinched for company fraud in 1928, October," he said. "He got three years at Kingstown. It was a baddish case. Forgery among other things. Now, we can get ahead."

I saw the chaplain at Kingstown Jail, a big, red-headed, humorous man, with a large crooked nose and a cynical jaw.

"Randall?" he said. "A nice gentlemanly chap. I remember him. The kind I dislike most."

"Pugnacious?" I asked.

"Sulked for a long time. Had one shot at a getaway. Then turned oily. I don't like those nice polite prisoners. Grousing's like sweat. You want to get it out of your system. He didn't. Was full of plans for what he'd do when he got out."

"Did he talk about his home affairs at all?"

"Not a word. Oh, you couldn't get him anywhere. Well, I didn't blame him for that. But I wouldn't mind betting he hadn't been out three months before he was at his old games. It's the fault of the prison system perhaps. You can't treat every prisoner as an individual case demanding particular treatment. You get accused of preferential behavior if you do, and the quiet, decently-behaved chaps that don't present a problem are the first to suffer. I mean, they don't need particular attention. Chaps like Randall learn nothing from prison except how to be a bit more careful the next time."

"Have you heard of him since he left?" I wanted to know.

"We gave him the usual D.P.A. letter. I saw him before he left, and he said, 'Thanks very much,' he didn't propose to publish to the world that he'd spent three years in quod. He didn't get remission. That almost successful attempt at a getaway did for him. Oh, I hadn't expected him to take any help. There are two reasons," he pulled out a tobacco pouch and for a moment was comically like the advertisement of 'Three Nuns,' "why a fellow doesn't want your help when he goes away from here. One is because he's resentful, he doesn't mean to label himself as a rescued convict— he's going straight, but he's going to try and blot out the past; and the other, the party to whom our friend Randall belonged, hasn't the slightest intention of going any straighter than a corkscrew. If I could have looked into that fellow's mind, as he was bored to tears by my jolly Sunday morning addresses, I'd have seen him twisting and doubling and working out plans to pay the community back for jugging him at all, and for making up for lost time. If he tried to trick people out of a couple of thousand pounds the first time, he meant to get them for a hundred thousand the next."

"Did he stand his trial on his own?" I asked.

"He had two partners. One got eight years, and is due out any day now; the other died in prison. Randall wouldn't wait for them; anyway, he wouldn't go in for the second time with a pair of blundering rogues. Randall's morality consists in not being found out. He told me once there was no justification for jailing him for any other reason. I don't know where he is now, but if he's alive you can take it from me he's a rich man, and he's planning how to be richer. The last time I heard of him he was down in Devonshire, secretary to a nabob. One of my fellows, a good chap who used to be a bricklayer and tried to slug the chap that stole his wife, saw him. He writes to me every three months and tells me how he's getting on."

"How long ago was this?"

"Oh, two or three years. Less than a year after Randall came away anyway."

"You don't know the address?"

"No. But Bennett might. I had a letter from him a couple of days ago. You could rout him out."

He found the letter, which gave an address in Poplar. "You can trust Charlie," said the chaplain. "Well, if anything eventuates, let me know. I didn't like Randall, but he's interesting, a dozen times more interesting than these fellows like Bennett. That's the worst of evil; it's an absorbing occupation and calls for so much more subtlety than virtue. So few righteous folk have the wit to recognize their opportunities. They're simple as doves, all right, many of them, but they can't combine that simplicity with the wisdom of the serpent, for all they're instructed to do so in Holy Writ." He shook hands with me and I walked out into the rain. The jail was a great gray building, devoid of hope. I thought of Randall, that energetic inventive man, walking away from it into the world, his mind full of the schemes he'd been planning during three years' incarceration. I agreed with the chaplain. He was an interesting beggar.

And there must have been something to make Fanny marry him. Something rich and forceful and individual. Just money wouldn't get her. My excitement rose as I neared London. I proposed to go down to Poplar that evening. It was now four o'clock and the lights of London were globes of gold in the wider streets, and arrows of light in the alleys.

Poplar, apart from the wide, central road that hums with trams and motor omnibuses, is a medley of small intersecting ways, some of them little more than court-yards. The once romantic Limehouse reveals itself as a squalid beehive of lanes and streets full of battered houses and broken window-panes. I inquired my way to Roland Street and was directed northward. The house in which Bennett lived was definitely outer-suburban; there were clean curtains at the windows, more ferns than usual, a handsome iron-gray cat stretching on a velvet-covered settee, an elaborate clock on the mantelpiece, a fur rug by the hearth. It was obvious that the Bennetts lived in comparative luxury. Mrs. Bennett, who let me in, wore a red silk dress and a pearl necklace that hadn't come from the Sixpenny Stores. Bennett was a spry little fellow, with pale blue eyes and long powerful hands. In spite of those hands it was difficult to believe he'd nearly killed a man.

Any embarrassment in the conversation was on my side. Bennett would have thought it far more shameful to take his case against his wife and her lover to court than to have bashed them both and done a stretch for it. Any chap, he told me a bit boastfully, has a right to go for any other chap that comes messing his missus about. I looked at Mrs. Bennett to see how she took this, but she was sewing, not the baby-clothes of righteous fiction but something flimsy and bright-colored—her own underclothes, I dare say.

Bennett saw the direction of my glance and explained quickly that that missus had died while he was in prison—a tactful woman, clearly, for all her misdemeanors—and this was No. 2. His victim, he added, was going lame all his life, which in some ways was more satisfactory than dying, from Bennett's point of view. He'd never be able to work again at the docks, which was his job; Bennett was pleased to remember that.

"Randall?" he said in reply to my question. "Oh, he was always different from the rest of us. Proper gentleman, you know. Didn't mix. Too low for 'im, we were, though 'e was put away for pinching. He didn't want a card or anything when he come out. Had slap-up friends, no doubt. Anyway, I was down at Romerton about a year ago doing a bricklaying job and there I see my lord walking through the village, bold as brass. Quite the gentleman again. Never ha' guessed he'd picked oakum in his time. He stopped to talk to the squire and the squire talked back. I went by, eyes right, if you understand, but he didn't know me. No one would ha' thought we'd ate the same skilly. I didn't say a word, of course, but the next time I saw him I stepped up and 'Hallo, Randall,' I said, 'going up in the world, aren't you?' I was a bit riled, see. After all, he might be a gentleman born but that's no call to look at a man like he was dirt. He looked at me when I said, 'On your feet again, aren't you?' and on my oath

I'll never be nearer death than I was that minute. I never saw a man look so like murder."

"What was he doing there?" I asked.

"Got some kind of a job up at a big house with an invalid gentleman called Kirby. Kind of secretary, I heard. I didn't grudge him his chance, and a nice soft job it was from all accounts, but I didn't see why he should put on such airs about it."

"How long were you there?" I asked.

"Matter of two months."

"And he was there when you left?"

"What do you think? It was a warm job for him. I used to think sometimes, all very well for you to look so high and mighty, but if your boss was to know the truth . . ."

"You didn't point that out to Randall?" I suggested.

Bennett's face turned crimson. "What do you think I am?" he demanded. "A dirty blackmailer?"

Up till that time I hadn't been sure. Now I was pretty certain. Men don't fire up like that, and put that type of suggestion on your lips, if there isn't some justification for it. I began to wonder just how much Randall's job had cost him, after Bennett came to Romerton. One thing, a bricklayer can't afford to live in the style Bennett was living in without some kind of additional help. I led him on to talk of himself; he hadn't been in the war, so there was no question of a war pension; he spoke of the bad weather that made bricklaying out of the question; he talked about unemployment, saying he'd had his share, though when there was work it was well-paid enough. At the moment, he said, he was out of a job.

"Bosses seem to think a family man can chuck up his home and go here, there and everywhere," he complained, "just at a minute's notice. That's all right for the single men. It don't pay for a man to leave his wife alone for weeks on end. I know. I've tried it. So when they told me there was a job out at Reading—new church or something—I wouldn't sign on for it. There's going to be work on that old site where they've been demolishing the rope factory in a matter of a week or two and I've got a promise from the foreman for that."

"And live on capital?" I suggested lightly, and added something about lodgers.

"No lodgers in my 'ouse, thank you," said Bennett. "I tell you, I've had some."

He told me the rent of the house was 27/- a week. It may have been worth it. But a man whose average wage varies between 60/- and 70/- can't pay that for rent and maintain the kind of home and table that clearly he did. Besides, Mrs. Bennett's clothes weren't made for nothing, and they spoke of a girl to help. It all pointed, to my mind, to a constant drain from another source, and that source seemed to me obviously to be Randall. In spite of everything my optimistic chaplain had said, I didn't trust one ex-convict any more than I trusted the other. They were both out for success and both looked to me as though they might overshoot their mark by being too ambitious.

I refused a cup of tea and walked down the street towards the station. At the end of the road I ran against an obvious laborer, whom I stopped to ask if he could tell me where a chap called Bennett lived.

"Charlie Bennett?"

"That's it."

He told me the number of the house. "Though you may not find him in," he warned me. "Out five nights a week, Charlie is. There's some of us would like his luck."

"Doing well?" I suggested casually.

"Well enough to give his wife a silk dress and chuck away ten bob of an evening at the Port of Call."

"Must have got a good job," I commented.

"And not the only one. Still, there's rainy weather, ain't there, like when they had that strike the other day. Proper put to it, most of us were. The ones with kids in work were the lucky ones. But it didn't worry Charlie, though his wife never has to put on a scrubbing apron and go out with a broom and pail like a lot of the women in this street when weather's bad and the boats don't come in. Says he's lucky with the dogs. Well, p'raps he is."

I placed my neighbor as a confirmed grouser; the tone of the voice, the long nasal pronunciation of the vowels, always gives them away. I bought him a drink and listened to his story of bad luck and jealousy and foremen squared—none of which did I believe. I was prepared, too, to discount about forty per cent of what he told me about Bennett, but that left sixty, which, with the sum total of my own suspicions, made a quite respectable amount on the debit side of the Bennett ledger. I came back full of ill-ease. I seemed to have traveled a long way from Plenders and my lovely Fanny in prison, and I could only hope I wasn't wasting my time. But I should otherwise only be hanging about waiting for news, and at least I had the consolation of feeling I was doing something. Besides, the recollection of that red hair on Rubenstein's clothes buoyed me up. No one so far had been able to explain it. And while I know coincidence has a long arm, and it's longer in truth even than in fiction, I didn't see how that hair could have dropped from heaven, while the only red-haired person remotely connected with the case was this mysterious fellow, Randall, whose trail I was on.

CHAPTER XIV

And ever since historian writ,
And ever since a bard could sing,
Doth each exalt with all his wit
The noble art of murdering.
W. M. THACKERAY.

I GOT back to find a message from Crook, whom I saw that evening. He said his expert had been over Plenders with a magnifying glass. There were no scratches such as would be inevitable had any one opened the windows from the outside with an instrument; there were no marks to show that the door had been tampered with. But there was a comparatively new scratch on one of the pillars of the veranda, such as a man might make with a boot.

"If the window had been opened from the outside . . ." I said slowly.

"So that has occurred to you? Point is, by whom?"

"Practically the whole household had the opportunity. We were all up there watching Bridie and examining the exhibits."

"And while every one else was watching Bridie, any one who knew the way the catch worked could have loosened it and left the window in such a position that it could be pushed open from the inside?"

"That's probably one half of the answer," I said,

feeling my feet grow cold. And then I told him what I'd discovered about Randall, and he said, "I expect that's the other half."

"What's your move then?" I demanded.

"When we've got the truth and if it turns out that the prisoner's guilty, that's when you need a lawyer. Thanks to our insane laws you can generally get a wife off if she's acting with her husband, even if all the ideas come from her and he's simply the tool. One of the privileges of the male. Don't look so gloomy," he added, clapping a hand on my shoulder. "These things can always be cooked, you know. If we do find that's the truth, I can suggest at least two explanations that'll free Fanny of an undesirable husband and a couple of sacks of quicklime. The difficulty in these cases is to get the truth. Give me that and I can make it look any shape to order." He winked, poured out something else to swallow, and lumbered off. I didn't like the chap, and I was damned glad it wasn't me he was after, but I was piously grateful to have him on our side.

The next morning I caught the first quick train to Romerton, in Somerset. Jonathan Kirby, Randall's erstwhile employer, lived at a house called after his family, a big stone house at the top of the town. Bennett had described it in some detail. But when I told the cabby to drive me there he stared and said, "The house is empty. Been empty for ages. The agents have the keys. Summertown and Bliss they are."

I said, "Drive me to Summertown and Bliss." Unless Kirby had sold the house they would presumably be in touch with the fellow, and I was prepared to go to Africa if necessary to get in touch with him, and having the trial postponed until my return. But Kirby had gone farther than that, he'd gone where even I couldn't get at him.

"Mr. Kirby has been dead for nearly three years," said Summertown, whom I saw in person, after I'd explained my errand to a clerk in the front office. "He died rather suddenly—in his sleep, I understand. The house has been to let since then."

"Hasn't it had a tenant all that time?" I asked.

"It was taken for a year by an American gentleman, but he found it out of the way. There's not a great deal going on in this village, not for an American. They're accustomed to a great deal of bouncing about."

"Quite," I said. "As a matter of fact, it's not the house but Mr. Kirby in whom I'm interested. I hadn't heard that he was dead. I've been abroad for some years, and I'm afraid I'm no model correspondent."

"Quite a shock," said Mr. Summertown sympathetically. "He was a great friend of yours?"

"Well, of course, he was an older man than I am," I said, and Summertown helped me out quickly, "Oh, of course. I suppose he can't have been very far off seventy when he died."

"I remember him when I was a boy," I said rashly. "He and my father. . . . But he was very good to me. . . ."

"He was good to a great many people," Summertown agreed soberly. "He's a great loss to the village. The church, the hospital, the old people here, they all miss him terribly. There aren't a great many rich men left."

"I ought not to take up your time," I said. "I dare say there are relations who could tell me. . . ."

"He didn't seem to have any. He was an only child, you see . . ." I nodded wisely, "and having no children of his own . . ."

"He was alone then when he died?"

"He had a secretary, a nice fellow from London. It was rather hard on him. He had to make all the arrangements. A very competent chap, a bit artistic, red hair and beard. The financial affairs were in a bit of a muddle, but he got 'em all straightened out. I remember his coming down here to see me about the house. He asked if I couldn't find any one to take over the responsibility."

"Wasn't there any one, some relative, however distant, who might have done something? Did no one turn up to claim his effects? You did say he was a rich man?"

"He'd lived very like a hermit for years. This fellow, Randall, looked after things. Mr. Kirby didn't go about much. His health had never been too good, though Doctor Meiklejohn said, after his death, it hadn't been so bad as he himself had supposed, certainly nothing like bad enough to justify the pessimistic view he took of life. But you know how it is with these elderly men who live too much alone—they get an idea into their heads and nothing will dislodge it."

"Well," I said, "I mustn't take up your time," I picked up my hat off the table, "but it has been a shock to me. One gets so out of touch when one's away, particularly when you're separated not only from your own country but from civilization generally, as I've been for nearly five years. There are gaps all round the table; people who seemed young and active when you went away have suddenly developed into old men, or they've forged new ties and they've nothing to say to you. One begins to get the impression," here I took up my gloves, "that one's no more than another of that maddening army of globe-trotters who only demand an appreciative audience and the best place by the fire in order to bore as many people as possible for as long as they'll stand it."

Summertown laughed ruefully. "It's bad being reminded that we don't get any younger," he agreed. "The Bible's right, it isn't good for man to live alone. If Mr. Kirby would have married again, he might have conquered this morbid impulse." He shook his head as over some inalienable tragedy. I only had one more question to put to him. "You've no idea where this fellow, Randall, is, I suppose?" I suggested.

"I heard he went back to London. He wrote to me once from some hotel there but he wanted to get abroad, to British Honduras. He said there wasn't much chance of getting on in an overcrowded country like this. And, of course, 1932 was the year of the slump, and even in 1933 things were still looking bad. No, I don't know what happened to him, but I shouldn't say he was the sort of fellow to go under."

I walked out of the office and asked for Doctor Meiklejohn's house. The doctor wasn't back from his morning round, but I was invited to wait in his study. I sat there staring at the sort of books a country doctor chooses—medical journals, Jorrocks, the *Pickwick Papers, Izaak Walton, Henry Fielding* and a couple of rows of modern detective stories—until the man came in. He was a square sturdy fellow who looked at me inquisitively and said, "What can I do for you?"

I said, "I'm not here as a patient. I came down this morning to see Jonathan Kirby. I'm only just back from abroad and I hadn't realized that he was dead. The house agent told me. He said you'd attended him."

Meiklejohn nodded, pulling at his long jaw. "A bad business," he said. "A rotten bad business. A woman said to me this morning, talking shop as women will—they think it flatters us, I suppose; you'd think they'd have enough imagination to realize we get so much of it we're choked with it—she said, 'I don't understand how you can go on just living among suffering and pain, doctor.' I might have told her, but I hadn't the time to spare, that what does nearly break you is all the unnecessary sickness and tragedy we come across. Take poor Jonathan Kirby, for instance. There was no more need for that fellow to be dead than there is for you or me. Less, I dare say, seeing he could afford to coddle himself. But he'd got it into his head that he had tuberculosis, and he poisoned himself with one of these damned trashy novels all the young women one meets seem to waste their time writing these days, instead of looking after the children they don't want to have. The book was mentioned at the inquest. I read some of it. Coroner asked me to. He's a nice chap, name of Bellairs. 'What the hell do these wenches want to pour their morbid slop on the public for?' he asked me. Well, I suppose they wouldn't do it if they weren't paid for it. It's the publishers you can get back on at the last. Anyhow, there were chapters about some poor devil who died of tuberculosis, and Kirby had absorbed the whole thing into his system, and was convinced he was dying and would presently peg out in agony."

"Had he got T.B.?" I asked in some surprise.

"Of course he hadn't. He'd got a lung he had to be a bit careful of, but good heavens, man, this country is thick with men and women with a delicate spot. We've all got one; so long as we don't know too much about it we're all right. But Kirby brooded and brooded till he really wasn't a sane man. They brought it in temporary insanity at the trial, of course. Well, everybody liked him and I will say he was damned generous, though some of us felt he might have done something for that secretary chap of his. The fellow can't have had much of a time during the year he was there, and Kirby didn't leave him a cent. Every ha'penny went to charities of some kind—war charities, mostly."

"He had no relatives at all?"

"Apparently not. Well, that's not so rare as you might suppose. You're always coming on these lonely folk. Look at the men and women who disappear and no one makes any inquiries. Look at that chap in the burning car case; nobody missed him. To this day nobody knows for certain who he was. And every now and again I'm called out to look at a dead body they've found in the sea, or poisoned in a wood. If the fellow's taken the trouble to cut the name out of his overcoat and empty his pockets, it's often the devil of a job finding out anything about him. Oh, Kirby wasn't an isolated case, but, of course, he brooded over that, too. He lost his wife, as you know, when the child was born, and then the boy, Ian, went down in the

181

war. I've often thought poor old Jonathan was never quite normal afterwards, and you couldn't get him to take any real interest in outside affairs. I remember he said in the note he left, 'I leave no one to miss me.' It's a pretty rotten confession for any man to make. Because that sort of thing is a chap's own fault."

"He took his own life?" I exclaimed.

Meiklejohn, who had turned aside for a moment, switched back. "You hadn't realized that? My dear chap, I'm sorry. I didn't understand. Yes. He was under my care at the time. Suffered badly from insomnia, as these brooding fellows often do, and I'd given him a sleeping draught. He swallowed a double dose one night. There were questions asked about that at the inquest. Having regard to the man's family history—you know, of course, that his father took his own life, too—shot himself one Sunday morning in his own gun-room—and the fact that I was aware that he suffered from melancholia, practically from delusions, in fact, did I consider it wise to put the means of suicide within his grasp? That's the kind of fool questions jurors like to put. As if you can stop a man taking his life, if he means to. He's only got to walk over the edge of the cliff or buy a bottle of aspirins or swallow some disinfectant out of the housemaid's cupboard. If you're going to put danger out of his way do away with gas-stoves and stop the tubes running and having all your windows hermetically sealed. The fact is that you can't prevent people accomplishing what they've made up their minds they will do at any cost. Jonathan meant to get out; he didn't feel he had much to live for and he was afraid of what lay ahead.

It's easy to condemn a man for cowardice, but—well."
He spread his hands. "There it is. *Nil nisi bonum
mortuis* And do you know what text they put on that
chap's grave? 'He giveth His beloved sleep.' I never
heard anything so impious with a chap who'd taken
his life into his own hands. But Raynes wouldn't listen
to any one. There wasn't any family to interfere, and
Raynes likes to feel that, under God, everything rests
on him."

"Raynes was the lawyer?"

"Yes. A local chap. Oh, not bad in his way, but he
seems to have made a holy hash of Jonathan's affairs.
Let him put money in all sorts of crack-brained schemes.
Lucky for him he didn't leave a lot of dependent
relatives. As it was, it was only the charities that
suffered."

"He's been doing it for years—speculating, I mean?"

"Chiefly that last year. He was in Switzerland before
that. He came back because Summertown wrote to him
that the house was falling down and he'd better come
and pick up the pieces. I dare say if he'd stayed out
there he'd be all right now. But the place is a deathtrap,
anyway; the rain seeps into the lower rooms during
the wet season and a dozen furnaces wouldn't make
that house warm. But he was an obstinate chap. He
used to moon about the hall staring at the pictures
of his ancestors. I dare say thinking about them helped
to send him off his head."

"What was the secretary like?"

"Oh, a nice fellow, with a bit of reddish beard. Distinguished sort of chap. I don't know where Kirby
found him, but I'll say he was lucky."

"Jonathan, you mean?"

"Yes. I suppose he paid him pretty well. Otherwise there was nothing to make the fellow stop here. It was a dead alley occupation."

"No romantic reason?" I suggested.

"I asked him once; he was the sort of chap you could talk to easily. He told me he'd been married years ago and it hadn't worked. He didn't say any more. Well, it's not the kind of thing a decent fellow wants to talk about."

I agreed. There were a dozen questions I was burning to ask, but Meiklejohn was obviously in a hurry, so rather reluctantly I came away. I went down to the offices of the local paper and told my fairy tale all over again. The clerk in charge turned up the record readily enough. I dare say he didn't mind having a stranger to instruct. He remembered the suicide perfectly well. It hadn't come as a special surprise; every one knew old Kirby was melancholy and suffered from ill-health. He had a mort of money, but what was the good of money to him? He'd sit about at home and fret and be no kind of company at all. I turned to the newspaper. It appeared that a servant called Bellamy had made the discovery.

I always took the master in a cup of tea, he told the court. That morning I took it in as usual and pulled back the curtains with the remark that it was a wet day. The master didn't speak, but that didn't surprise me specially. There were days when he wouldn't open his mouth, even to Mr. Randall, except to say: Do this or Do that. I took him over the local paper and said: You'll be sorry to hear Lady Webber passed away last evening, sir, and still he didn't look at me. I bent a bit closer. He seemed to be asleep.

Considering he had sleeping draughts—a fact of which you were aware—why should that surprise you?

Well, sir, he never did sleep late of a morning. Six o'clock was the latest he ever opened his eyes and here it was a quarter past seven.

When did you begin to get alarmed?

He had a sort of queer look. It wasn't just that he hadn't got any color; it was a limp kind of a look, and watch though I might I couldn't see him breathe. Besides, he was always the lightest of sleepers. He used to say he couldn't sleep for a minute with any one standing beside him. A sort of sixth sense warned him that he was being watched. I made bold to put out my hand and touch him, and he was cold.

Ice-cold?

Well, sir, not stiff, but cold enough to make me tremble. I went along to Mr. Randall's room and told him, and he came along with me at once. When he'd seen Mr. Kirby he said: Get Doctor Meiklejohn. There was a letter lying on the table by the bed addressed to the coroner. I didn't touch that. The doctor came in a few minutes and he said the master was dead.

Meiklejohn, in the box, had deposed that Kirby died of an overdose of strychnine. He (witness) had ordered the deceased a sleeping-mixture of which strychnine was an ingredient. Three days earlier the doctor had met Kirby who complained that the mixture seemed to have no strength. He had asked for something more powerful. This Meiklejohn had refused to give him. I can't give you anything stronger, he said, unless I want to find myself in the dock with a rope dangling in front of me. Kirby had become annoyed and had spoken of consulting another doctor. This Meiklejohn had told him he was quite at liberty to do. Subsequent evidence proved, however, that deceased had not carried out his threat.

Meiklejohn was asked certain technical questions as to the ingredients of the sleeping-draught and the chemist, a man called Bowers, had produced the original prescription. The draught was a usual one for a man in Kirby's health.

A juror observed that it was a pity the last witness had made the deceased a present of the fact that a double draught would prove fatal, but had been crushed immediately by the coroner, who remarked: In my opinion Doctor Meiklejohn would have been lacking in his duty to his patient if he had not so warned him.

The letter the dead man had left was then read out. It said:

I ask no forgiveness for what I propose to do, because there is no one to whom I owe any personal loyalty. I have made a failure of my life and I see no purpose in continuing it. I have nothing left to live for, and instead of being a burden on my friends and servants and an expense to my heirs, I prefer to take this way out.

I don't know how the jury will feel about this, said the coroner, but this letter seems to indicate that the deceased had reached a pitch where he had no further interest in life. He seems to have taken an exaggerated view of his own state of health and of his financial position. I propose to let you have more particular details of the position.

Then Randall went into the box, and agreed that he had been working for Kirby as his secretary for the past twelve months. They had met in London. During the first period of his employment Kirby had been cheerful and interested; he was a great reader and had a package of books sent from London twice a week. Latterly, however, he had become obsessed with the subject of his own health. He had unfortunately read a book giving in great detail the progress of a tubercular person, ending with a graphic description of the death-scene, and this had depressed him. He insisted on discussing his condition and practically lived with a thermometer in his mouth. He spoke from time to time of his personal affairs and would discuss for hours at a stretch his financial position. His money was for the most part invested in thoroughly sound businesses and companies, but he developed the notion that it was cowardly and unsporting to play always for safety, and he began to speculate.

He was a rich man, though. You were aware of that?

Yes. I asked him why he wanted more money. He said he didn't need it for himself, but he had to think of those who came after. That surprised me, as I understood he had no relations, but he said that he intended to leave his money to a Home for Incurables, chiefly war-shocked men, and that if he speculated boldly, and successfully, he would be able to endow a more ambitious foundation. I had the idea that he was morbidly conscientious on this point. A kind of feeling that by taking three per cent and not chancing eight he was putting himself on a level with the man who buried his talent for fear of losing it if he gambled.

Did you know anything of the businesses in which he invested this money, a good deal of which appears to have been lost?

I knew very little about them. He had a lawyer who presumably advised him. As a matter of fact, he got to the stage where he was more inclined to believe in his own instincts—hunches, he called them—than in any common sense. He said, Raynes wants me to play for safety. I've had too much safety and now that I'm getting near the end of my time I can afford to be reckless. It isn't as if I want to enrich myself.

You did gain the definite impression that he was— shall we say—inclined to be fanatical on the point?

Unquestionably. That and his health occupied all his attention. He used to take in a great many newspapers, and he would hunt through them or make me go through them, and mark with a blue pencil any reference to death from tuberculosis, or any tuberculosis statistics. It became a subject of comment throughout the house. I remember the housekeeper, Mrs. Marples, asking me one day why I encouraged him. I didn't; but after all, I was his servant and I couldn't refuse to obey his orders. It wasn't as if I knew him very well or was a friend of the family.

You mean, you felt your responsibility?

Yes. I urged him sometimes to have some one to come and stay with him. I thought it might take his mind off himself. But he always said he knew no one.

He used to quote Henry Vaughan's "They are all gone into the world of light and I alone sit lingering here." I couldn't persuade him to go out either. He said a man in his state of health couldn't afford to take risks; and there was always the chance of contagion if he went among other people. I asked Mr. Raynes once if there was no one we could send for, but he told me the same thing. He said Mr. Kirby had no relatives and no close friends.

He didn't have people up to the house at all?

No. He said that tuberculosis was very infectious. He suffered from bronchitis in the winter, and he thought that was tuberculosis too. He was a monomaniac on that point. I once dared to suggest that he should talk to Doctor Meiklejohn about seeing a specialist, going to town. Sometimes a stranger and a big name can work miracles. He asked me if I thought he was a damned malingerer. He said if I ever mentioned such a thing again I could leave his employ.

You never had any reason to suppose that the thought of suicide was in his mind?

Never. He had his melancholy fits, of course, when he said life wasn't worth living, but I didn't attach much importance to that. I didn't know he was especially bothered about this money he was losing. I'd done my best to warn him, but of course, I couldn't go very far. He did ask me once why I took so much trouble about his affairs. One doesn't like to be accused of self-interest. . . .

But it made no difference to you—financially, I mean?

He might have thought that I expected to be left

something in his will, provided I was in his service at the time of his death.

And you can't recall anything that happened that day that might throw any light on this sudden decision of his?

Absolutely nothing; but then I didn't see him after lunch. I don't know how he spent the afternoon. He told me I could go off. I had some business of my own to attend to. I caught the last train back and wasn't in till half-past eleven, when I had a drink and went up to bed. I glanced under his door as I went by and the light was out, so I supposed that he had taken his sleeping-draught and settled down.

What time did he generally have it?

I generally gave it to him about eleven o'clock. He took to going to bed quite early, about nine, and at ten he would ring and I'd come up. He liked to drink tea last thing at night and while he drank it he would tell me his plans for the next day. And at about eleven he'd settle down. He always had breakfast at half-past eight, and got up about seven-thirty, as soon as he'd had tea.

You didn't pour it out for him that night before you left?

No. His servant did that, I understand.

(This part of the evidence was subsequently confirmed by Bellamy.)

You don't happen to remember how much sleeping-draught was left in the bottle?

I had a note in my diary to order some more the following day, that is, today. There were, I think, a couple of doses left.

Here a sudden interruption provided the sensational element that is so often lacking from inquests on suicides. From the body of the court Meiklejohn's voice said: I beg your pardon; two doses would not have been fatal. Yes, I am aware that I deliberately gave Mr. Kirby that impression, but that was for our mutual safeguard.

Every one seems to have turned and stared, Randall among them.

Not? Then . . . and he hesitated.

The coroner asked him if he were sure there were no more than two doses and Randall said, Well, honestly, I wasn't sure there was more than one. I don't say I'd have hesitated to leave a fatal dose on a night when I was going to be out, but I'm sure I should have thought about it.

And you didn't?

I didn't. I'm sorry. That seems to complicate things.

It did. It held up the inquiry while further investigation was made. Meiklejohn, in reply to a question from the coroner, said that three doses would be fatal, and when it seemed absolutely proved that no strychnine had been bought by any member of the household, the general feeling of the court was that Randall must have been mistaken and that there had been more in the bottle than he remembered.

I stopped at this point and tried to see how Randall could have got hold of strychnine and introduced it into the bottle but if he had managed to do it he'd been infernally clever. In spite of the most searching inquiries there wasn't an atom of evidence against him. A servant said that Mr. Kirby kept the stuff locked and carried the key about with him. You could argue that Randall had had strychnine in his possession for a long period and had merely been biding his time. But you'd never get any proof of that. I went on with the record of the inquest.

Mrs. Marples, the dead man's housekeeper, said she had been troubled about her employer for several weeks. He seemed to get more and more morbid. He was queer about money matters, too. He took all his money out of a firm of armament makers, on the ground that he didn't want to make a living out of the blood of other men's sons.

How did you know that?

He told me himself, sir. Very queer he was, as white as a sheet, sitting bolt upright in his chair and waving his hands at me. Mr. Randall was there, standing behind him. He looked at me as much as to say, don't pay too much attention, but the master turned his head and said: Isn't that what you said? Don't you agree? and Mr. Randall said, Yes, Sir, of course. Afterwards I said to him, It's a pity, sir, to encourage the master, and he said, Can you tell me any way of stopping him? Has he always been like this? He used to hunt round after books that weren't good for him, medical books and the like. These last few weeks we haven't been able to do a thing with him. And fussy about his food. Wouldn't have this, wouldn't have that. That's poison to me, he'd say, and he'd thump some magazine he'd discovered. Mr. Randall asked me more than once if he hadn't got any friends. He was proper bothered about him.

The lawyer, Raynes, gave evidence, too. He said

that he'd been looking after the dead man's affairs for a number of years, giving him personal attention ever since the death of his partner, Simpson, about four years earlier. Up till the last twelve months of his life Mr. Kirby had never taken much interest in the way in which his money was laid out, accepting the fact that it brought him in a good return, and leaving the business side of it to the experts. During that last year, however, he began to get restive— Other men get eight per cent, he'd say, why shouldn't I? My secretary was reading out the financial news to me this morning and he mentioned one company after another who pay far higher dividends than I ever receive.—Did he tell you that you have to pay something for safety, Mr. Kirby? I asked him.—Well, I think I've banked too much on safety, he said. I think I'll take chances. I may be only a steward of all I possess, but there's no reason why I should be a spiritless steward.—He brought out a lot of prospectuses that, he said, he'd written to town for. A number of them were frank speculation and so I told him. Of course he was one of the people who could afford to speculate. If a poor man loses his bit he's probably ruined. Mr. Kirby only had himself to think of. He got a bit excited when I talked of the dangers of speculation and asked me how anything would prosper if there weren't certain people always prepared to take a risk. He asked if I realized how the motor industry had been built up. Not by the men who wanted to be on the safe side, he said, but by the speculators you disapprove of. Well, you can't argue with a man like that. He gets an idea into his head, like this idea he had that he was ·dying rapidly of T.B., and nothing short of the Judgment Day is going to get it out. I let him change those investments; there were some others that I couldn't recommend. They had a bad name. He flew into a towering rage and stalked out. The next day his secretary, Mr. Randall, came to see me. Look here, he said, can't you do anything with Mr. Kirby? He's simply bent on pitching his money down a drain. I can't move him, naturally, but you're his adviser. I don't want to get the sack and I shall, if I say much more, but can't you persuade him that it's no true charity to let his money silt into the pockets of rogues? I was a bit dubious, but I said I'd do what I could. I went up to the Grange next day and tried to talk to Mr. Kirby, but he took the wind out of my sails by telling me that, since I was so chary of acting for him, he'd written himself for shares in certain companies advertising huge dividends, enclosing checks for the requisite amounts. When did you do that? I asked him, and he said, The same night as I came to see you. I said, Did Randall write the letters for you? and he said, No, he's as fearful as yourself. I wrote them with my own hand and Bellamy took them to the post. Well, there was nothing much I could say. I kept my hand as well as I could on the rest of his investments, but there's no doubt about it that his affairs were beginning to look bad. I had an appointment with him for this very morning. I was to go up and see him. He'd got the idea that it was bad for him to go out. He said, on the telephone, I suppose you're going to try and scare me, and I told him there was no question of my trying. I was afraid I might be going to give him something of a shock.

And what did he say to that?

If you like cold feet, stick to them. Then he rang off.

He didn't seem alarmed?

No. Angry, perhaps. Of course, that may have been bluff. That didn't occur to me at the time. I was puzzled. I couldn't understand this sudden hunger to make more money, and, incidentally, to make ducks and drakes of what he had. It wasn't as if he were getting married or had to make provision for any one, nothing of that kind.

I take it that he wasn't ruined?

Nothing like it, though he had had heavy losses. In any case I only warned him that he mightn't like everything I had to tell him about his investments. Any man with my experience knows how necessary it is sometimes to warn clients in advance about unpleasant news.

Exactly. And, of course, it didn't occur to you that he had any thought of self-destruction? You'd never heard him use any such threat?

Never. And certainly I should have expected him to keep the appointment with me first.

That was the end of the evidence and after a short pause, the jury decided that Randall's memory was at fault as to the exact quantity of the sleeping-draught left in the bottle and brought in suicide while of unsound mind.

CHAPTER XV

*Some circumstantial evidence is very great—as when
you find a trout in the milk.*

THOREAU.

"YOU remember this?" I said to the young man as I
shut the paper.

"Caused a lot of stir at the time," said he.

I asked why.

"Well, Mr. Kirby being one of the old gentry here,
and his father having killed himself before him. You
know how people talk."

"What did they say?" I produced my case and offered
him a cigarette.

"Oh, nothing special. Just it must have been bad
for that chap, Randall."

"What happened to him?"

"Went back to London, I think. He wasn't a local
chap. But it's been a bad thing for the house. It was
lived in for a bit under a year by an American gentleman, but he didn't like it."

"Ghosts?" I asked lightly.

"Not that, I think. Anyway, these Americans don't
believe in ghosts, do they? But when a yarn like that
goes round, a house gets the name of being unlucky.
This one has, anyhow. There was a gentleman came
down some time ago to look at it, representative of

some charity, I understand, that profits from Mr. Kirby's will. He went to see Mr. Summertown about selling the place, I believe, but it seems there's something in the will that won't let you sell."

"Was that deliberate, I wonder?"

"I don't see why it should be. Seeing there was no family to come back to it, you wouldn't think anybody would care. It was just the way the will was written out. Not that anybody 'ud want the house, so old-fashioned as it is, but the land might be worth something."

I went along to Raynes's office and luckily found him at a loose end. I told my story again. "I've been looking up the report of the inquest," I added. "It's a pretty bad shock. He never gave me the impression of being that sort of a man."

"None of us supposed he was," said Raynes. "And anyhow, I'd have expected him to wait until he'd seen me. I could have reassured him. It was bad luck on Randall. A lot of work fell on his shoulders. He had rather a worrying time with the old man altogether, always trying to keep papers and books away from him because of this morbid obsession of his. He told me once he didn't dare leave a medical journal in his own room, because the old man might lay hands on it. He used to try and skip the medical bits of book reviews, but of course, half the time you're in the soup before you realize what's coming. He'd look ahead and try and skim, but Kirby was as sharp as a needle. 'What are you leaving out?' he'd say. And he'd ask him, 'Did you ever know any one who died of tuberculosis?' As a matter of fact, Randall's mother died

197

of it, and Kirby wormed the whole story out of him, inch by inch. If Randall said, when they were making up a book list, 'Oh, I shouldn't include that one, you won't care about it. It hasn't been well reviewed,' Kirby would immediately suspect he was being hoodwinked, and he'd read that book the first of the bundle, and go through it with a toothcomb. That happened more than once, I know. Randall used to try hiding the papers sometimes, but Kirby used to come stealing after him and unearth them again. I believe there were one or two scenes. I know at one time Randall thought of throwing up the job. He came and spoke to me about it. I urged him to stay on."

"It was a good deal of responsibility for him," I agreed. "Had he known Kirby long? I don't remember the name."

"I don't think so. I told him to hang on a bit longer and see if things got better. I had an idea that if we could get through the autumn we might persuade the old man to go abroad for the winter. When I arranged to come up and see him that morning I was going to tell him that he really couldn't afford the expense of this large house—it simply ate coal and light—servants' wages, Randall's salary."

"You hadn't said anything to him?"

"I hadn't had a chance. I'd only arranged to see him the afternoon of his death."

"You telephoned him?"

"No, he rang me up. He said it was important."

"He didn't say why?"

"No. It was to do with money, of course. He seemed a bit distracted. I think he realized he'd have to cut down expenses, because he spoke of getting away."

"Funny about the sleeping draught," I suggested.

"Oh, I don't know. It's easy to make a mistake. Two doses or three, there's very little to it."

I didn't agree. There had been meticulous descriptions of that sleeping draught, and when a man makes a note that it's time to order a fresh supply he knows pretty well where he stands. Moreover, a careful fellow like Randall, who's accustomed to pouring out the doses himself, doesn't miscalculate. And Meiklejohn had said that two doses wouldn't be fatal. Looking through the notes I'd made of the case other considerations engaged my attention. For instance, Randall's persistence in explaining how difficult it was to keep from his employer papers or books whose tendency was to enhance his natural morbidity. There was no need, surely, for him to leave about medical journals dealing with Kirby's particular obsession; and the more I thought about it the more I doubted the story that Kirby had invaded his secretary's bedroom and carried away thence a magazine that didn't belong to him. Far more likely that Randall, of set purpose, had left the magazine where Kirby would be bound to find it. And I knew well enough the gambit that by a show of hesitancy is designed to draw a sick man's attention to the one subject most dangerous to himself. I could see Randall ferreting through those damned papers till he found a suitable book review, starting to read it with great gusto, becoming obviously embarrassed, skipping, coloring, bringing the column to an abrupt close until the attention of an imbecile would be arrested. Oh, an astute fellow, this Mr. Randall. And wherever he had gone he had made his point—calling up Meiklejohn, going to see Raynes—everywhere speaking of Kirby's unfortunate preoccupation with himself. All the same, I had to admit that that was only evidence of indirect murder. You can kill a child by starvation as well as by suffocation, and so you can actually murder a man by driving him to suicide—as blackmailers do—or driving him out of his senses, as clearly Randall had tried to do—without having to answer at the criminal court on a capital charge. Not that it would have surprised me to learn that Randall was guilty on that count itself. Only I didn't see how, if he'd been out all the afternoon, he could be accused of poisoning his employer. I played with a number of ideas. He might have crept in unperceived, gone to talk to the old man as usual, and given him the triple dose; and then I remembered that Kirby hadn't taken his own medicine; a servant had poured it out for him. The man admittedly didn't know what the correct dose was; but he had said he was sure there wasn't much of the mixture left in the bottle. Nor could you suggest that, after the servant's departure, Kirby had added to his draught, because the bottle had been emptied. The problem was a stiff one, and I was less inclined than the jury had been to accept the version that the servant, being unaccustomed to pour out the stuff, had inadvertently dosed his master to death.

I went round and round the case like a dormouse going round its wheel, and still I couldn't detect the flaw. Of course, although the engagement with Raynes had not been made until after Randall's departure at midday, Randall may well have been aware that such an appointment was to be made. Equally, it might be proved—though here I foresaw a good deal of work before I could hope to make my point—that Randall simply didn't dare let his employer realize his own financial position. It was hard to believe that any man, short of an imbecile, would have put good money into some of the concerns Kirby had with apparent enthusiasm chosen to back. But suppose, I argued, he hadn't done anything of the kind? Suppose there had been a long system of fraud, of forgery even—and I remembered that at the original trial forgery had been one of the counts for which Randall had been condemned—and Randall couldn't allow Kirby to know the truth? If that were the case, then he had only one solution. Somehow Kirby must be got out of the way. And Kirby had been got out of the way. He'd been found poisoned, apparently by his own hand. I realized that the burden of proof still lay upon me. There wasn't a note in the report of the inquest to show that Randall could be guilty. He hadn't poured out the fatal dose, and the evidence had gone to show that Randall hadn't had access to the bottle on that day (the old man kept it locked up); if he'd added strychnine the day before, then Kirby would have died of the previous dose. Besides, when had he been able to get at the bottle except in his employer's presence? Even allowing that somehow he'd supplied himself with strychnine, I couldn't see any answer that would hang Randall. Nevertheless, I clung to my theory that Randall was responsible. I got a pencil and jotted down notes of everything I could remember. And this was the picture that I got.

For several days after he began to take the sleeping draught Kirby had complained that it had no effect upon him whatsoever. Then he took the final dose and it had too much effect. I examined the prescription that had been quoted in full at the inquest. The principal drug was strychnine. I kept saying that to myself over and over again. The principal drug was strychnine. And then I saw light and I applauded Randall's cunning and skill; I believed, recklessly, that he was responsible for Rubenstein's death, and I wondered whether he'd get away with that as he'd done with this one.

Because strychnine, in a mixture, sinks to the bottom of the bottle. The mixture has to be shaken each time. And if it isn't shaken, what happens? The strychnine stays at the bottom of the bottle and when you come to the last dose you get a fatal quantity. It was as simple as that. Oh, clever Randall to be out of the way when the last dose was given. Cleverer still to point out that he hadn't left enough stuff in the bottle to poison the old man; that was the sure way of averting all suspicion from himself. Again I applauded Randall's cunning. It was improbable that any one would think of this explanation, and even if they did they'd never be able to bring the crime home to the man. And how safe for Randall to creep back at midnight, steal into the doomed man's room and make sure that the fatal dose had indeed been taken, leave the note. . . . I had seen in the paper a facsimile of the actual letter. The writing would be easy for any one to copy; for a convicted forger it would be child's play. And he'd got away with it completely. It was the perfect crime. You couldn't in law suspect the man. More, he had left the neighborhood, taking with him the sympathy of every one who had known him. And now, after two years, that security was being disturbed, not because of latter-day suspicion, but because, like so many successful criminals, the fellow couldn't be content with committing one crime and getting away with it, he had to get himself involved in another.

As soon as I got back to town I went to see Crook. I thought there might be some news from his end, but there was none. He hadn't been able to establish a single alibi for any part of Fanny's story.

"Matter of luck," he boomed, rubbing his hands, and refusing to look dejected; indeed, he seemed to invite congratulation. "Well, well, mustn't take a gloomy view. What about your luck? You're the hope of the side now."

I told him my story. "I wish that young woman of yours had a bit more respect for truth," he grunted when I'd finished. "I'd give a lot to know just how far she was involved in all this. Does she know anything about the Kirby affair? Or does she suspect? If she knows, she's an accessory after the fact, and for her own sake—and I wouldn't put Miss Fanny down as an altruist—wouldn't dare speak. On the other hand, it's possible," he stressed the word a little unpleasantly, "that she's as innocent as the proverbial new-born babe."

"None of this is any proof that she knows anything about the Rubenstein affair," I interrupted.

Crook was bland. "No proof at all," he agreed. "We've yet to prove a connection between Randall and the affair. I don't mind taking chances, my dear Curteis, but I don't want to look a prize fool in the courts, and

there are some stories a sane man doesn't offer a judge
—a story that rests on a hair," he grinned apprecia-
tively at his own nicety of phrase, "is one of them."

I said with a groan that if Randall were mixed up
in the case, that presupposed an accomplice in the
house, and there was no need to guess whose name
would be on every one's lips. It was difficult even
for her sympathizers to escape the conclusions aroused
by Fanny's button found in the dead man's hand.

"Quite," said Crook, calm as ever. "Any idea where
the fellow went after leaving Romerton?"

"Came back to town—oh, a vague address, I grant
you. And it's two years ago. I've got a man out after
him. And also after some of the companies into which
Kirby was—h'm—persuaded to invest so much of his
capital. It would be instructive to discover whether
Randall by his own or any other name was concerned
with them."

"You do like miracles, don't you?" said Crook, admiringly. "Well, good luck to your hunting, but it
sounds to me as though the fox might still be several
fields away. We're still, so far as evidence goes, no
further on than the original idea—original to the police,
I mean—that Rubenstein never reached Kings Benyon
at all. The crown have quite a good case to date. I'm
not at all sure your Fanny isn't making a fool of
herself trying to pull learned counsel's leg, to say nothing of the judge's. They take 'emselves seriously, these
chaps."

"If you can persuade Fanny to change her story at
this time of day I'll eat a judge's wig," I promised
him. But he said he didn't think I need start worrying

about that. My digestion wasn't likely to be taxed. "There's one thing about your scoundrel," he said as we parted. "He seems to have come down on Fanny's from what we can learn, immediately after Kirby's death, but to have left her alone since. You might argue from the first that he left Romerton without a bob, which is the state of an honest man. But if he was so infernally broke, why has he never attacked her again? Of course, he wouldn't be able to lay hands on the money, even if he'd been cooking the accounts, or forging signatures, directly the trial was over. He's a gentleman with a healthy concern for his own neck, but later he could collect his ill-gotten gains and live happily ever after—or until he'd blued the cash. Our Fanny may have guessed the truth, or he may have told her, knowing she was safe enough, and that did give her a scare. She cleared out at no notice at all. People who stick at nothing else do, I find, boggle a bit at murder."

"Not Randall," I muttered. "His experience seems to have taught him that murder's a profitable speculation."

"Don't forget one thing," said Crook, the expert. "If he did do this old boy in, what in heck was his motive?"

CHAPTER XVI

We want nothing but Facts, sir, nothing but Facts.
THOMAS GRAGRIND.

IT was late afternoon when I came away from Crook's chambers, still brooding on his problem. A saffron light flowered in the sky above the housetops. The people I ran against in the street seemed to be of two dimensions only, like those black cardboard silhouettes you find at parties. I couldn't discover anything real about any of them. Only Fanny was real and our problem, with Randall as a wild red-headed ghost slipping in and out of shadows, as intangible as they. I got back to my flat and found no message from Stokes, the man who had promised to find out about Kirby's speculations. I had been back for about an hour when he telephoned.

"They were mostly stumers," he said. "You anticipated that? I could have told you within fifteen minutes of your inquiry. It isn't so easy to discover who's behind them. Most of them are operated from a single room in Black Lion Square. You know the place? It's small and suspect, and mostly accommodation addresses. Siver Square, Finchley, was another address. Of course, technically, every company had a different office and different directors; but most of the names were spurious. I'm on the track of some of the fellows who really were flesh and blood. A man called Marriott was behind several of them; an outpaced wrong 'un. He found it convenient to clear out of the country about a year ago. There were others, of course, but they mostly hid coyly behind pseudonyms and don't care about the daylight."

"No mention of a fellow called Randall?" I asked without much hope, and he said no, there wasn't. But he was still inquiring.

Sitting late before my fire, the blinds undrawn, watching the interplay of leafless branches against the dim sky, I continued to wonder what motive Randall had had for this murder. I was being more and more drawn to the conclusion that it hadn't been planned. If you mean to do a man in you provide your own weapon, and in this case one had been snatched up at random. My own reading of the case was that X had got into the house through the window that had been left unlatched for him, and had set to work to remove something of value. Picking the lock of the cases had been a longer job than he had supposed. The fact that they didn't show marks of rough usage didn't impress me. In my time I've known men who could open the most delicate lock without leaving a trace, and I didn't see why Randall shouldn't possess a similar capacity. Rubenstein had returned early and gone straight to the Chinese Room. Perhaps he had seen a light under the door; he couldn't have heard anything for the room was sound-proof. He had walked in, warning the intruder, by the necessity for turning the key in the lock, of his coming, and before he could raise the alarm had been stabbed and silenced. X might have staged

207

the rest of the scene himself and gone backwards through the window, but for that fatal wad of cotton-wool. That, unquestionably, had been supplied by some one who knew the house, and again, it could only have been supplied by a confederate. It seemed to me it was one of those cases where you can argue all round the point and meet yourself going to bed. Every version I propounded came back to Fanny as the accomplice.

The question of the motive, however, remained. I'd have to suggest something. I brooded. Presently I dragged up the telephone book and began to hunt through the TES's. There were more Testers than I had expected, and though I could eliminate several I was left with a handful, any one of which might be our friend from the British Museum. The trouble was I didn't know his initial.

I allowed patience, however, to have her perfect work, and my fourth telephone call discovered for me the man I wanted.

"How's your mystery?" he asked me.

"As mysterious as ever," I said, and asked if 'there was any chance of seeing him that night. He was sufficiently intrigued by the position to come over to my flat for a latish dinner. He looked more cadaverous than ever, and was one of those people who are silent when not permitted to talk shop. Fortunately on this occasion I wanted him to talk nothing else.

"I don't envy you or the police," he said with his first mouthful of soup hot on his tongue.

"I dare say you have your troubles, too," I said.

It was the kind of remark to which he sprang like Noah's dove making a beeline for the olive twig.

"That, of course," he said, "is true. There are precautions, anxieties even, in connection with bequests like Mr. Rubenstein's. A certain responsibility cannot be avoided. We have had our difficulties since the discovery of the body." I grinned. I was beginning to enjoy myself. I liked the fellow's moderation, his careful dignity. "The papers, naturally, have been giving us a good deal of advertisement, calling the attention of approximately eight or nine thousand thieves to the value of the collection that, incidentally, we were not at once allowed to remove. What, after all, is the chance of two years for burglary against the possibility of getting five—ten—fifteen thousand pounds for your loot? We have kept men on the premises—until we were able to remove the collection, you understand— and had doors and windows hermetically sealed."

"But you've been allowed to take the stuff away by now?"

"Certainly. But we had a period of anxiety. Perhaps," a stiff smile stretched his lips, "the police anticipated that the criminal would return, like the repentant villain of an early Victorian novelette, to the scene of his crime to atone for it."

"You've had it vetted?" I asked. "The collection, I mean."

He looked at me sharply. "Why do you ask that?"

"I'm wondering if it was perfect. You had the inventory, of course."

"Yes, we had the inventory."

"And everything was in order?"

He pushed back his chair; his spoon lay forgotten in his neglected soup.

"Mr. Curteis, you've asked me here for a purpose tonight?"

"I have. I'm working for the defense. You had gathered that. I want to know if that collection had been tampered with."

He regarded me in a considering fashion, as though discretion suggested silence would be best here. But his eyes were smoldering.

"You won't get my story from any other source," I warned him. "Whereas I can approach the police and put my question to them, and in the interests of justice you'll be officially questioned. . . ."

He drew his soup towards him. "That would be one explanation," he said, calmly going on with his meal.

"And the other?"

"That even Rubenstein sometimes slipped up, was misled, or suffered from a not quite perfect judgment."

"You can wash that out," I said curtly. "What is it?"

He said, "There was a pair of jade bracelets," and stopped, because I could feel myself go as white as a sheet, and I was desperately cold. It had to be these particular bracelets, of course. Tester went on to describe them, but I didn't listen. I didn't need to, I knew which they were. They were the bracelets that Fanny and I had seen in Rochester Row that now lay among the actual treasures of the Rubenstein Collection at the British Museum.

I went to Parkinson. "The bracelets," I said. "Do you know when Rubenstein bought them?"

He said he could give me actual details if I could wait a few hours; he'd have to get at the papers. Presently he phoned me. They'd been bought at X———'s

Auction Rooms, where first-class stuff was often kept for Rubenstein to look it over. His reputation was as big as that. I went down to X's. I hadn't a doubt in my own mind that the bracelets Rubenstein had bought had been the genuine ones, and that the others had come from Rochester Row, but you can't in cases like these take a single chance. And there might be two duplicates. We had to wait a bit at X's until some one realized what I'd come about, and then I had all the attention I wanted.

I saw a man called Bywaters, who asked in a curt sort of voice if I was calling the authenticity of the bracelets into question.

"Hardly that," I said, "but the fact remains that the bracelets found in the Rubenstein Collection are not originals, but only very brilliant fakes. They've been submitted to a number of experts," I reeled off a list of names, "all of whom are agreed."

"And all of whom, with one exception, were called in consultation on the bracelets bought by Mr. Rubenstein and were unanimous that they were genuine."

"That gives us two alternatives. Either Rubenstein sold the originals and substituted the others, which is quite unthinkable, or they were substituted unknown to him either before or after his death."

"Mr. Rubenstein is, of course, free to do what he pleases with his own possessions," Bywaters pointed out a bit pompously, "but as you say, it's incredible that he should deliberately perpetrate a fraud, which is what this would amount to. Besides, there's the question of the insurance. He paid heavy insurances for each article as he bought it."

"We could inquire about that," I agreed, "but only to verify suspicions that are practical certainties."

"Where did the second pair of bracelets come from?" Bywaters wondered, and I said, "If my ideas are right, Rochester Row. I'm going along now to see what I can learn at that end."

I called for Crook and we drove down in a cab. The shop was unchanged; it looked to me as though the same China dragon reigned from the same carved bracket, the same antique silver spoons and sugar bowl were grouped round the fine old silver tea and coffee-pots in the window. There was an old Persian mat hanging like a tapestry at the back of the window, and some old English china, of a kind that personally I have never been able to admire, lining one side of the window. Only the bracelets were missing; some fine Chinese jade necklaces had replaced them. I went inside. The shop was a cavern of shadow; the occasional small lights that cast little pools of brilliance here and there intensified the general gloom. The man moving from behind a counter as I entered was like some genie. His features didn't seem to stir as he spoke.

Crook left the talking to me; he gave the impression of pricing everything in the shop.

"In November," I said, "I saw some Chinese bracelets in your window. I thought they might be genuine. I came in to see them."

"With a lady," he said at once, and his voice seemed to have neither depth nor echo. It was like watching a shadow-play, and the surroundings approved the situation. "The lady realized that the bracelets were only a very fine copy."

"Since then," I told him, no longer surprised at his memory, since it was clearly Fanny whom he particularly recalled, "those bracelets have appeared in the Rubenstein Collection."

The man put out his hand and took a carved crystal elephant from a shelf.

"With Mr. Rubenstein's knowledge?"

"I fancy not. But those bracelets of yours—you've sold them?"

"Some weeks ago."

"You know the name of the man who bought them?"

"I can't tell you."

"Inability or discretion?"

"Inability, as it chances, though discretion would suggest the same reply."

"Why be so secretive?"

"It wouldn't be etiquette to reveal a customer's name," he told me suavely.

A certain rather garish light burst upon me. "In case I'm a professional thief out for swag and asking for information? As it happens I'm not. But—the fakes were found in the Rubenstein Collection."

Some men can express a whole mood with a single feature, by a twist of the mouth, a droop of an eyelid, sketch a complete change of thought. Our friend used his eyebrows; these shot up in twin peaks—long pale brows they were—to convey incredulity, shock, perplexity.

"There is no question of the accuracy of the report?" he hazarded.

"Absolutely none."

He was silent for a moment. Then, "I knew Mr.

Rubenstein," he observed. "Once or twice I was able to be of service to him. He was the artist par excellence. He would certainly never have allowed the bracelets I sold to be placed in his collection. Besides, as I happen to know, he had the originals."

"Who else knew that?" I asked curiously.

The fellow shrugged. "Every one who is interested in the subject could answer an examination paper as to the whereabouts of choice pieces. A man's house is regarded as almost as much public property as if it were a museum."

"And you still don't feel able to tell me who bought the bracelets?"

The man hesitated. "If I don't?"

I shrugged in my turn. "It'll be a matter for the police, naturally. This substitution means a heavy loss to the British Museum, quite apart from the—artistic aspect of the case."

"Yes," agreed my companion rubbing his hawk nose. "That's right. Then—it was some one I didn't know. In a place like this you soon learn to differentiate between the man who's out for something unusual, perhaps to sell again, and the genuine collector. This man was the first type. He came in, just as you did yourself, and asked to see the bracelets. He said to me, 'They're not genuine, are they?' But any one would swear they were. I told him you would need to be an expert, and he said, 'Yes, but what's their percentage of the population?'"

"Did you say anything about the originals being in the Rubenstein Collection?"

"No, sir, he said that. He asked me if I had ever

seen it, and I said I hadn't had the privilege. There have, of course, been photographs of some of the prize specimens from time to time in magazines like the *Connoisseur* and the *Art Collector*. He said, 'That fellow, Rubenstein, is a very fortunate man. Not many of us can afford to indulge our hobbies on that scale.' It passed through my mind that not many men have hobbies worthy of indulgence."

"And he bought the bracelets?"

"Yes." He named a sum.

"He paid for them by check?"

"No, sir. By cash."

"Didn't that strike you as odd?"

"He spoke like an American. I thought he was an American. They often pay in notes."

"You didn't keep the notes, of course?"

"They were one-pound notes. Not even a five-pound note in the whole bundle."

"And that didn't arouse your suspicion?"

Perhaps I sounded impatient. I was stiff with anxiety, I know.

"I'm a shopkeeper, sir, not a policeman," said my friend. I tried to reassure him with a hasty laugh, but he was like a hedgehog with all its prickles out. It took me some time to gentle him into amiability again.

"I was thinking it was rather a large amount to be carrying about with him," I speculated, "but he may have been in a plot. You'd had other inquiries, of course?"

"Several."

"So he'd know the price. Yes, that's quite a notion. He was no one you had seen before?"

"No. I couldn't even give you his name. He was a baldish man, with a fringe of silky reddish hair, and a rather short red beard. Fortyish, or perhaps a little more. I remember another thing. He kept his right glove on all the time."

As I turned to go Crook remembered to ask the date of the sale. It .was forty-eight hours after Fanny and I had looked at the bracelets.

"That cooks our goose very nicely," remarked Crook gloomily, hailing a taxi for which ultimately I should pay. "Now—how are we going to fool the law? It's got to be done somehow."

CHAPTER XVII

There's danger in a single hair.

I DON'T want many more nights as bad as that one was. I lay awake, drinking brandy and smoking cigars, and putting two and two together and making it four every time. Who else knew where the originals of the bracelets were to be found? Dozens of people, according to Field (the fellow in the shop in Rochester Row). Who knew where these copies were? Quite a lot of people, including Fanny. Who had had a chance of substituting them? The answer seemed written on every wall to which I turned; at about five o'clock I gave up the puzzle and went for a walk. It was a cool, gray morning when the world seemed transparent as a bubble; I found my way to one of the quiet London squares, where no one moved; through black iron railings I saw the flowerless shrubs in their dark beds of earth, and the shabby green wooden seats that next spring would be repainted for the benefit of dwellers in the square. A dachshund, an ungainly beast, whose back legs seemed fastened on wrong, peered at me from a first-floor balcony where the dead spines of Virginia creeper made a natural barrier. A white cat was curled outside a public-house. I walked round and round the square, trying to fit my pieces into some other pattern. The red-bearded man must be Randall, and if so, Fanny couldn't escape. Every one would argue that Randall had got his information direct from her. For when had Randall known so much about Chinese ornaments? Some one, some expert, had told him. I dreamed wildly of getting in touch with Randall, dragging a confession out of him at the pistol point, and shooting him if he tried to involve Fanny. I was full of bold notions. The devil of it was I had no idea how to pull them off. Round and round the square I went, under the windows of the sleeping garage, the shutter green and white and dark blue, of the picturesque little houses, stepping carefully past the sleeping cat, walking under the black buds of the ash tree, until I became aware that I had attracted the attention of a policeman who stood on a corner of the square, stroking his black mustache and looking at me with a calculating stare. I began to realize that I was behaving in a most suspicious manner. The next time I passed him I hesitated, wondering whether I'd turn sharply about and go back to the quiet high road where the first vans of the day were speeding past on their way to market. It was too early for the first omnibuses but soon they'd be on the street, too. I was still hesitating when he came across to me.

"Lost something, sir?" he asked sympathetically.

I grinned in spite of myself. "Nothing I'm likely to find in the square," I said.

"If you know where you lost it . . ." he began, but I shook my head.

"That's my trouble."

"And when?"

"About two years ago."

I could feel him stiffen. "I don't understand, sir."

"It isn't a thing," I explained. "It's a person."

He put his hand over his mouth to conceal a smile. "A lady, sir?"

"No, damn you. An ex-convict."

"Have you tried the Yard?" I might have lost a notecase for all the feeling his calm voice betrayed.

"How can I go to the Yard and ask for a man whose present name I don't even know?"

"It's awkward, sir."

I realized that he thought I was drunk. "Damn it, I'm as sober as you are," I exclaimed violently.

"Quite, sir. If you know some one who was in touch with the person . . ."

Light flooded upon me. "Charlie Bennett," I muttered.

"I beg your pardon, sir?"

"Nothing. I said that was a very good idea."

You can't tip policemen, but I tried to look as grateful as if I'd given him half a crown, and he nearly succeeded in looking as lofty as though he'd had it. I went away from the square at a quick step, wondering how soon I could get in touch with Bennett, and how, when I did find an excuse, I could extract the man's address from him.

I didn't know whether Bennett met Randall, or whether he got his money by post. If he got it by post it was going to make things difficult. I thought of various ways of fighting my way into his house, representing a vacuum cleaner, a brush manufacturer, but I abandoned those. I'd have to be more subtle than that. I went round to see Crook, and we got in touch with Marks, the man who had done some inquiry work for us already in this case. But Marks was now engaged on one of these divorce jobs that, for private detectives as for barristers, are much the most paying things there are.

"We can get some one else," said Crook, but I said no. I could do the job myself. When Crook looked doubtful I asked him if he realized that for years I'd had to assume a second personality at the shortest possible notice. I'd learned to write two hands and speak in two different voices. I'd even, hardest of all, contrived to adopt two totally dissimilar walks. It's a man's walk that betrays him as often as not; I've recognized a criminal before now from his back view, where I've been deceived by his face and manner.

Crook said soothingly, "Yes, yes, I had forgotten the bloody spy. Very well then."

That night, the 27th of February, a stranger came to the Port of Call, was very jovial at a very low cost. He got stood a drink or two when he explained that he was just down from Carlisle and had tramped the whole bleeding way.

"What for?" some one asked him, and he said, "Work, of course. Nothing doing in the north."

"Nothing doing 'ere," several voices assured him. "Three days dock and three days dole, that's a good average."

"Make it two and four," said another voice.

The stranger looked impressed and dejected. "Stands to reason there must be more work down south," the stranger argued.

"Not enough to go round," said the sullen ring of voices.

"Well, there seems to be plenty of brass here," said the stranger, speaking with a broad Lancashire accent. "To judge by the way it's flowing the wrong side of the counter."

"Oh, that's Charlie." The temper of the crowd changed. " 'Es a ruddy millionaire, ain't you, Charlie boy?"

"Lucky with the dogs," said Charlie boy.

"Yus, and what kind of dogs?" asked some one and raised a laugh.

Charlie seemed untroubled.

"Troof is, 'e's one of these perishing capitalists," one of the drinkers confided to the bar at large. "That right, Charlie?"

The chorus swelled. "What's in those envelopes that come round first of every month? Dividends, eh?"

The chaff went on. Bennett seemed flattered by it. He winked and nodded, and gradually filled himself up with beer, but he didn't really resent all this fun at his expense. You could see that he thought himself a hell of a fine fellow to be able to throw the cash about at a time when half his mates were lining up at the relief office. I disliked him more and more; it was a pity the chaplain from Kingstown couldn't see him. It might have made him revise his estimate of what constitutes a good fellow.

As he got fuller he became boastful; he had, he said, had his misfortunes like other men, but a wise chap learned something even from his bad luck. A parson he knew (I recognized the chaplain) had once said to him that nothing need be wasted, and by gum, chaps, that

221

fellow was right. Keep your weather eye open and you could turn anything to good account.

There was nothing to be done after that but wait until the first and hope that there had been truth underlying the chaff of the men at the bar. On the 1st of March, a Friday it was, I remember, the postman went his morning rounds in Argyle Road at 7.45 as usual. He knocked twice at No. 4, and Mrs. Bennett, who seemed to be expecting him, came to the door and took in a registered envelope. A man lounging on the other side of the street, looking through a betting list, saw clearly the oblong envelope with its red seals and blue chalk cross. At 8.15 a man in the uniform of a post office official came to the door of No. 4 and asked Mrs. Bennett if she had had a registered envelope delivered that morning. Mrs. Bennett, looking surprised but not yet alarmed, said that she had.

"And were the contents in order?" the official asked.

"Well, it isn't for me, it's for my 'usband. 'E's out on a job now. 'E won't be back to his dinner neither —gone over to 'Ounsditch, 'e 'as—but 'e'll be back this evening. Why, there's nothing gone wrong, 'as there?"

The official tapped his teeth with a pencil and then said he didn't know. "We've been having complaints from several people in this district about registered packets having been tampered with. Did you notice any sign of interference with yours?"

The obliging Mrs. Bennett fetched the letter and showed it to the visitor.

"Looks all right to me," she said. "Lor, I 'ope it is all right. Charlie'll carry on something awful if anything's gone wrong."

The official weighed it thoughtfully in his hand. "You know what ought to be inside," he said.

"Well—money, I reckon," said Mrs. Bennett, hesitating a bit about committing herself, as any wife might.

"What time d'you say your husband will be home?"

"A bit after five, I dare say. He generally comes back in good time on the first of the month, if 'e 'appens to be in work then."

"Because of this?" The official was still balancing the envelope in his palm.

"That's right."

"I'd best come over and see him then," the visitor decided. "It wouldn't do for you to open it, and see what's in it, and if it's right?"

Mrs. Bennett said at once that it wouldn't. "I don't want to roast before my time," she said.

The official nodded sympathetically. "Will you tell your husband I'll be over between five and six and ask him not to open the packet till I return? We're having a lot of trouble, and there's the chance that the culprit's one of our own men."

Mrs. Bennett said she would, and the official departed, to resume ordinary dress, to walk restlessly about the streets of London, to fight down a sudden desire to go and see Fanny on some pretext, and finally sat and slept alternately through one of the worst films that ever came out of Hollywood at a cost of a quarter of a million pounds, if fifty per cent of current rumor can be believed, until it was time to go back to Poplar High Road.

Bennett was in, and his manner was a mixture of perplexity and alarm. "What's all this?" he said. "What's wrong with my money?"

"Nothing, I hope," his visitor told him. "It's just that we want to be certain everything's all right. You know how much there ought to be in that envelope?"

"Twenty-five, same as it always is."

"It's always been correct?"

"Yes."

"And to time?"

"First of every month. Well, there'd be trouble if it was late."

"It's been coming for some time now?"

"More than two years now."

"Always the same amount?"

"It began at ten, and it's gone up——"

"And it might increase again?"

Bennett was thoughtfully slitting the envelope that he now threw upon the table. It was addressed to Mr. Charles Bennett in a tall sloping script, a hand that would baffle any board of experts. I remembered that Randall was a forger.

"It might increase?" I repeated.

"That depends," said Bennett, laboriously counting a thin wad of pound notes.

"On Mr. Randall?" I asked.

At first the shock was so great that Bennett didn't speak; only his hands tightened on the notes and he stopped counting. At last he lifted his head.

"What the 'ell . . . ?" he began.

"Keep quiet," I told him. "It's common knowledge that Mr. Randall sends you hush-money every month, ever since you discovered him working for Mr. Kirby and thought it might upset his plans—his carefully-laid plans—if the old man knew he wasn't long out of Kingstown Jail. That's your private arrangement with Mr. Randall. If he thinks it's worth twenty-five pounds a month to shut your mouth, that's his affair. If you can make him believe it's more, that's yours."

"I know 'oo you are," cried Bennett in sudden fury, "the low 'ound that came skulking down 'ere with 'is story of wanting to find Mr. Randall . . ." His manner became threatening.

"I wasn't stalling," I told him, "and you needn't look around for a bread-knife, because murderers hang, and no one would think any the more of you for having half-killed another man a few years back. Blackmail's an ugly word. People don't sympathize with black-mailers."

"You're calling me a blackmailer?"

"I didn't come here to exchange compliments."

"Then why the 'ell did you come 'ere?"

"For the same reason as I came before, to know where Mr. Randall is."

"I don't know," said Bennett sullenly.

I shook my head. "You're no fool, Mr. Bennett. You know well enough. Where is Mr. Randall?"

"Why don't you go to the police?" he demanded with feeble truculence.

"It seems my last alternative," I agreed. "Though I'm surprised at the suggestion coming from you."

"They can't touch me," he exclaimed defensively.

"I don't see how you can keep out of the picture," I warned him. "They'll come to you for information."

"I tell you, I don't know."

"Meaning, he's given you the slip?"

"I don't mean that..." The fellow stopped, with bitten lip.

"You're asking me to believe you're a fool," I said. "If you didn't know where he was, if you didn't make it your business to know where he was, you'd never be able to count on your monthly dividend. Oh, I don't expect him to put his address on the slip of paper in which the notes were wrapped, and the postmark on the envelope doesn't help much—thousands of registered letters must go out from the S.W.1 district every day —but you know where he can be got at if anything goes wrong with the supply."

"I don't know where he lives," said Bennett grudgingly. "And I don't never see 'im...."

"I expect he wouldn't want that," I agreed. "But you have an address."

Very reluctantly he gave it to me. Silver Square, Finchley—my heart leaped. At last, I thought, we were making a little headway. I knew the district by repute, small mean shops and office buildings, little snug suburban houses with porticoes and plush curtains and stone figures in front lawns the size of a handkerchief. It was now six o'clock, and I determined to go to Finchley before Bennett had time to warn any man that I was coming.

I went to Silver Square that night, but I didn't, after all, go up to Randall's office, though it would have been easy enough. I was dining with Crook, and I explained the reason for my sudden withdrawal, trying to make discretion sound the only reasonable course. He cocked a bibulous eye at me.

"Confess it, Curteis," he said, "lawyers hear a lot of truths that would astonish a court. You came away without trying to see the fellow because you wanted to preserve a whole skin."

"I shouldn't be much use to Fanny with a punctured brain," I urged, and he chuckled and offered me a second cigar.

"What a versatile fellow you are," he remarked. "There are so many professions you might have adopted —a diplomatist, politician, novelist . . . and you'd have made an excellent journalist."

"Meaning?" I said, a shade haughtily.

"That in your shoes I'd have felt inclined to stay in the fried-fish bar, too. When your story began I was all for tearing up the stairs. You've converted me. That's a journalist's first job," and he clapped me heartily on the shoulder.

This is the story I had told to Crook.

On leaving Bennett I went along to Finchley and found Silver Square easily enough. Randall's office was in one of those drab blocks I had pictured, a number of little dreary rooms like rabbit warrens let out for the most part in single offices, with a communal bathroom in the basement, where odd-looking women washed tea-cups and mopped down smeary tin trays. I should need no subtlety, I realized, to discover Randall's whereabouts, for almost the first thing I saw was a shining brass plate inscribed:

MR. RANDALL,
Private Enquiry Agent,
Second Floor.

227

I stood still for a minute or two considering this.

"There was always the chance," I pointed out to Crook, "that the business was a genuine one. It would suit Randall's book admirably, if it were. The fellow is a born scamp, blackmailer, all the rest of it. If he could get in on the ground floor on a number of domestic scandals he'd be in clover, comparatively speaking, for the rest of his days."

"A chap like that isn't satisfied with clover," Crook pointed out in his turn.

"No, but clover's something to be going on with. Besides, he'd get inside private houses, be on terms of peculiar intimacy with his clients. I thought it quite likely that the business was a going concern."

"But didn't go up to find out?"

"No. I had intended to, when it occurred to me that I was behaving with the folly that exasperates me in films and detective stories, where the hot-headed hero dives out in a fog in response to a telephone call from the heroine, that it never occurs to him to verify. I had come posting hot-foot from Poplar to Silver Square, without warning a soul of my plans. I was unarmed; it seemed to me more than probable (1) that Randall kept a revolver on his premises, and (2) that he was expecting me."

"The faithful Bennett having telephoned as soon as you were ought of sight?"

"Precisely. And so astute a rogue would certainly have some good explanation for the police if he did happen to shoot fatally a man who was becoming a bit of a nuisance to him."

"What did you do? So ardent a lover certainly

wouldn't come posting back without even discovering if he was on the right trail."

"Oh, I did my bit of sleuthing," I assured him in as jaunty a tone as I could contrive. "You know the way these offices are built? A row of little shops, and three stories above them—offices—and, on the top floor sometimes private flats. Most of the first floor goes with the shops. I went into a stationer and asked for some postcards that I didn't want and some ink that I did. It isn't always easy to get stationers to gossip—tobacconists are the best market for that sort of thing—but I did work the woman into a conversational frame of mind. I asked for blue-black ink, and she only had bright blue. I filled my pen, made marks on a little scribbling pad, objected to the color, which gave her a chance of saying that all the people round there preferred the blue. That got us on to the people themselves, and I soon worked in Randall's name. He's a newcomer to the flats, only taken the room quite recently. She doesn't know him, not even by sight. I asked for the address of the landlords, said I wanted an office in the neighborhood myself. Luckily they lived just round the corner, and I went along to see them. They simply confirmed what the old woman had told me. He'd been there about a week, and they knew nothing of his business. I asked what sort of leases went with the buildings and they said mostly they were rented by the month. I asked if there was another Randall on the premises and they said no, and never had been. I got them to look through the books for me, which proved that whatever name the chap was using at the time of Kirby's death and afterwards, when the prospectuses were being sent out, it wasn't his own. "On the whole," I added doggedly, "I think I was wise to avoid paying my first call alone and unarmed. There was a fried-fish bar opposite the newsagent, and I went in and ordered some food. I could keep Randall's window under observation. It was quite dark, which either argued that he wasn't there, in which case I had lost nothing by not calling, or else that he was there, waiting for me in the dark. I've had some unpleasant experiences of this kind of thing. There's a very ingenious trick by which you attach a cord to the door-handle and leave the door slightly ajar. When your inquisitive visitor arrives he gently pushes the door, sees that the room's quite dark, and, as it opens and he hesitates on the threshold, he gets a bullet through his heart. Even if he isn't killed outright he's a nasty mess, and certainly not capable of arguing with a plausible Randall in the presence of a police officer. The man in possession holds practically all the cards; he only has to say he was threatened, producing a revolver from your coat pocket, where he's just slipped it, to justify himself; Randall knows all the tricks of the game."

"Do you know if he was there?"

"Yes, silent as a cat at a mouse-hole. I'd had two plates of fish and was wondering how much longer I could stand the stink of frying skate, when I saw a wavering light at the window; it was faint and circular, the beam thrown by an electric torch discreetly used; then the blind was drawn aside and a figure appeared. It was too dark for me to see anything except a wedge of beard and a glimpse of a dark suit. I got the impression of a dark hat pulled over a face that was completely hidden by shadow. The fellow looked up and down the street; he stayed at the window perhaps half a minute. Then the blind dropped back into place."

"Did he know you were in the fish bar?"

"I've no idea. Of course, he has this tremendous advantage over me, that he knows what I look like and I don't know precisely what I'm after. I can't stop every red-bearded man in London."

"Did you see him come out?"

"No. He may be there still for all I can tell."

Crook regarded me critically. "This has shaken you a bit," he said.

I felt myself color. "I'm growing a fool as I get older," I told him shortly. "Five years ago I'd have had more sense. But I give you my word that until this happened I'd regarded myself as being in the position of a man playing solitaire. If you've seen them, as I have in out-of-the-way corners of the world, you'd be amazed by their absorption in the game. The rest of creation can take its own sweet path; it can sing, weep, love, loathe or die; the solitaire player doesn't care. I'd forgotten that practically every game is for two or more players; while I've been carefully stalking Randall he also has been stalking me. The devil of it is I'm like a man who has lost his compass. I've no idea where I stand. Does he know how much I've discovered of his past history? How much I've guessed? Does he know how much Fanny has or hasn't told us? I confess frankly I had cold feet over the whole business. In fact, when I saw a policeman in the opposite doorway I nearly got up and went over to ask for protection.

For a moment Crook the imperturbable looked

alarmed. "You didn't do any such dam'-fool thing?" he exclaimed.

"No. I know the spirit of the London police. There's a right and a wrong way of doing things, and you have to do 'em the right way. You can't go bursting in on a man because you suspect him of murder twice over—half a dozen times for aught I can guess."

Crook looked thoughtful. "There's one thing," he said. "You've still got Randall guessing. I agree with you. We'll keep away from that room for the present. Sooner or later he's bound to come into the open. I'm inclined to leave the next move to him."

He wanted to call a taxi for me when I left him, but I told him I'd feel safer in some public vehicle. "There's something a bit sinister to a man who isn't sure whether he's being shadowed or not about a taxi at night," I said, "with the light switched off and a barrier of glass between himself and the driver. Besides, Randall may be able to drive a taxi. Every gambit I've ever encountered or remembered from the thousand odd crime yarns I've read in various spots of the world warns me to avoid taxis." I jolted home in a brightly-lighted bus. For the first time since my return I was careful about the bolts and bars in my flat, and I even got out the little revolver I didn't expect to have occasion to use ever again and put it conveniently beside my pillow.

And to make things doubly sure I stopped awake all night.

We didn't after all have to wait long for Randall's next move. When I came down next morning I found a letter in a plain white envelope on my plate. It was addressed in the sloping script that had distinguished the address of the registered letter; inside was a half-sheet of unheaded cream-laid notepaper on which was written in the same dark spidery hand:

"If you want to keep a whole skin stay out of this."

Folded inside the message was a long red hair.
The postmark was Finchley.

CHAPTER XVIII

He'd make a lovely corpse.
                    Mrs. Gamp.

IT now appeared, as Crook pointed out, that my life might be a mere matters of hours unless I adopted the suggestion contained in the anonymous letter. A man with one murder at least to his credit isn't going to hesitate at another. Besides, murder's like everything else. You pull it off once successfully, and you see no reason why you shouldn't go on pulling it off successfully whenever it suits your book.

"And you can bet your boots it'll suit Randall's book to get you bumped off," Crook assured me. "There are risks that only fools take."

"And there are risks that even sane men have to take," I retorted. But Crook chuckled and said no man in love is ever sane.

I felt like a distracted puppy that has got locked out of its house and doesn't know how to get it. I ran down any little alley that seemed to offer the minutest clew. I had Bennett shadowed in the hopes that he'd meet Randall, but he never did; I even went to the room in Silver Square, but I only rattled the handle of the door in vain; there was nobody there. I asked a neighbor when Mr. Randall was at home, and he said he didn't know. He'd never seen the man. I went back to the

estate agents and asked for the name of the last man
who had occupied the flat. He told me Russell. I asked
what Russell had looked like, and he said vaguely he
was a fair man, youngish. I dismissed my idea that
Randall had had the flat ever since Kirby's death, in
varying names, and came back to Crook, disheartened
and nearly desperate.

"Take it easy," Crook advised me. "There's one
avenue that doesn't seem to have occurred to you. I
don't say it'll give us our answer but it's worth
exploring."

"And that is?"

"Has it occurred to you to wonder where the bracelets
really are?"

"I'll tell you where they aren't," I said promptly.
"They aren't in the murderer's possession."

"And equally they aren't at the bottom of the
Thames. A man doesn't commit a murder and then lose
the fruits of it so lightly."

"Whoever has them must realize their value," I
argued.

"Where's the logic of that? If you ask me I'd say
whoever has them has no notion of their value. And
when the stink has died down, the murderer will reclaim
them at the modest price for which most likely he
popped them. My idea isn't to try the collectors, the
experts, but the pawnshops where, so long as you pay
the interest, your goods can lie hidden for months."

"And if the man doesn't know who left them?"

"I don't suppose the murderer would give his own
name, but we may be able to trace him. After all, he
has to leave some name and address—he has to pay

interest—of course, we'll make the usual trade inquiries, too."

"That means the story will leak into the press," I said sharply.

"Any objection?" asked Crook. "Most men like a little free advertisement."

I damned the press heartily.

"Don't be so free with your curses," Crook reproved me. "Suppose the bracelets are in the hands of a collector? Once the public knows they're missing you've got your fellow on toast. It's just a question of time."

I began to see light. "Meaning, that if they're on view no man in his senses will dare withdraw them for fear of exciting comment? And if he does, some one will start putting two and two together? That's a notion."

He smacked me on the shoulder. "Got it in one."

"But surely once the hunt is up, whoever has 'em will come forward?"

"Little Arthur or the Sunday School lesson-book," jeered Crook. "Where did you get off, my boy? Haven't you ever met a collector? Don't you know the species? They're like all monomaniacs, not altogether human. Their consciences don't work in the same way as the consciences of other men. They wouldn't do what, according to the facts, it might be suggested that Rubenstein did, substitute a fake for a genuine article, but they'll jump at the chance of acquiring the antique and not too many questions asked. Like the body-snatchers of old, who turned a virtuous deaf ear to the suggestions that perhaps there was a leetle—just a leetle violence used in procuring specimens."

"And, of course," I said eagerly, "X didn't expect the crime to be discovered for months, if ever."

"By crime you mean the substitution of the bracelets, not the murder, I suppose?"

"Precisely. You see, that's a specialized form of crime. Numbers of people can commit murder, whether they do or not; not every one, I grant you. There are some people who couldn't take life not even in the hottest blood. But murderers are by no means rarities. You need no particular knowledge to shoot off a man's head or even put prussic acid in his coffee. Once you've overcome the initial difficulty of procuring the weapon, laying hands on the poison..."

"And neither of those presents much difficulty if you know the ropes," Crook assured me dryly. "Guns can be bought as easily as gramophone records, if not at quite so many stores. And I could name a dozen haunts between my office and Trafalgar Square where you could get enough morphia or cocaine to finish off ten men."

"Well," I said, "once we find the bracelets we ought to be able to trace the course they've taken since they left Plenders...."

"And when we've done that the path of the thief to the scaffold should run as straight as that of the righteous towards the perfect day. Now I'll get to work."

As he had suggested, he made the usual trade inquiries, which got us nowhere. The press jumped at the story, having no particular crime to feature at the moment.

FURTHER MYSTIFICATION IN RUBENSTEIN MURDER

I read, and

SENSATIONAL DEVELOPMENT IN PLENDERS CRIME

It has now been revealed (exulted the press smugly) that the famous Chinese Collection bequeathed to the British Museum by the late Sampson Rubenstein, the circumstances of whose tragic death are still being investigated by the police, was tampered with, presumably by the murderer, before actually coming into the possession of the authorities. This gives a new motive for a crime that has hitherto appeared a little pointless. The missing articles are two Chinese bracelets of jade of very ancient manufacture and of considerable value.

I had somehow expected news at once, and as the days went on and nothing happened I became terribly restless. I couldn't sleep at night for thinking of Fanny in her cell; I didn't dare go and see her without fresh news and fresh hope. I badgered Crook till he told me to get out. I remembered what a man in Borneo had once said to me: "Tarrying the Lord's leisure is difficult enough, but tarrying a lawyer's leisure becomes intolerable." This wasn't really fair to Crook, who was doing all he could. If there's any man living who knows more about the holes where human rats hide I've yet to meet him; he had any number of people on the job—mostly ex-cons., I think—who could dive into dens that would be suicide

238

to you and me. Cables went to New York and the Continent; we had spies of a more reputable kind keeping their eyes skinned. But it was one of the ex-cons., who found our first clew.

It was ten days after what Crook liked to call our intensive campaign that I got a telephone call from him saying, "There's a chap coming to see me at six o'clock. Says he has news. You'd better come on."

I went and found Crook full of hope. On the stroke of six a little fellow pattered in, his pale face worked by anxiety. He was a German Jew from North London, a sober-looking, elderly man with an intelligent bald forehead and a thick fringe of dark hair. His eyes, dark and set very deep in their sockets, never left Crook's face except to stare into mine. He didn't smile once; he stood like a statue. But it was his hands that arrested my attention. They were more revealing than any facial expression; long, sensitive, intelligent hands grasping a shabby bowler hat. That man could speak through his hands, when his face was like a wooden mask.

He said his name was Hermann; he kept a small jeweler's and pawnbroker's shop in —— High Street. On the 10th January a man had come in with a pair of carved jade bracelets, not to sell but to pawn. He had asked eight pounds on them.

"Have you got them?" I asked promptly.

His mournful eyes bore into mine. "No, sir." His accent, though not markedly Teutonic, was obviously foreign. "They were taken away from me."

"Then how on earth do I know they're the bracelets we're after?" Crook demanded.

"There's the photograph in the papers, sir."

We both groaned. "Have you any notion of the number of dealers who have brought us bracelets that in their opinion resemble the missing bracelets?"

The little German said, "No, sir," and he said it in a manner so respectful that I, at least, was momentarily abashed. I don't think the Judgment Day will abash Crook.

"Well," he told the little chap in a rather brutal tone, "there have been hundreds."

"I only thought, being about the right time," said Hermann apologetically.

A new thought struck me. "Did you say they were pawned?"

"Yes, sir."

"Do you remember the name?"

"Robinson, sir."

Well, of course, you wouldn't expect a man to use his own. "The address?"

"Some hotel. The name I do not remember. I remember it was a hotel because I thought most truly I would not see my money again. I thought that perhaps no one would care for them."

"If they were what we're after they were worth a small fortune," I assured him dryly. "Did you say he only asked eight pounds?"

"Yes. Eight pounds. But, of course, I could not give him so much as that."

"You didn't think they were worth it?"

The little man twined his fingers and laid them thus linked on the surface of the table. "It was the hotel address," he explained. "Always we lend less on an

240

hotel. A man may leave a lodging—we do not know—
but always a man leaves an hotel."

"How much did you give him?" said Crook.

"Half of what he asked. I did not know then that
they were valuable."

"When did you guess?"

"When the policeman came."

I started. "Policeman?"

"Yes. He told me they were stolen goods."

"What was the policeman like?"

Hermann made a vague gesture with those wonderful
hands of his. "Just a policeman," he said disappoint-
ingly. "He said, 'There has been a big robbery round
here. I wish to know if you have . . .' and he read out
a list of jewelry to see whether any of it had come to
my shop. When he spoke of two bangles of jade I
stopped him. 'There was a man—he had a red beard—
yes,' for by an incautious movement I had stopped him.
'a man with a red beard.' He asked me what else he
had brought but I said nothing. He asked for the bracelets; he said they were very valuable; he asked what
I had paid for them. I told him four pounds. He said,
'I am the police. These are stolen property.' I said I
did not know. How should I? He was stern, but he
took the bracelets away and left me four pounds. He
said, 'When the man with the red beard returns, tell
him to come to the police.' "

"And did he return?" asked Crook cynically.

"No, sir. Never. I wait and wait—but, of course, if
the goods are stolen, naturally he will not come back.
Perhaps he is already in prison."

I shook my head. "No such luck." We tried to get a

definite description of the man but Hermann was vague. He remembered the red beard, but he remembered nothing more. It was useless to press him, and we had to let him go. Down at the local police station they knew, of course, nothing of the bracelets or of the fictitious jewel raid. That was what I had anticipated.

I came back cursing myself fluently. It was the G. K. Chesterton argument once again. A policeman had spoken to me in the square and had learned from him the gratuitous information that I proposed to tackle Bennett; a policeman had come down the steps and halted in the doorway of the block of offices where Randall had an apartment; and here was the ubiquitous policeman again.

"Are we much further on?" I asked Crook.

"We know one of his disguises," Crook reminded me, "and he doesn't know that we know it."

But he did. When I got back to my flat I was greeted with the news that a gentleman had been waiting for some time to see me. I experienced a spasm of nervousness. Strange gentlemen were beginning to be something of a menace to my security. I went up, opened the door and stood aside for a moment, so that if anything so inhospitable as a bullet were to greet me it could find some more suitable target. But nothing happened except a movement from the other side of the door, and then Parkinson's voice exclaiming, "Hallo! What on earth..."

I came in. "Oh, it's you," I said.

"Yes. I was beginning to fear he'd got you."

"He?"

"I've brought something to show you," he said, shoving his hand into his pocket.

Before he brought it out I knew what his exhibit was going to be, and I was right. It was a white envelope addressed in black spidery writing, and inside a single long red hair.

I stood staring at it. "But why not?" I stammered.

"Presumably the owner dislikes my activities. This business about the bracelets, you know. A bit rash, perhaps, in the circumstances, seeing he's already given us a taste of his mettle. But much as I value my life, I could hardly refuse when Crook asked me . . ."

"Crook asked you?" I stared.

Parkinson seemed taken aback, even a little put out. "Yes. Why not?"

I recovered. "Sorry. As you say, why not? You're much more likely to be useful to him than I am. It was just that I didn't see why you should be expected to risk your neck. . . ."

"Have you had one of these?" he demanded.

"Heavens, yes. I dare say there's a crop waiting for me somewhere. It does look as though the gent means business."

"I thought you recognized it very rapidly. I fancy Crook's idea is that if we can lure the fellow on he may betray himself through sheer vanity, like that beggar, Neil Cream, who was so anxious to show the police where they got off that he put his own head in a noose."

"Was there a message with yours?" I asked.

"Keep out of this if you value your life."

"You can't say the gentleman wastes words," I observed.

"Or that he doesn't give us fair warning. My idea is to put the matter in the hands of the police. I think he's dangerous."

"So are the police," I told him. "There have been altogether too many of them to please me to date."

He looked at me inquiringly from under his slanting fair brows.

"Meaning?"

"What I say. That I could do with at least one policeman less in this."

He nodded. "I dare say you're right. In any case, we're probably too late. Clearly we're up against an enemy who knows the primary law of warfare. In aggression, attack first."

"And that means?"

"Unless I'm much mistaken, we're already under police surveillance. Or at least I am."

I started violently. "What's the fellow like?"

"Oh, just a bobby. Of course, it may be a delusion but when I came out of the telephone box after ringing you and being assured that you'd be back any minute there was a bobby carefully studying my movements; when I went down the tube steps he came behind me; as I crossed the street I saw him or his twin brother loitering on the other side of the road; and when I went and looked out of your window there, a constable went casually past."

Suddenly hot with anger, I dashed across the room and flung up the window. My room was on the ground floor at the back; its window looked over a dark yard in which some clumpy shrubs made a black patch against the evening. I put my hand on the sash, but even as I raised it, I heard a yell that I didn't recognize as Parkinson's voice, and simultaneously I swerved. That swerve probably saved my life. There was a muffled sound, and a feeling of shock rather than pain. I heard without recognizing Parkinson's cry of horror, felt his hands grip my shoulder; and then I suppose I fainted for a minute. I came round to find him stuffing a handkerchief into a wound that was bleeding too freely for my taste and, as it subsequently proved, for my landlord's. Luckily every decent creature loves a murder, even if it's frustrated, so I got off more lightly than I had anticipated, considering the damage done to the carpet.

"That was a near shave," said Parkinson, who was looking pretty white. "Might have been your heart." He stood up and went to telephone for a doctor. "Now what do you feel about the police?" he continued, slamming the receiver down.

"I'm more convinced than ever we've got more policemen than we want in this game," I told him grimly. "By the way, what happened to him?"

Parkinson ran to the window. "Gosh, I never thought about him. Oh, he's got away all right. Probably he thinks he's done you in. Obviously it's you he's after. I've been standing at that window for some time, and he didn't attempt to pot at me, though of course," he added politely, "he may be keeping me for the second round. After all, I might recognize him, and I am, willy-nilly, in your confidence over this, so probably he'll consider it best to put me out of the way, too."

"He didn't try and get us both together," I reflected.

"He'll wait and find out if he's polished you off first.

245

No point wasting ammunition. Was that our red-haired friend in fancy dress?"

"I suppose so," I said.

"That complicates matters, because that fellow hadn't got a beard. Which means that normally he's a clean-faced man. Pity about that. London's lousy with the type." We grinned at one another sympathetically, and then the doctor arrived.

He was casual and reassuring. "Only a flesh wound," he said. "How did it happen?" He looked sharply from one to other of us."

I said quickly, "I was fooling about with a revolver, didn't realize it was loaded."

He put his hand on my sound shoulder. "Take a tip from an old hand at lying," he urged. "Don't make the mistake of supposing the other fellow's a fool. You couldn't have shot yourself."

Parkinson chipped in, "Curteis is trying to save my face," he explained. "It's his gun but I was mucking about with it. Neither of us knew that it was loaded."

"The asylum's the best place for people like you," grunted the doctor. "I've known fellows stand for a manslaughter charge for no worse folly than that." He gathered up his things, told me to get to bed, that he'd be round in the morning, and cleared off.

"Are you all right for a few minutes?" asked Parkinson. "I want to make sure the fellow's gone."

He came back a minute or two later. "Not a sign. I spoke to the regular fellow on the beat. He's been on duty for some time and won't be relieved for some hours. That skulking chap is a fake, like the bracelets the British Museum have got. Let's have a look at the bullet." It had passed through my shoulder and struck the edge of the marble mantelpiece, that had blunted its nose rather badly. It was a commonplace .32.

"I'd hate to have to guess how many hundreds of those there are going about London," I remarked. I had one myself. "You've only got to read the papers to see how many people keep guns, apparently for swatting flies."

"And occasionally for polishing off their enemies. Well, if you won't have the police in . . . ?"

"How can I?" I asked reasonably. "Can't you see their attitude? Here's a murder mystery. We've solved it. If these adjectival amateurs choose to try and upset our case they deserve to be shot."

Parkinson laughed. "You do like paddling your own canoe, don't you? Have it your own way, if you must, but I hope Crook will make you see sense. Personally I'm all against these killers being allowed to roam the streets. No, not altruism, just pure self-interest. After all, I'm probably marked down for the next target, as I pointed out just now."

I said impulsively, "He'll overreach himself one of these days. The trouble with most criminals is they're too infernally clever. They leave nothing to chance."

"If you're holding it out as a consolation that my death will be the means of bringing a ruffian to justice, let me repeat that I'm no altruist. I'd feel a lot happier if I were on the high seas."

I wouldn't give way. "I'm damned if I do," I said. "Given enough rope, the fellow will hang himself. The fact that he's started to distribute his souvenirs is significant. He's beginning to panic and he wants to warn us off the grass."

Parkinson looked at me sideways. "Jealous?" he asked, and I admitted gruffly that I was.

"We're getting near the end of the case, I'm convinced of it," I said. "Yes, you can say I'm jealous if you like."

"Meaning, you don't only want to see Fanny rescued, you also want to be her rescuer in person?"

"Well," I exclaimed, "you know as well as I do she wouldn't think much of me if I threw in my hand the first time things looked a bit uncomfortable."

Parkinson shrugged. "All right," he said. "But if you take my advice you won't go prowling about after dark. Next time you'll get a crack on your skull or a knife between the shoulder-blades. A man who's for the rope if he's caught anyway isn't going to have conscience pangs about another body or so. I'll speak to the bobby on the beat, the genuine one," he added from the door, "and tell him we heard suspicious noises at the window a few minutes ago—there must have been a silencer on that gun or it would have made much more row—and ask him to keep his eyes skinned. I'll ring up in the morning and make sure you're still alive."

For days I was *hors de combat*. I fretted passionately at being out of the picture, and the doctor threatened me with a couple of weeks' seclusion. He talked of a nursing home, but I told him to get out. I spent a good deal of my time telephoning Crook, who still had his birds out, like a flock of vultures, and on the afternoon of the fourth day we got news. Crook himself came round to bring it to me.

"Got something to show you," he said in his abrupt manner. "Ever seen these before?" And he dumped on my bed the missing Chinese bracelets.

At first I couldn't believe my eyes; I thought they were some first-rate fake, but they weren't. We got Tester's opinion presently and he called some other experts into play and every one agreed they were the genuine article.

"Where did they come from?" I wanted to know.

A lady called Harper brought them along. She says she bought them from a Chinese shop off Bond Street. I know the place. That is," he grinned and jabbed the bedclothes, "some of my boys do. Lots of artistic junk and an occasional first-class thing by accident, as these." He handled the bracelets lovingly, not because they meant anything to him as works of art but because they might be instrumental in bringing his case to a successful and, if possible, a sensational close.

"When was this?" I asked.

"About a month ago. Of course, she'd no idea of their real value. She thought they were attractive jade bracelets and would go nicely with a new evening gown she'd just bought."

"But the fellow who keeps the shop?"

"It's one of these gentlemanly married couples, youngish people with a little capital and large, refined ideas. Sometimes it's an eating-den, sometimes it's a picture-shop—but it's generally one of these amateur businesses where the books are never quite accurate and losses go down as sundries."

"Where did the couple get them from?"

"Some man came in, said he'd just returned from

China, offered them a lot of little carved ivory ele-
phants, some bangles and neck-chains, embroidered
table mats, all bazaar stuff, and these among them.
These, he said, were the star of his collection. They
told me they'd been so much impressed by their appearance that they'd given forty pounds for them. Their
mouths were like a couple of tankard-tops when they
told me that. Forty pounds! Ye gods!" He threw back
his great scornful head and shouted.

"Oh, well," I said, hoping my tone conveyed my
meaning, which was that until the beginning of this
case he probably would have thought forty pounds an
extortionate price for the goods himself. "How badly
Randall must be hating us. Forty pounds!"

"I'd value my life above these." He weighed the
bracelets in his huge hand and whistled. "Why didn't
they come to us in the first place?" I asked. "The China
shop couple, I mean? Or are they too refined to read
the papers?"

"Oh, they're not a very knowledgeable couple." He
dismissed them carelessly. "They'd no idea what they'd
got. I fancy some customer was shown the bracelets
and said, 'But aren't these the ones for which they're
combing the country?' Then they looked at one another and thought perhaps they were."

"Did you get any description of the man who called
himself a returned trader?"

"A tallish fellow with a black mustache and a bandage on the fourth finger of the right hand. That's not
much to go on. Why, what's the matter?"

I had shifted upright; the wound was healing well

and anyhow I couldn't think of such a triviality at such a moment. "A black mustache? That's beginning to be familiar. Even a policeman's helmet takes off, you know."

"If that's all you've got to go on," scoffed Crook. "Black mustaches are cheap enough. You can get them for as little as fourpence-halfpenny, I'm told."

"Exactly. Anything else strike you? Then listen. This man has a bandage on the fourth finger of his right hand. The man who bought the bracelets in Rochester Row kept on his right glove. What's the reason? To hide some characteristic disfigurement. Well then? Who has any noticeable mark on his right hand, some one likely to be involved? What about the collectors you spoke of a few days ago, the men without conscience?"

Crook struggled upright. He was lying along his spine in a deep chair and the effort and his surprise combined nearly brought on a choking fit.

"Graham?"

"Who else? When I was sorting the household to start with I picked on him. He was so damned afraid of being accused. A guilty man can't believe that the whole world doesn't suspect him. And he dissociated himself so violently from Fanny."

"Hold on," said Crook sharply. "Where precisely does your Fanny come in? As Graham's accomplice? And voluntarily or involuntarily?"

I stared at him, gaping with a foolish, slack jaw. "Not voluntarily," I said, after a minute.

"What made Rubenstein invite the fellow down?"

"He said he'd invited himself."

"Through Fanny?"

"I—don't know. No, I think not."

"He'd fit in quite well, provided you stick to the two-man crime theory. He was infernally jealous of Rubenstein—insanely jealous in fact. Did he know about the bracelets?"

"I remember him saying something rather derisively to Rubenstein the first time we met about some bracelets —I don't know if they were these."

"So both he and Fanny knew about them. They knew where the originals were."

"I don't think Fanny did. She didn't say so."

Crook looked at me oddly out of his large light eyes. "Would you expect her to?"

"I refuse to believe she's involved," I said in loud tones.

"Then let's concentrate on Graham, see the sort of case we can make out against him. He was on the premises, he was fiercely jealous, he knew about both lots of bracelets, he insisted on coming down, though he can hardly have thought he was a welcome guest, he answers to the physical description given by the Rochester Row chap of the purchaser of the fake bracelets, he's money-mad—what was he doing that evening?"

"Before dinner? I think he went to write some letters. He sent some letters off. He didn't play bridge. But I can't vouch for him, as I wasn't there myself."

"And he's been a bundle of nerves ever since. That might be the answer. He'd be the one person whom you could expect to know about Randall and be able to turn his knowledge to account. But all this is guesswork; we haven't a blade of proof."

"Leave that to me," I said harshly. "I'll get it if I have to hold a pistol to Graham's head and shoot the admission out of him."

CHAPTER XIX

It is the ray of rays, the sun of suns, the moon of moons, the star of stars. It is the light of Terewth.
DR. CHADBAND.

LATER, Crook remembered that random remark. Not much later, either. Less than twenty-four hours, when London buzzed with the news that some one, presumably Graham himself, actually had put a gun to his head and blown out his brains all over his polished desk and the cheap stained Axminster carpet on the floor. I discovered the fellow and gave the alarm. It was like this. I spent a sleepless night laying plans, wondering how I could entrap the man, when my difficulties were solved by his voice on the line asking me to go and see him. That was ten-twenty. Graham asked me to be there at eleven. At ten minutes to the hour, to be on the safe side, I rang up Crook and told him where I was going.

"Don't go," said Crook at once. "It's a trap. If he invites you it's because he smells danger. He's had one shy at your life, and it didn't succeed. He's much too desperate not to try again. It's suicide to go."

"If I don't I see no chance of getting Fanny out of that infernal cell. I've got to go, Crook. I told you before, there are some risks that must be taken."

"Then don't go alone. Take a couple of men with you. . . ."

"I can't," I said again. "My one hope is to trip the fellow up, make him admit his complicity, get the truth out of him by fair means or foul. I'll heckle him all I can. . . ."

I could hear Crook's groan. "Are you mad, man? Have you forgotten he's still got the gun with which he shot at you, and he won't hesitate to use it again?"

"Self-defense?"

"That'll be his story."

"You'll be able to give evidence that I telephoned you and told you of his invitation."

I could hear Crook cursing softly and fluently at the other end of the line. "You may be excellently equipped to be a lot of things, including a damned fool," he said, "but you're no lawyer. Don't you realize I'm your solicitor, Fanny's solicitor? And what's a solicitor for but to cook evidence where he doesn't manufacture it, to lie and steal and, if necessary, commit murder on his client's behalf?"

"He won't shoot on sight," I consoled the fellow. "He'll want to know what I've guessed, what I've proved, how many other people are involved. I'm his chief mine of information at the moment. He'll try and wring every scrap of news out of me, and then ungratefully fill me up with lead. I know the type."

"And you propose to go there and be filled up?"

"No, that's where you come in. Give me, say, a quarter of an hour, and then come along. I'll see to it that the door of the flat is left ajar. They're cheapish sort of mansions, it won't be difficult to fumble the latch. I've had experience. I'll try and jockey him into an admission. When I hear you—or when the hands of the clock point to the quarter—I'll get excited, make him repeat anything incriminating he's said, and you can come in as witnesses."

"It's like one of these damned films. You're crazy, Curteis. One thing, I hope there'll be enough in your estate to pay expenses; they're about two hundred and fifty per cent above normal already. The nervous strain you've put on me. I'm accustomed to doing my best for accused killers, but I don't expect my client's defense to try and add to the list of crimes. Good God, man, haven't we had enough buckets of blood to satisfy you?"

Which wasn't really fair. Considering we had had under review three corpses and a fourth murder attempt, the quantity of blood shed had been remarkably moderate. This, however, was to be remedied in the very near future.

As the clock chimed eleven I stepped into the lift at Ravenswood Mansions with a large lady in a fur-collared coat and shot up to the third floor. The door of Graham's flat was on the latch, and though I rang no one answered. Crook would have said another trap, and I went through the usual precautions of pushing the door wide and then leaping back against the wall, but nothing happened and I walked in. Graham was there, though he didn't rise to greet me. He couldn't. He lay slumped over the table, as dead as a stone though less cold. The room was so appallingly hot it was odd that I should shiver so.

My first shot at the telephone got me, not on to the police, but to some mysterious female who said, "Did you want Mrs. Salter?"

"Good God, no!" I cried violently. "I'm telephoning from Ravenswood Mansions. A man's shot himself. I want the police."

I'd just got through to the police and explained the position as Crook arrived on the landing outside. He pushed open the door and stood staring on the threshold, ejaculating, "My stars! What's this, Curteis, in God's name. . . ."

"Oh, don't be a bloody fool," I cried, slamming down the receiver, and neither experiencing nor displaying a scrap of that reverence for the dead that is supposed to be customary in such a situation.

"There's blood all right," Crook agreed somberly, striding across the room to that disheveled smashed horror in the leather desk-chair.

"Well, you wanted it, didn't you? Buckets of it. Aren't you satisfied even now?"

My nerves were as raw as rags. "Oh God," I exclaimed, "will the police never come?"

"What happened?" asked Crook.

"I don't know. There are letters on the table there. They may help us. I haven't touched a thing. I've not whiled away interminable voyages with detective yarns without learning that the wise man leaves everything immaculate for the police."

Crook shuddered. "Immaculate! The words you choose." He stood staring with a kind of appalled fascination at that crumpled disfigured heap, half of whose head had been blown off. There were even drops of blood on one of the envelopes, and the fountain-pen that lay at his elbow.

"Hallo," he called out, "one of these letters is addressed to you."

"I know. His sense of the artistic, presumably."

"Meaning he knew he was for it, and thought he might as well save the State the expense and anxiety of hanging him. I wonder if the police will be pleased or not. They do like to get their man." He put his hand on the shoulder of the dead. "Not cold," he said. "What time did you arrive?"

"Eleven. That was the hour he suggested."

"Hear anything?"

"No. But if he used the same gun as that with which he tried to polish me off it has a silencer on it. I shouldn't expect to hear unless I were outside the door at the time."

"They'll save a couple of sacks of quicklime," remarked Crook. "Ah, here they come."

And at last they arrived, a sergeant called Fletcher, and a stubby, blue-chinned tough called Bryce, who turned out to be the police-surgeon. Fletcher looked at Graham and then at me and from me to Crook; Bryce only looked at the body.

"Well?" snapped Fletcher to Crook.

Crook waved to me. "This is Mr. Curteis, sergeant. He found the body and telephoned to you."

Fletcher asked all the usual questions as to time of arrival, nature of the appointment, my relationship to the dead man, possible motive for suicide.

Crook intervened. "He left letters, sergeant," he said.

Fletcher regarded him with suspicion. Crook said, "I am Mr. Curteis's legal representative."

"Why did he want to bring his lawyer to this interview?"

"For this very reason. I suspected we might have a corpse to deal with—but not this corpse."

"You mean Mr. Curteis's?"

"Exactly."

"Then why . . . ?" His dark suspicious eye turned to that frightful body.

"Perhaps the letters would help you, since neither Mr. Curteis nor myself is in a position to do so," suggested Crook, blandly. He wasn't the sort of man to be intimidated by any sergeant of police living.

There were a number of formalities to be observed, but presently I was allowed to open my letter. It was a very bulky and hysterical document, and as melodramatic as any reader of the Sunday press could hope for. The other letter, which was addressed to the coroner, was a facsimile of mine—both letters had been typed on a machine that was subsequently found in the room and identified as Graham's property—with a covering note.

This was the astounding document I found inside the envelope.

"Well, Mr. Curteis, so the last card lies with you, and I hope you're satisfied. Even now I don't know how you got on my track; I thought I had stopped every earth; perhaps it was just that odd card that fate likes to play in hands like this. But I'm at the end of my tether now. I can't last much longer and I prefer to take my own way out. But there are two things I must put on record before I go. The first is that Fanny isn't to blame; she couldn't help herself; she was never a murderess in intention or deed, and this letter should at once set her free. That it should set her free for you is a bitter thought, but at least I shall no longer be there to care. The second is that Rubenstein, morally speaking, is his own murderer. If ever a man asked to be killed he did. He was arrogant and exclusive and those are sins to be forgiven in no man. I will explain what I mean.

"I know what Rubenstein thought of me; I know the jokes he made at my expense—the middle-man, the profiteer, the man who wouldn't take risks, the man whose god was gold, the man to be laughed at, sneered at, gibed at. He had intelligence and even sensitiveness in some degree—where his work was concerned, say—but he hadn't wisdom. Only a fool makes enemies of a man like me. He told you, I dare say, as he told others, that though I cared for the things he cared for, that he squandered his fortune in buying, I cared for the money more. He made me a byword. It's hard to forgive a man for that. But he did worse. He bought, for the money he affected to despise, the things I loved, the things I spent my life discovering and rescuing; and having bought them he shut them up, he called them his, he turned the key on them, he refused to let the rest of us in. Mine, he'd say. Fool! Beauty's not to be bought. A man may be privileged to house it, to cherish it, but who was he, that little gray man, to own the miracles of bygone centuries? He was mad, I think, as too many possessions make too many men mad. He put on airs; I found that last robe he bought, but he owned it. I said I wanted to see it at home, in its right place, in his gallery, and I had to plead for my invitation. That enraged me. I thought I must somehow be revenged. But not by his death. Never that. What profit was it to me that he should die? But he believed himself—almost—a god, and when a man reaches that pitch he is mad. He was driving me mad, too. I thought I must be revenged. And I schemed how to achieve this. And then I saw my chance. When I found those bracelets in Rochester Row I saw my chance. He was always so sure of himself, so sure that he was right; he, the man who could never be wrong. And I thought, now he shall be wrong—wrong, wrong, wrong. I bought those bracelets and I took them with me down to Plenders. I knew that the originals were there, and I thought, I will wait my chance, I will substitute these that I had brought, and for the rest of his days, Rubenstein, that man of pride, shall have nestling among his treasures that faked treasure. Oh, I never meant to tell him, and he would never guess. Only an expert, examining carefully, would know they were not genuine, and when a thing is yours you pay less heed to it. He would pore over it, but as a lover, a possessor, not an expert. And I—I would keep the real bracelets, sometimes I would take them out, and I would gloat over them. I would think, 'That poor fool,' and I would know that I was even with him at last.

"I didn't want to sell them. People may not believe this, but it was true. I have money enough, and no money in the world would buy those treasures back from me. Every time I handled them I would see in them the proof of Rubenstein's downfall, of his folly

—he, the fool, with faked ornaments in the collection he believes, and with truth, to be unequaled. Oh, it seemed to me a fine jest, so fine that I was never afraid of possible consequences. I had no time to think of consequences.

"I laid my plans so well. While I pored over the gems, I was examining the locks of the cases. I went across to Rubenstein and I said, 'May I see so-and-so?' and he handed me his keys. 'Lock the cases afterwards,' he said. 'These things are priceless.' The man of gold, the Jew, the merchant who thinks his stinking money can buy eternal life. I turned the key, I opened the case, but I couldn't make the exchange then, it was too dangerous, there were too many people standing round me. Besides, Rubenstein might be watching. But when I turned the key again the lock didn't catch. I saw to that. Then I moved across to the window. I had been in the garden that morning; I had seen the windows, and the veranda beneath the windows. I had said to Parkinson, 'Isn't that dangerous?' and he had laughed and said, 'Say that to Rubenstein. It isn't safe for any man to suggest to him that he doesn't take proper care of his gallery. Those windows are locked from the inside. I believe the device really is burglar-proof.' I laughed too, and we moved on. But that afternoon, in the gallery, I slipped the catch of one of the windows. Rubenstein, the conceited man of straw, was showing us how they worked, after you, my dear Mr. Curteis, had so assiduously accompanied our hostess down-stairs. It was so easy, when he turned back to gloat, to slip the catch for the second time. Then down we all came. My stage was ready, my window unlatched, my showcase unlocked. Fanny helped me by quarreling with her hostess and taking Rubenstein out of my way. This luck I had not anticipated. The gallery, I knew, was kept locked. Rubenstein kept the key. He must be out for an hour at least. I would be circumspect and careful. I said I had letters to write and went upstairs. But not to my room. Before the household separated, while still they stood staring and whispering in the hall, my task should be accomplished. I went down by the back stairs. I saw no one. I went through the garden door, that was unlatched. I came under the windows of the gallery. The night was dark, but not so dark that I could not see a glimmer of light on the long, shadowy panes. The curtains in the billiard-room were drawn, and the click of the balls, the voices of the players, would distract them from any sound. I was quite without fear—it is strange to remember that, I, who have never been without fear since that night. It was easy to get into the room; I had brought a torch with me, and I held the light low so that no gleam should be seen if any one passed. I found the case, I made my exchange. I could not, of course, lock the case again, but I knew that when Rubenstein discovered this he would merely curse the ineptitude of his guests; he would suspect nothing. Why, he did not even know of the existence of those duplicate worthless bracelets. And then, then, with the case shutting gently under my careful fingers, I heard something that turned my heart to stone. First I heard footsteps, but I paid little heed to them. No one but Rubenstein had the keys and he was speeding on his untrustworthy way to Kings Benyon. But the footsteps stopped, there was the rattle of a key in the lock, the door was flung open, and he stood on the threshold. He stared—oh, God, how he stared! In my private vision he has been staring at me ever since. Wherever I turn I see that face—in shadows, in the patterns of carpets and curtains, it peers at me in trains from the shoulders of young and old men, it looks at me in crowds, it follows me up and down the stairs, it comes peeping into my windows. Perhaps even in the grave it will watch me through the clods.

"He stared. And I stared back. This I had never thought of. He said, 'I had forgotten...' but I shall never know what he had forgotten. A kind of cry broke from me. He would not turn those eyes away. He came closer. He said, 'You are a thief.' I couldn't explain. I stood there, with his bracelets in my pocket and the bracelets from Rochester Row in his case. I think even at that minute I was glad to remember that. This might be my hour of humiliation, but my triumph lay ahead. He came closer, he said, 'You were going to rob me.' I said, 'Look at your case. Nothing is touched.' He didn't move any nearer. He said again, 'You were going to rob me.' I hated him then but I didn't mean to kill him. What use was his death to me? He said. 'This is the end of you,' and he came a step nearer. I was afraid in that minute. I said, 'What do you mean? What are you going to do?' He said, 'All London shall know of this.' And again he called me a thief. I then tried to explain. I tried to tell him. I said he was arrogant, vain, greedy. He didn't listen. He stood there like a statue; his eyes burned in his head. He said, 'If I had not forgotten . . .' and suddenly rage swept over him like a storm. He swayed, it was so powerful. And then he came towards me, saying again that he would ruin me. Hate and fear engulfed me. There was a knife, the knife that killed him, lying by. I can remember now the cold feel of the handle as I clutched it; it slipped in my damp palm. I said, 'Keep off. I'm no thief.' And he came closer. He said, 'All London . . .' and 'Ruined . . .' and then he was twisting at my feet, twisting with the knife in his side. I stared at him stupidly. I didn't understand yet. I looked at my hand and it was empty. I looked at him and the knife was in his side.

"Then Fanny came. She came running up the stairs. I knew her step. I knew I had only to move and shut the door—it closed automatically; it was only from the outside that it had to be unlocked. But I couldn't move; I watched the gibbering figure, and Fanny came in. She stood in the doorway without speech. Then she came across and bent above him. He clutched at her; he tried to speak but there was only a bubble of froth at his lips. She tried to hold him up, but suddenly he died, sprawling at our feet. He must have twisted the button off her coat then, but neither of us thought of it. She was quite calm, white but very calm.

"She said, 'You killed him?'

"I said, 'I didn't mean to.'

"Then she saw the open case. She said, 'You were robbing him?'

"I said, 'Nothing's been touched.'

"She said, 'No, he came too soon.'

"I said, 'What are we going to do?'

"She said, 'We must call some one. You can hide a lot of things in life, but you can't hide murder.'

"I said, 'I won't die for him. I never meant to kill him. It was an accident.'

"She said, 'You can tell that to the judge.' And then, 'You fool, couldn't you have waited?'

"I said, 'Why did he come back?'

"She said, 'He thought he had left the window unslipped. He couldn't remember. These things were his life.'

"I was suddenly angry again. If I'd had a knife I could have plunged it a hundred times into that still body. I understood that maniac who once stood in the moonlight sabering his enemy's corpse. I said to Fanny, 'And his death too.' And then, 'You're in this. You can't get out.'

"She said, 'It's nothing to do with me.'

"I said, 'Who's to know that?'

"She said, 'You wouldn't tell such a story.'

" 'Making you my accomplice?' I asked. 'Why not? I'd be believed. No one understands why you went away so suddenly.'

"She said, 'I had a reason. It had nothing to do with you or Rubenstein.'

"I jeered in my turn, 'Tell that to the judge. It's a question of which of us he believes.'

"She said, 'I don't know what you mean.'

"I said, 'Who knew about the bracelets in Rochester Row? Fanny Price. Who's been associated with me for years? Fanny Price. Who's been here before, knows the run of the house? Fanny Price. Who got Rubenstein out of the way by a trick? Fanny Price. Ring,'

I told her, 'call in the world, and let them see how our plot has failed. They won't hang you, pretty Fanny,' I told her. 'You'll only be shut up for years—twenty perhaps. You'll be fifty when you come out, Fanny,' I said. 'You'll be quieter then. You won't drive men mad. You won't be involved in murder again.' She threw back her head in that defiant way of hers. I've never seen Fanny cowed. I've seen her beaten by life, bruised and humiliated. I knew about that husband of hers. He nearly killed her once, but he couldn't break her spirit, though he broke an arm when he was drunk. She looked at me—she has eyes like a snake—and she said, 'Call the whole world in. I'll take my chance.'

" 'As you please,' I told her. 'But first, listen to what I shall say. I shall say that I was in my room and I heard steps come up the stairs. I heard the Chinese door unlocked. It was nothing to me. I didn't move. Then I heard feet, voices, a sound, a fall, and I came in and found you standing over him. Do you see, pretty Fanny, what every one will believe? You cajoled him out of the house for your own purposes. When he was supposed to be clear you persuaded him to come back. You remembered seeing a window open. He came back, you followed him. You were the thief. I came in and found you. Which story do you suppose they'll believe?'

"For a minute I thought she would defy me, even then, but she didn't. She said, 'You win,' and then we talked rapidly of ways and means. It was her notion to hide Rubenstein in the Chinese coat. She said, 'It'll be days before they discover him, weeks perhaps.

They'll think he took Lal at her word. They won't
search for him here.' And she told me to wipe the
blood off the knife. Rubenstein didn't bleed much.
Fanny went into his room and fetched the cotton-wool;
she mopped up a little pool of blood from the floor,
but he died from hemorrhage. Then we arranged the
tableau. We hadn't much time, but we were fighting
for our lives. It was Fanny again who thought of
sending the car over the cliff. She said, 'It's mad and
it's wicked but it's our only chance. I don't see why
I should die because Sammy has been stabbed.' She
thought of the boots, too. Then she re-latched the
window and I went back to my room, and she went
down and drove away. It was a long series of chances
and but for you no one would have learned the truth.
I say, but for you, but that's not honest. It was that
infernal button clutched in the dead man's hand. Why
did neither of us notice it? We were working at too
high a pressure, I suppose. They got Fanny for that.
She didn't speak, I knew she wouldn't. How could
she? If she told her story who would believe her?
She hadn't an atom of proof against me. I simply
had to deny it, and no lawyer would have dared to
come into court with the accusation. I wouldn't have
come forward—be sure of that. What was the use
of two of us suffering? You were working for Fanny
—I knew that—but I didn't think you'd discover me.
Mind you, I didn't want her to hang. I did all I could.
I knew about her rascally husband. I thought we
might shelve the blame on to him—at least that we
might raise enough doubt to acquit Fanny. I didn't
think she'd get off completely—how could she? But

the public would bawl their applause of her when they realized she'd been defending her husband. Sentiment is more value than eloquence still, and they're both worth more than cold fact. But somehow—I don't know how—you got on to my track. Did I betray myself by those anonymous warnings I sent to you, and to Parkinson when he began to interfere? Who was it who said it's the passion for security that destroys most murderers? I meant to kill you that night. It was my luck again that Parkinson should be with you, to pull you aside. I'd have tried again but once the bracelets were discovered I had no hope. You meant to get me, didn't you? I hoped you'd fix on Randall. . . . Well, you win, and while I hate and fear death I hate most of all the suspense, in a double sense, of the kind of death to which you'd send me."

Here followed his signature, and underneath he had scribbled in a black spidery hand with which I was by this time familiar, "At least count it to my credit that I've saved Fanny for you."

The reading of this amazing document took some time. I felt nothing but the stupor of relief; I hadn't known till that moment how terrified I had been that things might ultimately go wrong in spite of all my efforts to prevent it.

I said, in a dazed sort of voice, "This lets Fanny out," and the sergeant said shortly, "Maybe." Crook put a hand on my arm. "Pull yourself together, man," he said. "Here's a corpse at last that's some use to you."

We parted outside the station; he had to go and

see some one else—"You're like all the rest," he said with a grin. "Comes as a shock to realize that I've other clients beside yourself." I went home and walked irresolutely up and down the floor. I rang up Parkinson and told him the news. He said, "My God! Graham! The last chap you'd have thought capable of the job." And then, in an irrepressible chuckle, "I'd like to have seen the old boy shinning up those veranda posts."

I couldn't think of anything but Fanny. I wondered how soon it would be before they let her out. At about six o'clock, after an interminable day, I telephoned Crook.

"Will she be out tonight?" I asked.

Crook snapped my head off. "Don't be a fool. How can she? She's committed a crime."

I was staggered. I hadn't thought of that.

"She's guilty of complicity in a murder, isn't she?" he said. "You can't do that kind of thing and get away with it."

"Do you mean, she'll stand her trial even now?"

"Bound to."

"And—what sort of sentence will she get?"

"Ask the judge. Honestly, I can't tell you. She's had a bad time—I dare say she'll get off light."

I said furiously, "Half the court will believe she was Graham's mistress," and he replied, "I doubt if that will trouble that young woman much."

An hour later he rang me up again. "Hell's bells," he said. "Something's gone badly wrong. Tell me, you didn't murder Graham and fake the letter, I suppose?"

"No," I said. "I didn't murder Rubenstein either. Why? What's up?"

He said, "I've just bidden farewell to the man who stood your lovely Fanny coffee and saveloys at 10.40 on the evening of Sunday, January 6th."

CHAPTER XX

I'm Gormed—and I can't say no fairer than that.
　　　　　　　　　　　　　　Mr. Peggotty.

THE ancients who depicted fate as a woman were quite right. She's ingenious, devilish, mocking and quite without conscience. Here for weeks on end had we been laboring to free Fanny from the frightful accusation of murder. Here at last we had succeeded, and within twelve hours fate plays a trump that she'd had up her sleeve all these weeks in the shape of a bunfaced little rat called Bligh, who had emerged from hospital the previous day and for the first time realized the tremendous importance of his own existence.

Immediately on parting from Fanny, he had contrived to walk under a motor lorry, and "I wish to heaven it had finished its job," I said savagely. As it was, the beggar had been pretty badly mangled— he explained sheepishly that his mind had been so filled with memories of Fanny that he'd forgotten every London street may be a death-trap, even on a Sunday evening. So under the wheels of the lorry he had rushed and what was left of him was carried off to the Westminster Hospital, where for a long time he took no interest in life at all and forgot all about Fanny, until Graham's suicide, reported in the evening press, startled him into recollection. He had

272

apparently telephoned the paper in which he read the news; he was naturally during the following few days a much-sought after man with police and newspaper representatives on his doorstep and fine offers for interviews and music-hall stunts, though most likely he couldn't even stand on one leg for more than five seconds. Still, he was copy, and for those few days he was topical. I dare say he quite enjoyed it. The fact of his accident gave his evidence a value it could not otherwise have had. There were police records to show that he was knocked down at precisely one minute to eleven, that is, four minutes before Fanny's second train arrived at Victoria.

We had, now, two incontrovertible alternatives that could not possibly be reconciled. If Graham's story was true, then Fanny couldn't have caught the 6.28 and if she hadn't caught the 6.28 then she couldn't be Bligh's girl. And, conversely, if she was Bligh's girl, then she couldn't have been concerned in Rubenstein's death. Graham being dead, and having left behind him that astounding confession, the onus of responsibility to prove the truth of his yarn lay with Bligh.

"And I hope to God he can prove it," said Crook to me. "Otherwise it looks as if we've paid over a fiver to help our bitch over a stile."

But Bligh proved his case up to the hilt. The police worked over his evidence a bit; they didn't much like him for some reason; I didn't like him myself, come to that; he was a swaggering, self-important little beast, full of his own significance, and not really giving a damn whether Fanny swung or not. It was pointed out to him that because he remembered the name of the picture he claimed to have seen that night, and could name its central character, even the fact that he had bought a girl a meal afterwards didn't show that he had been at the cinema at the time he said he had or that the girl he fed was Fanny.

"And what price this?" drawled Bligh, who needed a kick in the pants more than any man I've ever met. This was a round pearl earring set in a peculiar gold clip. "When my girl had gone that night, and she went off in a bit of a hurry, I found this under her chair. I'd noticed she was wearing big pearl drops in her ears, and I thought I'd hurry after her and ask her if she hadn't some more use for it. But the barman stopped me, wanted his money, wouldn't listen to me. By the time I'd settled the account and got my change the girl had gone. I didn't know where she'd be, but I came out into the road and saw her on the opposite pavement. I started to go across to her, got bowled over by the lorry and that's all there is to it."

The police remarked coolly that large pearl stud earrings were as common as flies in July, but that didn't let them out. The companion stud was found among Fanny's jewels, and she identified the missing bauble as soon as she saw it. Indeed, she described the setting to the police so minutely that the only answer they could produce was to the effect that hers wasn't the only pearl earring in London. The jeweler who had set the studs, however, remembered them well; the setting was most unusual, and he had made a special alteration to suit Fanny who had complained that they weren't very comfortable. He was prepared to come into any court and give his evidence. So, reluctantly, the police had to accept his story which immediately had them upsides with Graham's. Because, if Fanny hadn't had anything to do with Rubenstein's murder, why on earth should Graham say that she had? If he had an accomplice why not name him? He'd told us definitely that the mysterious Randall wasn't involved. Nothing he said could affect Graham himself, who was getting out before the confession became public property. There was one answer that met the case, and soon we were all giving it.

"I hope this pleases you," I told Crook. "You've got a really bloody murder at last."

"A murder isn't a murder till it's been proved," snapped he.

I told him that wouldn't take long.

The police came round to see me again and again. They seemed to blame me for not being able to tell them more.

"I'm sorry," I said, "but I didn't hear the revolver explode, I didn't meet any one in the lift except the elderly lady who has confirmed my story and who was on her way to the fifth floor."

"And you didn't see any one on the stairs?"

"No. But that isn't proof of anything whatsoever. If I killed a man on the third floor I should immediately go up, not down. Then I could give the impression that I had been visiting at the top of the building."

"You're getting nice practice," Crook assured me sarcastically. "Both in dealing with policemen and in picking up hints for concealing tracks if and when they're ever after you."

"Are you sure there was no one on the premises when you arrived?" Fletcher continued.

"Of course I'm not," I said. "I didn't see any one, but there's more than one room to the flat. There's a communicating door to the bedroom, and that leads to a passage going down to the servants' quarters. I know that, because, when I was looking for a flat a few months ago, I went over one in this building."

The police were on to that like terriers after a rat; they examined the carpet, the polished wood of the corridor, the furniture, they fired off questions at the concierge as to visitors to that building that morning, but nothing got them very far. The concierge explained that at that hour he was generally occupied elsewhere; the electric lift was worked by the tenants themselves and it would be pure chance if he had seen any one special. Appealed to, I had to admit that he hadn't seen me when I came in, and any one else could have arrived without being specially noticed.

"Well, but if he escaped down the backstairs, as has been suggested, he'd be noticeable," the police argued.

The backstairs led to the domestic offices of the flats, and at that hour of the day a number of tradesmen would be taking or delivering orders. As many as possible were questioned but none of them could be of assistance. They had noticed no one in particular; there were always people messing about in the yard during the morning. The tenants of the flats were appealed to, in case any of them could remember seeing a stranger on the stairs or in the lift, but nothing happened for two or three days when a Mrs. Fraser from the top floor said timidly that she did remember seeing a policeman outside Mr. Rumbold's door, but she didn't suppose that had anything to do with it. After all, policemen are so respectable.

I smote my thigh with annoyance. "I don't deserve to get Fanny out of jug," I acknowledged. "Why didn't I think of that at once? I'd got it so firmly into my thick head that Graham was himself the policeman that I'd forgotten how much of our original case went by the board when Mr. Bligh butted in and upset the position. Of course, a policeman is never listed as a visitor. If he's met on the stairs no one pays any particular attention to him. If he's seen in the yard it isn't anything out of the ordinary. There was even the chance, if there proved to be no other way of escape, that he might pretend to be the real article and walk out under all our noses. My gosh!" I exclaimed more angrily still, "to think that twice at least I've had the fellow under my hand and I've let him walk out on me."

Mrs. Fraser was asked whether she had spoken to the man and she said, "Yes." He was a tallish man with a heavy mustache; he had stood at Mr. Rumbold's door for some minutes, knocking and ringing. She had chanced to come to the door of her flat and seeing him there had said that she believed Mr. Rumbold was always out at this hour. The policeman had asked when he returned and had then gone away saying he would call again.

Mr. Rumbold, a short gingery man, said violently that it was all bunk. He hadn't been expecting the police and they could search the local records from now till Christmas and they wouldn't find a mention of his name, which proved to be true. Presently this story of the policeman was confirmed by an errand-boy who had been cautioned about leaving customers' weekly books, containing money paid at the door, in his basket. Putting temptation in the way of other lads, the copper had said. He hadn't noticed the man's appearance. A copper was a copper. 'Nuff said.

The next point was to time the policeman's visit. Mrs. Fraser unhappily couldn't be more definite than "between twenty to eleven and eleven o'clock." The dead man's solicitor, a fellow called Wood, said that the dead man had telephoned to him at 10.45 speaking of the possibility of bringing a case for libel. His name was being mentioned in connection with a notorious criminal case; he proposed to take steps to stop this at once. That was the last man who came forward with a story of having heard Graham's voice. The next incident was my discovery of him at eleven o'clock, stone dead and, as the villains of melodrama liked to put it, weltering in his gore.

"Allowing the letter is a forgery," said Crook, "who's your man?"

The typewriter on which the letter had been typed was found in Graham's room, and a test was taken to prove that this was indeed the right machine.

They also found a packet of typewriting paper and a box of carbons in a drawer in the writing-table. The carbon used for the confession was found in the waste-paper basket.

"What becomes of our red-headed friend?" I asked. "Surely this was his final throw for safety. He couldn't foresee the advent of Mr. Percy Bligh, of 23, Stanstead Villas, Peckham Rye, S.E., solicitor's clerk at two hundred pounds a year and a thorough damn nuisance."

"Look out for yourself," was Crook's laconic warning. "You aren't going to be popular with that man."

"No point his smothering me," I urged. "The police have got the job in hand now."

"Still, unreasonable though it may appear, when a fellow's going to be hanged, he often likes a companion or two in the death-chamber. By the way, do you like flowers on the coffin or do you prefer the cash to be sent to a hospital?"

The question of the revolver was also raised. This was the same type as the machine turned against me a few days previously. There were no marks on the revolver to identify it or differentiate it from a thousand others in the city of London; but an examination and a comparison of barrel marks proved beyond all question that this was actually the revolver used on the previous occasion.

"Well, if our friend has parted with this, there's a chance he may be unarmed," I said with more cheerfulness than I felt. As I've observed before, few things are simpler, in spite of the red-tape entangling us all, than getting hold of a gun.

"Has any one ever heard of Graham owning a revolver?" Crook wondered. When we went to see Fanny who might, we thought, be able to answer the question, she said, "What unoriginal minds you all have. The police—the real police—have just left after putting exactly the same question. I can't lay my hand on my heart and swear, naturally—Graham's personal life never touched mine, and I don't think I was ever inside his flat—but I'm pretty sure he hadn't got one just the same. He had a nervous terror of firearms. He wouldn't even go to the Naval and Military Tournament at Olympia; he didn't like to hear the guns popping. I remember asking him once if he wasn't afraid of going about with so much money on him, and he said he had a stick with a loaded handle and he'd never hesitate to use it. I don't think he ever did though."

I was inclined to plump for Randall as the murderer —the letter had acquitted him so definitely it would arouse suspicion in a moron—with Graham as his accessory. The bit in the letter about getting even with Rubenstein had, I said to Crook, a ring of truth.

And who would know that secret poison-well in Graham's heart but the man who had been his accomplice? Who else, I urged, would be so anxious to disprove the existence of the red-bearded man? We knew the fellow was alive, because he was still paying blackmail to Charlie Bennett; we knew some one, who used the room taken in Randall's name, was masquerading as a policeman; no one concerned in the case, excepting Fanny and Graham, would be likely to know either of his existence or his past history. The two criminals had hoped that they would never be suspected; when Fanny was taken they began to see security ahead; then I came along stirring up dungheaps, making things damned uncomfortable for them, and fresh trouble eventuated. At length, with discovery in sight, Randall had taken a long chance, put his partner out and bound the guilt on his shoulders. Graham made a fine scapegoat; and what was it to Randall if he involved Fanny? Probably he thought he'd done rather handsomely by her. It was a lot of luck for him that Rubenstein had got that button clutched fast in his hand.

"All very well," grumbled Crook, "but this is mere supposition. We've no proof that we can dare bring forward in court that Randall is connected with this affair at all. Don't quote the red hairs to me. Any one who knew the fellow would know he had red hair, and there are such things as wigs."

"I'll quote you an authority," I answered. "Sherlock Holmes laid it down that when you have eliminated all the people who cannot conceivably be guilty, what remains, however improbable, is the solution. I admit Randall is a far-fetched answer, but what other is there?"

I hadn't one for the moment nor had Crook; but next morning I was made to realize that Randall had by no means finished with the case. When the man brought in my letters I saw that the top envelope was white and smooth and addressed in a now familiar black writing. Inside was the equally familiar red hair and a message. It said, simply:

"You have been warned."

At this point I came to the conclusion that I didn't like the case one little bit.

CHAPTER XXI

*Hasn't a doubt—zample—far better hang wrong fler
than no fler.*
THE DEBILITATED COUSIN.

ABOUT a quarter of an hour later, as I ate a fragmentary breakfast, rather expecting to see the noses of revolvers poke through walls, or the painted judge over the mantelpiece step down as he did in Bram Stoker's story, a rope in his hands, the bell of my flat pealed and Parkinson came in.

"Look here," he began with more violence than I commonly associated with him, "this has stopped being a joke."

"Graham found that out before you did," I agreed. "You, too?"

"I've had another of these infernal letters. . . ." Then his eye fell on my envelope and he started. "He's got it in for both of us, hasn't he? Where do you imagine this is going to end?"

"In the morgue, so far as we're concerned. What does your note say?"

He showed it to me. "If you want to know the truth, come to 72b, Silver Square."

"Randall's rooms, office, whatever you like to call it," I exclaimed. "Well, that's as obvious a trap as ever I saw."

"So obvious one feels there must be something behind it. I never saw a clearer 'Keep Off the Grass' notice. It makes me feel one ought to go to Silver Square."

"To meet our deaths? I can't see that we should be much use to Fanny as corpses."

"If you don't mind my saying so, I can't see that we're doing her much good staying alive. And if, as your letter seems to suggest, we're going to be bumped off anyhow, we may as well have some idea of the fellow responsible."

"Thanks very much," I said. "I've had him under my hand more than once. I fancy he changes his appearance to suit his company."

"And you feel you'd be safer here? I'm sure you're right. But all the same, I shall go to Silver Square."

"With a squad of police?"

"No. I want to make him betray himself."

"Take care he doesn't betray you. I went to see Graham with precisely that intention, and look at the outcome. Make sure Randall doesn't realize the game is up and has decided he'll have a fellow-corpse at the mortuary."

But neither mockery nor argument could move Parkinson.

"You do as you please," he said, "but I'm going."

"All right," I said at last, "then I'll come with you. I've always despised the man who reads a book to the last chapter and then sends it back to the library with the solution unread because he's afraid of a grisly ending."

At least, I told myself, I could go armed, but when

I crossed to the drawer of my desk I found the revolver had gone. I stood staring at the place where it had been—I had never bothered to lock the drawer —and then rather foolishly back to Parkinson.

"Well," I remarked, "it looks as though Randall has kept an even closer watch on my movements than I realized.

"I've got a gun," said Parkinson. "A nice new one." He took it out and balanced it on the palm of his hand. "After that fellow shot at you through the window I thought I'd better be on the safe side."

We went along shortly afterwards. We met no one on our way up—I'd phoned Crook of our intentions— and when we pressed the bell outside Randall's door no one opened it or answered it.

"See if it's locked," I whispered.

Parkinson tried the handle. The door opened easily, and we looked into what appeared to be an empty room. We had no more than crossed the threshold, however, before I stopped with a sort of gasp. I saw Parkinson's eyes turn towards me and then he followed my gaze. Dark curtains hung by the windows, and between a crack in the curtains a face peered out unwinkingly at the pair of us. A ghastly, an unearthly face, plaster-white, with huge, gleaming eyeballs and a fork of red beard jutting into the room.

"Look out," I exclaimed, but Parkinson had had enough of risks. Without a word he lifted his gun and the shot shattered both the silence and the face, that crumbled like the plaster it resembled.

"That's the only way to deal with that sort of gentleman," said Parkinson grimly, standing his ground deathly-pale, the gun smoking in his hand. He turned to me. "Let's sit down."

I moved forward; with the firing of that shot the red beard had become detached from the mask to which it had been fastened, and now it lay, foolish and sinister, on the floor.

I heard Parkinson's voice behind me. "The last lap, I think," he remarked in a peculiar voice. "Didn't you once say you liked a long run for your money, Curteis? Well, you've had it. But now it's over. The last earth's stopped."

I turned quickly, only to feel the icy barrel of the revolver pressed in the small of my back.

"Sit down," said Parkinson, "and I'll tell you the truth. You, if you're so disposed, can fill up the gaps."

We sat down facing one another, he nursing the revolver that pointed ominously in my direction.

"What a clever chap you are," he began, "and what a lot of experience you must have had. It's the new technique, of course, to commit your crime and then, instead of retreating, occupy the limelight, consort with police and lawyers—was Crook in this, by the way? No? That was cleverer still. Of course, it has its advantages. No man can know that better than you. The fellow who hides from the light of day is literally proceeding in the dark. He's no idea what the police's next move will be. But the man who stands in with the authorities has complete information of their plans; he can openly follow in their tracks, discover the lie of the land, do the necessary delicate tweaking and adjusting that's so important if he isn't to swing for his crime, and all this, mark you, in an atmosphere of sympathy and condolence. How damned sorry every one has been for you, doing your utmost to get Fanny released. What a courageous beggar you were to put your head time and again in the lion's mouth and chance having it snapped off! That red-headed villain, for example! Didn't Crook advise you to keep away from this room, if you valued your life? And when the letters kept coming, didn't people think you a pretty fine chap to take no notice of their warning, but go on risking your precious skin for darling Fanny's sake? I bet they did—and how you must have reveled in it. And all the time you could have answered the questions of the police, giving them chapter and verse, as to the actual hour Rubenstein was killed—you and your mistress, Fanny Price, who went down there to rob Rubenstein, though to do you justice, I don't suppose either of you intended to include murder in your program."

Rather skillfully he contrived to light a cigarette with one hand.

"A bigger fool than you, or shall we say," here he laughed softly but there was something jarring and violent in the sound for all its smoothness, "a man who was rather less of a knave, would have sat back in an uncomfortable security and let the police make what they could of the case, let 'em find their own hare and go lolloping across country after it. You took the bold step, provided a hare none of them had ever heard of —that poor devil who married Fanny and, I'll dare swear, has spent the rest of his days regretting it. I suppose," he added curiously, knocking the ash off his cigarette, "if he had been taken for the job neither of you would have cared. Let him hang! What's a scape-goat for? And when there didn't seem much likelihood of his conveniently putting in an appearance, and the shadow of the scaffold loomed uncomfortably near, you pitched on Graham, poor unlucky devil, and saddled him with the murder."

All this time I'd sat like a rock; I thought I'd been pretty clever; now I wasn't so sure. It seemed to me that for all my scheming I might die yet. I was aware of sounds around me, but I didn't dare turn my head; I supposed Parkinson had got men behind those curtains, waiting for me to throw in my hand, give myself away. . . . Some pulse in my brain was beating furiously; I heard my mind say to myself, "He's got you here because he thinks he'll make you commit yourself. He's got a case, but not a complete case. If he had he wouldn't be going through this elaborate charade. Let him talk; every word you say is weighted with iron; he can afford to chuck them away, or believes he can." It was like walking on the edge of a crumbling precipice, where the smallest false step meant instant and horrible death. I asked if I might smoke. Tobacco clears the brain.

Parkinson leaned forward; he put a cigarette between my lips, struck a match.

"It's all right," I told him. "I'm not armed."

"I know that," he said. "I know where your revolver is."

"How well informed you are," I mocked him, my mind obsessed by a vision of myself and Fanny in the dock, with an irrefutable case against us. Even now I didn't see how I was to save my skin.

"It's in the hands of the police who found it in Graham's flat, soused in his blood. God, when I think I might at least have saved him if I hadn't been so keen to give you enough rope to hang yourself! Oh, I've been after you for some time, ever since I heard about the substitution of the bracelets. I remembered then how you'd called to Fanny in the gallery, saying that here were the originals. Who else knew where the fakes were? That was a good point in Graham's letter. It was pretty brilliant of you," he added in grudging tones, "to tell so much of the truth. That's your experienced criminal's way. Tell the truth to a certain stage and then twist its tail; your reputation as a candid man is established by then, you see. That's the great secret of diplomacy; you get credited on a double count—reliability and statesmanship."

"This is all pure supposition," I said, as quietly as I could.

He shook his head. "Not quite. I'm not that much of a fool. It was the act of a clever scoundrel to arrange for the attack on your own life, with a witness standing by, too. I'd been suspicious up till then, but I had no proof, and when you were shot I came to the conclusion I must be on the wrong path after all. But there was something just a little odd about the way you dashed to the window, believing there was a man in the yard who was after you, gave yourself to him as a target, in fact, a black silhouette against the lighted room. You were cautious enough when it came to creeping into this room, into Graham's room; you suspected traps then, but this time you offered yourself. And when I went out to look for the enemy I didn't find him, but I found the revolver, tied to the clump of bushes, with the long black string dangling from the trigger, and a bit more string fastened to a hook under the window. As soon as the window was opened the revolver exploded. If I'd had any idea what was in your mind I'd have collected the gun and gone to the police then and there, but I wasn't sure. . . ."

"That I'd killed Rubenstein?" I filled up the gap for him.

"Oh, I was sure of that." He shied the stub of his cigarette into the fireplace. "I wasn't sure that even that arranged tableau would be enough to prove it. You might say that some one else had arranged the plot— so I waited. And I waited too long."

"Quite twenty minutes too long," I agreed, and he stared.

"You mean this explanation? Oh, I felt I owed you that. After all, you showed skill enough, and no man can be on his guard against luck. You couldn't know about Mr. Bligh. You thought you'd saved both your necks, by involving Fanny, and he must have been a nasty surprise for you. Because, you see, that let Fanny out altogether and destroyed your case. I've tried to work out a solution, and I've found a rough-and-ready one. You'll be able to correct me on the various points. I suppose Rubenstein came back before you were ready for him, and found you on the job. Luck's queer," he brooded, repeating his trick of lighting a cigarette with one hand, "any jury would swear Fanny was involved. Actually I believe she's innocent from start to finish, and can't prove it. That button was damnable luck."

"Yes," I agreed smoothly, "how are you going to explain that?"

"I should say that as Fanny jumped out of the car in a tearing hurry, and as she slammed the door, the button caught in the hinge, and Rubenstein found it and brought it in. I can think of no other explanation that meets the case."

I shrugged my shoulders. "If you think a jury will accept that. . . ." My mind worked like a weasel that can escape from almost any trap.

"I fancy they will. As for the car, you were very keen to run down to the gate when you thought you heard Rubenstein coming back. You came in with mud all over your shoes. The car had to be moved from the back entrance, you see—and no one on a foggy night would find it in the lane beyond the house."

"You're very persuasive," I agreed, "but even you are going to find it difficult to prove that I killed Graham. How are you going to make any one believe that a letter like this was written in—what was it?—about ten minutes—that is, between eleven o'clock when I arrived and eleven-ten when I called the police."

"I'm not going to suggest that it was," returned Parkinson coolly. "I'm going to suggest that he was killed before you went into the flat—for the second time. No, don't argue. I'm telling this story. You cleverly staged your alibi with the lady from the fourth floor; she could come forward, if necessary, and swear that it was eleven when you arrived. But—who opened the door to you? Graham? No, because he was dead. But do you think, in order to save trouble, he left it open for you to find him in his sensational attitude?

That might wash, if it hadn't been established that Graham's death wasn't suicide but murder. When did he telephone to you?"

I said heavily, "Ten-twenty."

"And when did you telephone to Crook?"

"Ten-fifty."

"Yes. I wonder why you phoned from a call-box quite near the flats, instead of using your own instrument."

"Because it wasn't till the last minute that I thought of letting him know where I was."

"I see. Well, the jury can make what they like of that. Have you got an alibi for your movements from 10.20 to 10.50?"

"I walked down from my flat."

"I said alibi."

"I walked alone, if that's what you mean. To the average man in the street, one passer-by is the counterpart of another."

"Isn't that unfortunate?" said Parkinson. "Let me tell you the story as I see it. You got the telephone message, went over at once, realized your danger, shot Graham, and then wrote out his confession on his machine, using his paper and his carbon. You thought of practically everything; you even rang up his solicitor to establish the fact that he was alive at 10.45. If any one had passed the door and heard the sound of typewriting they'd have supposed it was Graham himself, hard at work. Then down you came—it was clever to send the letter to yourself—as I say, you thought of practically everything—telephoned Crook from a call-box, and on the stroke of the hour stepped into the lift and made your sensational discovery."

He chucked the stub of the second cigarette after the first.

"Almost," he said with a kind of grudging admiration, "you deserved to win. That master stroke of getting on to a wrong number before actually calling the police to establish your alibi yet more firmly. And you gave all the details, didn't you, address and everything? You were right," he added, grinning maliciously. "You promised me the murderer would overreach himself, and, sure enough, he has."

The movements behind me became more definite. I was aware of Burgess's blue spaniel face against the dark wall. He said. "Game's up, Mr. Curteis. That letter. Got it on you?"

I had. I took it out of my pocket and passed it to him. He crossed to Parkinson's side. "Look here, Mr. Parkinson," he fluttered the sheets, turning to the last one, "this bit in ink. That was the clinching touch. Because, look. . . ." He turned back to me, "Got your pen on you? Write your name on this bit of paper, will you? Thanks. Now you, Mr. Parkinson. Now I will." He drew a pen from his own pocket and bent over the sheet. I didn't know what he was driving at. As it happened, the pen wouldn't write. He scratched futilely, then threw it down.

"See that?" he said. "That was Mr. Graham's pen. And there wasn't any pen and ink in his room. Notice that, Mr. Curteis? So if he didn't sign with this pen (and it's broken; no man living could sign with it) what the devil did he sign with?"

"He didn't sign at all," said Parkinson. "We've established that."

Burgess turned a dour eye upon him. "We don't say established in our job till we mean established. Guesswork, pure deduction, aren't good enough for us. Well, then, if he didn't, whoever signed that letter was the author of it. Agreed?"

"Of course."

"Then," he picked up the sheet of paper, "how d'you explain this? Mr. Curteis's signature is bright blue. The signature on the paper was black. Well—any suggestions?"

Parkinson leaped to his feet, but Burgess's men were on either side of him. The revolver fell to the floor with a clatter, and Burgess stooped and picked it up.

"You were right, Mr. Parkinson," he said. "The cleverest criminal overreaches himself sometimes. Well, I think we have all the evidence we need at last."

"There's just one more thing I'd like to know," said a familiar bland voice at my shoulder. "Perhaps, inspector, you will allow me to ask Mr. Parkinson a final question. I wonder, Mr. Parkinson, how you knew that Mr. Curteis rang up a wrong number before he got on to the police? It wasn't in the press, it wasn't in any edition of the evidence that has so far been made public property. I don't see—really, my dear fellow, I don't—how any one could have known that unless he was actually present. Of course, if Mr. Parkinson can persuade us of any really good reason why he should have been hiding behind the curtain. . . . No? Then let me make a suggestion. He was there because he knew the game was up and we were on his tracks. We were bound, with all our spies out, to show that he was not only the murderer of Rubenstein, but also Arthur Randall, murderer of Mr. James Kirby and potential murderer of Simon Curteis, because that's what it was meant to come to, if it was another hand that manipulated the drop." And here Crook, who is a gross foul-minded old vulture at heart, leaned forward and twitched away the thick yellow wig from the head of the helpless man, revealing a new person altogether, a man about fifteen years older than the Parkinson I'd got accustomed to, a man whose colorless face worked with rage and humiliation, a man with a baldish forehead and a fringe of red hair.

"You had to stay, of course, Randall," Crook went on. "You see there was always the chance that some one would telephone to Graham, and if he didn't answer, questions might be asked. Some one even might burst into his room through the door you so conveniently left ajar. And it was necessary to show that he was alive up till the time Curteis was due to arrive. That flat is an ideal place for a murderer to hide; he only has to stand behind the communicating door, and then when the police had come and everything was in a state of turmoil, slip off by the back way. What a lot you thought of, Randall. And how clever to implicate as chief suspect the man who actually had committed the murder. As you told Curteis just now, that's the new technique. There's no surer way of throwing the chase off the scent."

CHAPTER XXII

Let us be moral. Let us contemplate existence.
MR. PECKSNIFF.

"IT'S vanity gets them every time," said Crook earnestly to me the next day, "that or funk. It was both that got Parkinson. By chance, and these things always do happen by chance in spite of the chastening warning of one John Keats who, like most poets, took full advantage of his poet's license, he'd committed a perfect murder. There was no reason that I can see why any one should ever have suspected him; even if his name was mentioned in connection with the crime, there wasn't an atom of proof against him. No one thought of linking him up with Randall—no one had ever heard of Randall. He simply had to sit back and let the police blunder ahead. The finding of Fanny's button crossed his last T. It argued, naturally, that Rubenstein had been killed, not after his return but before, practically speaking, he'd left the house, and it argued that Fanny was involved in his murder."

"Suppose Fanny had spoken up, had said that this was Randall?"

"It might have been unpleasant for him, but still there would have been no case. He'd worked for Rubenstein for nearly a year, there'd never been a word of complaint against him; at worst, he was a man who'd taken a wrong turning and now wanted to go straight. He'd have had everybody's sympathy. The world would say that a wife like Fanny was enough to put any man wrong. Parkinson had a perfect alibi for the time up till seven o'clock; he was playing bridge; he had two witnesses at least who could confirm that. Fanny's sudden move was a gift to him. It meant clearing the house of Rubenstein till, say, seven-fifteen, and while he was away Parkinson meant to substitute those bracelets. He knew about markets, knew where he could pick up the cash for them and not too many questions asked. And I dare say he needed money pretty badly. Rubenstein wouldn't overpay him and he had Bennett battening on him like a great hungry bug."

"And what about Graham? Was he in it? And was he killed because he was weakening and Parkinson was afraid of betrayal?"

"I should say not. Wouldn't have the guts, my boy. You talk big about murder, but it isn't everybody's money."

"You think Parkinson intended murder?"

"No," said Crook. "Honestly, I don't think he did. I don't see why it should be necessary. He'd be the last man Rubenstein would suspect if the substitution were discovered. With you and Graham and Fanny in the house, Parkinson would have had a pretty clean sheet. Only—Rubenstein came back too soon. Probably did come by Black Jack, and he found Parkinson in the very act. There was no question then what the fellow had to do. It was jail for him and he knew it. But he kept his head. He did everything possible to hide the traces of the crime, concealed the car temporarily while you were all dressing, and sent it over the cliffs during the night. And in all this he left no trace but that single red hair on Rubenstein's coat. But for that I doubt if he'd have moved, and he'd be as safe today as he was the night before Rubenstein's murder. But that red hair was discovered, you got busy; you were dangerous to him. You hunted about till you realized the existence of Randall, and once you'd found out about him rats weren't in it. You went for him head down—and Parkinson lost his nerve. When you know a thing yourself it's always hard to believe that other people don't know it, too. Parkinson, of course, was following up every move of yours. You can't blame him for that, his life depended on it. And there came to him the brilliant notion—here's a busybody looking for Randall as the murderer. We'll give him Randall. That's when the red-hair campaign started. He sent them to himself to put you off the scent; that's also part of the new technique. Of course, he fixed up the revolver outside your window and came in person to make sure it polished you off. It was sheer bad luck that you weren't killed. If you had been he'd have phoned for the police, slipped out through the window and unshipped the gun, chucked it away—or better still, rubbed it clean of fingerprints and returned it to the drawer where he found it."

"He took a chance, didn't he? I might have come in any minute."

"He'd phoned your flat, remember, and learnt when you were expected back. Oh, he thought of most things. When that didn't work he played his last desperate card. Graham was suspected; in a manner, if I had a conscience I'd feel responsible for Graham's death, but a lawyer loses that very early in his career. Graham, therefore, should be the scapegoat, and but for Mr. Bligh, Mr. Parkinson's skin would have been safe. He must have felt at the end of his tether when that story came out; his last throw was you. If you come to think of it, there wasn't any other choice; I suppose at the back of his mind he'd been keeping you as a last hope if everything else failed. He didn't realize that any one might connect him with the real Randall. That was bad strategy on his part. You don't use a man's name if there's any likelihood of his coming forward to deny your evidence. Either Randall was dead, and we'd proved he wasn't, or Randall was in the very middle of the picture, so large and so obvious that he was being overlooked. If he hadn't been so keen to get you we should never have caught him. For he was clever. In fact, I'm inclined to think he was intoxicated by his success. Remember, he'd murdered Kirby and no one had suspected him; he'd murdered Rubenstein and no one had suspected it; he'd tried to murder you and no one had suspected it; he'd murdered Graham, and still he was at large. But he didn't know how much longer he'd be safe. You remained. So long as you were alive you were a danger to him. You had to be eliminated, and he went about it pretty neatly. It's an object-lesson of how easy it is to put up a case against an innocent man, though actually you'd never have got as far as a verdict of guilty, not with me as your lawyer," continued Crook conceitedly. "He tripped himself up on one trifle—the blue ink—for which he might almost be forgiven. Nearly everybody uses blue-black. But when he began to boast, he lost his head and because of that he'll hang as he deserves. Otherwise he'd thought of everything, and you helped him at every turn. You helped him by telephoning me at the last moment, instead of ringing up from the flat.

"Of course, the button was pure luck for him. Your being there was luck for him too. Skillfully twisted, the facts might make a very pretty pattern in your disfavor, and he did twist them skillfully—only to give himself away by a piece of stupidity for which he deserves to hang, as he certainly will."

"You mean his remark about the wrong number? That's a bit slim—that and the pen. If he gets a man like Rubens to defend him..."

"Rubens won't. He won't get the chance. There are the fingerprints. They'll clinch the case. That's the reason why you were allowed to risk your life. He'd got to incriminate himself. The police examined the envelope in which the fake confession was found, for fingerprints; they found some, but they weren't Graham's. They weren't yours either. They were Randall's—Randall's, mark you—not Parkinson's. They hadn't got Parkinson's fingerprints then. They didn't know the two men were identical. But when they got an expert on to it he ran the fellow to earth...."

"You being the expert?" I suggested.

Crook grinned. "So you say. Well, there's your case. And an awful warning against the folly of subtlety. That's another of the discoveries of the new age."

"That's what Fanny said," I ejaculated. "She said subtlety could be spelt in four letters—R-U-I-N."

"And quite right. That girl knows her onions. I will say that for her. She's an odd creature, Curteis. She'd take lovers as you and I might take sugar in our tea, but just commit a murder and she'll stand by you till death. And it would be death, too. It's precious hard to get away with it. That's another of the discoveries of the new age."

"She didn't know Parkinson was guilty," I defended her warmly.

He smacked me on my uninjured shoulder. "That girl can add two and two together as well as the next man. Well, good luck. If I were a younger man I might envy you, but at my age you like something a bit quieter," and he complacently patted his comfortable paunch as the car set him down at his door.

THE END

〉〉〉 If you've enjoyed this book and would like to discover more great vintage crime and thriller titles, as well as the most exciting crime and thriller authors writing today, visit: 〉〉〉

The Murder Room
Where Criminal Minds Meet

themurderroom.com

www.ingramcontent.com/pod-product-compliance
Ingram Content Group UK Ltd.
Pitfield, Milton Keynes, MK11 3LW, UK
UKHW040434280225
455666UK00003B/56